M000196895

About the Author

Debra Ison lives in Frankfort, Kentucky, USA where she enjoys flower gardening, time with family and friends, and travel. She came to writing after retiring from a healthcare career. A lifelong and avid reader, she has loved mysteries from an early age. This penchant for the genre inspires her writing.

The Confession

Debra Ison

Debra Ison

The Confession

Olympia Publishers
London

www.olympiapublishers.com
OLYMPIA PAPERBACK EDITION

Copyright © Debra Ison 2022

The right of Debra Ison to be identified as author of
this work has been asserted in accordance with sections 77 and 78 of
the Copyright, Designs and Patents Act 1988.

All Rights Reserved

No reproduction, copy or transmission of this publication
may be made without written permission.
No paragraph of this publication may be reproduced,
copied or transmitted save with the written permission of the publisher,
or in accordance with the provisions
of the Copyright Act 1956 (as amended).

Any person who commits any unauthorised act in relation to
this publication may be liable to criminal
prosecution and civil claims for damage.

A CIP catalogue record for this title is
available from the British Library.

ISBN: 978-1-80074-653-4

This is a work of fiction.
Names, characters, places and incidents originate from the writer's
imagination. Any resemblance to actual persons, living or dead, is
purely coincidental.

First Published in 2022

Olympia Publishers
Tallis House
2 Tallis Street
London
EC4Y 0AB
Printed in Great Britain

Dedication

I dedicate this book to my late husband, Kenneth, who taught me so much about life and love.

Acknowledgements

Thank you to my dentist, Patrick Peters, who suggested the plot while I was in his office. That nugget of an idea took hold in my imagination. I also must thank pharmacists Aaron McIntosh and Glenn Stark who researched drugs for me.

Dr. Matthew Brooks was a gambler and faced bankruptcy, but was he capable of murder – for money?

Chapter One

Matthew Brooks finished shaving, chose a Brioni shirt and tie, and dressed for the day. His wardrobe had cost a small fortune, but he considered it an investment intended to impress his elite clientele. He checked his image in the hall mirror and decided, at forty-five, he still had it. Athletic good looks, deep blue eyes, and sandy blonde hair epitomized the professional chic look he carefully crafted. He reached for his keys on the table by the front door and dislodged several pieces of mail. With a sigh, he picked them up and thumbed through them. *Bills, all bills,* he mumbled to himself. He pulled out a drawer and stuffed the bills on top of others. *There, go join your friends!* A clench in his stomach reminded him of how deeply in trouble he was. He could probably hide the problem from public view for another month, maybe two, then he would be ruined. His dental practice, his house, everything he had worked for would be gone.

Since his costly divorce, he had cleaned out his retirement accounts, second-mortgaged the house, and used his dental practice for collateral to pay off his crushing gambling debts. He had a big problem, and he wasn't sure how to fix it. With another look at his image in the mirror, he straightened his shoulders and fixed a smile on his face. No one would believe he had a care in the world – at least for a few more weeks.

He opened the door of his leased Mercedes SL and slid

behind the wheel. He checked his mirrors, waited for a passing jogger, then backed out of his driveway.

His home and office were located in a prestigious bedroom community just outside of Chicago. The prime location gave him a fast commute and he pulled into the small parking garage next to his office ten minutes later. His practice was housed in a professional building that boasted some of the most successful blue-chip professionals in the Chicago area. Brooks, along with investment advisors, attorneys, and physicians catered to the wealthiest of clients and the building reflected it. Polished marble floors and walls of etched glass in the lobby were a prelude to the pampering each client could expect. Yes, Matthew Brooks had made it to the big time and had made a small fortune in his fifteen-year career. Bolstered by his father's social and business connections, he had attracted wealthy clients quickly and established himself as "the" dentist to see. It would all be perfect except for one small detail – Matthew gambled – big.

While his father was still alive, Matthew could count on his dad to bail him out of his gambling debts. After his father's death, his portion of the considerable estate was tied up in a trust with a contingency. The senior Brooks must have realized that tough love would be the only thing to turn his prodigal son into a more responsible adult. So, in death, he did what he could never bring himself to do in life; he cut his son off from the family wealth until Matthew could show the old man's attorney that gambling was a thing of the past.

Matthew brooded over how to get his hands on what he felt was rightfully his. The trust fund had millions in it. He could clear all of his debts, save his practice and his reputation, and continue his high-flying lifestyle with no intention of giving up gambling. It gave him a high when he won, and when he lost, well, it could always be made up, right?

These thoughts occupied him as he pulled into his designated parking spot in the building's attached, three-story-garage. As he exited his car, a familiar voice called to him from behind. "Hey there, Matt, did you watch the game last night?"

"Oh, hey Brian; yes, I caught most of it," he lied.

Encouraged by his friend's response, Brian continued. "That last shot at the buzzer was a real heart stopper!"

"Yeah, it was something to see." Matt only had to agree with Brian to keep up his part of the conversation as Brian was more than willing to give a blow-by-blow of the entire Chicago Bulls game. Fortunately, the walk into the building took only a minute, so they parted at the elevator. Brian ascended to his fourth-floor law office, and Matt continued down the hall to his first-floor dental practice.

He opened a door marked PRIVATE and turned the knob. He made his way to the reception area to check in with his staff.

"Good morning, Dr. Brooks," the receptionist cooed. Ever since Matthew's divorce, the attractive and very young woman had made it clear she was interested in her boss. Matthew dismissed her with a wave and a grunt, and headed to his office. Here, at least, he was shielded from his creditors. No one had dared send bills or leave angry messages at his place of business.

Matthew glanced outside at the enclosed courtyard that ran along the back side of the posh businesses. Exotic plants, statuary, and fountains reflected the luxury which clients had come to expect. Matt smiled. *It will all work out; I'm sure of it. I have enough left to score big at the poker and roulette tables this weekend. I might get enough to carry me for a few more months until I can figure out how to get at my trust fund.*

A timid knock on the door pulled Matthew away from thoughts of his dismal financial situation. He turned from the garden view and sat down at his desk. "Come in," he said in his most professional voice.

Sylvia Bennett, a petite brunette, timidly entered the office. "Dr. Brooks," she began, "I have a-um-a problem."

Matt waited, familiar with his dental assistant's inability to get at what she wanted to say quickly.

"Dr. Brooks, I need help with something. I don't know what you can do, but I thought, well I was hoping, we could work this out together." Sylvia released her breath, obviously relieved to have gotten this far.

"Okay, Sylvia, how can I help you?" Usually dismissive, the aloof dentist grudgingly admitted to being curious. He waited for her to explain.

"Well, I was thinking maybe I could help you if you help me."

Matthew wondered how in the world this mere assistant could be of any help to him, but he answered politely. "Just how can I do that, Sylvia? Is there a problem with someone in the office? Has anyone said something to upset you?" Matt asked with as much sympathy as he could muster.

"No, no it's nothing like that. Everyone here gets along very well. My problem, uh, is at home."

Matt raised a quizzical eyebrow, surprised at the admission. While nearly everyone in the office recognized the signs of a battered wife, Sylvia always chatted about happy things at home. More than one co-worker wondered if the stories were just that – stories.

"At home?" Matt asked.

"Yes, you see my husband, Ron, drinks a good bit. Sometimes he isn't very nice when he drinks."

"Does he hit you, Sylvia?" Matt asked with genuine concern now reflected in his voice.

"No, at least not all the time. He's always sorry afterwards, once he sobers up."

Matt had heard it more than once from his wealthy clients over the years. Net worth and social status seemed to have no bearing on this type of behavior. He sat up a bit straighter in his chair. "Sit down, Sylvia. How do you think I can help you?"

Sylvia assumed one of the polished leather seats in front of her employer's desk. Matt could see that her hands were shaking. It must have taken a lot for her to come to him. He waited yet again while she seated herself and arranged her hands primly in her lap, her head down.

When she spoke, she raised her head and looked directly at Matthew, searching his face. "I want you to help me kill my husband."

Chapter Two

Matthew stared at his assistant. "What did you say?"

"I said I want you to help me kill my husband. He's such a brute, and now he has started hitting the children. They are so young, only three and five. I can't stand by and let him kill one of us, can I?" Sylvia added the question in an effort to garner support. She stared wide-eyed at her employer, but he gave away nothing of what he was feeling.

The two sat there for several moments, neither speaking. After what seemed an eternity to Sylvia, Matt asked, "Why don't you go to the police, get a lawyer, and divorce the idiot?"

Sylvia sighed as she remembered past attempts to report Ron's behavior to the police. "It would do no good; I've tried. Ron is friends with half the department. He just tells them I'm being over emotional, that I'll settle down in a day or two. Most of the police force buy cars from his dealership and it doesn't help that he gives deep discounts on new and used cars to them. He also handles the fleet business for their patrol cars. No, I can't expect any help from the police."

Matt leaned back and absorbed what Sylvia had said. Matt had heard stories of corruption in the small town's police department. Cash inducements guaranteed special treatment if one happened to be caught speeding or committed some other low-level crime. He studied his assistant's face for a moment before responding. The desperation he saw there was genuine.

"How do you expect me to help you?"

"Well, I was hoping you could decide how to do it so it looks like an accident, or a heart attack, or something."

"Or something? Are you crazy? You'd never get away with it. I've seen him; he looks as if he just stepped off the defensive line of a pro football team!" Matthew protested.

Sylvia was non-plussed by the outburst, "You're a very smart man; I'm sure you'll think of something, Dr. Brooks." Having delivered the shock wave, she sat quietly and allowed the flattery to take effect. She knew that stroking his ego would smooth the way for her. Her employer was a vain man; everyone in the office knew it.

"Why do you think I would risk my license, my very freedom to do this for you?"

A slow smile tugged at her lips. "Because you need money, and I'll get a very generous settlement from my husband's life insurance. I'm willing to share it, fifty-fifty."

The mention of money got Matt's attention, "How did you, I mean why do you think I need money?"

"Well, I happened to overhear you talking to your bookie last week. You're in big trouble, Doc. Don't think the entire office is blind to what's going on with you; everyone knows you gamble. You need money and my offer could help you with that." Suddenly, the mousy, quiet assistant Matt thought he knew looked quite different to him. He thought he had been so careful around the office. He had given his creditors his cell phone number and had made it clear he would respond only to calls to that number, never his office phone. Apparently. More went on in the office than he knew. He wondered what else the office gossips knew, or thought they knew.

His musings were interrupted by the office intercom. His first patient was Hazel McIntyre, one of the town's elite, and she never expected to wait. He looked up, startled to see Sylvia still sitting in front of him. "Sylvia? Oh, yes, right, well let's talk later – after the day is over, shall we?" Without waiting for an answer, he rose and walked briskly out of his office, leaving Sylvia still sitting in front of his desk. After all, Mrs. McIntyre couldn't wait.

Sylvia went through the routine of her day, but she wondered if her boss had taken her proposal seriously. Would he turn her down, or worse, tell the police of her plan? She could always claim she was only kidding if she was questioned, but that wouldn't solve the problem. Ron was a mean drunk, and lately he was always drunk. Her mind raced through various scenarios even as she completed her assigned work tasks.

At the end of the day, she tarried in the breakroom, taking time to gather her belongings. Finally, she was the only employee remaining in the office. Once the door closed behind her co-workers, she retraced her steps to Dr. Brooks' office. She knocked softly and waited to be invited in. There was no answer, so she knocked a bit louder. "Dr. Brooks? It's Sylvia. You said we could talk after work, so I'm here."

Matthew sighed and leaned back in his chair and closed his computer. "Come in," he called. He wasn't sure how this conversation would go, and he was a fool to even listen, but the lure of fast money had him interested. Sylvia approached his desk and sat down uninvited. Her expression sent a clear message: *I'm here to talk business, let's get to it.*

***

An hour later Dr. Matthew Brooks pulled into his driveway. Usually, after a full day at the office, he enjoyed a drink at a nearby pub, but not tonight. Tonight, he needed time alone to think about his conversation with Sylvia. Until she came to his office at the end of the day, he had not really taken her proposal seriously. As the day had worn on, he had become convinced it was all a hoax, something his staff had dreamed up. That would have made sense; murder-for-hire did not.

Sylvia was more confident during the second meeting with her boss as she provided more detail to her plan to murder her husband. Not wanting to seem too eager, he didn't interrupt her as she shared the details of the insurance policy. The payout was a million dollars – each; not chump change.

Matt replayed the conversation as he wandered into his study and poured whiskey into a tumbler. The bottle of Pappy Van Winkle had cost a small mint, but it had been worth every penny. He slowly sipped the amber liquid as his mind raced. The money was tempting, but the risk was high. He had done some pretty shady things in the past, but this was a first for him. Murder – was he even capable of taking another's life? For money?

***

Matt awoke Saturday morning after a fitful night of sleep. He donned jogging gear and headed out for a five-mile run. He needed to clear his head. With each passing mile, his mind returned to The Plan, as labeled by Sylvia. *The Plan,* to kill another human being and make it look accidental or natural. *Huh! There is nothing natural about murder,* he admitted.

At the end of five miles, his head was anything but clear. It was crazy to even think of going through with this; he wasn't even sure he could. He walked another mile to cool down and headed home. He took a quick shower and donned navy-blue shorts and a white silk-blend tee. He knew he should go into the office and catch up on paperwork, but his mind was too unsettled. With a heavy sigh, he walked to the entry hall table and pulled out the bills.

He placed the invoices on his desk and turned on a small calculator. With each invoice entry, his anxiety increased. *How did I get into this much debt? What was I thinking?* He felt trapped and had trouble breathing. Sweat broke out on his brow and under his arms. In front of him, detailed on each page, was his future, or what would be left of it. He shook his head, dazed by how quickly he had slid from having a successful dental practice, a healthy bank account, and a beautiful wife to the black hole he was staring at now. His gambling, his former wife's heavy spending, and the divorce had brought him to the brink of bankruptcy.

He stuffed the invoices back into the drawer and slammed it shut. *Blast it all! Maybe I can sell the house, my Mercedes, and my gun collection. That should carry me a bit longer,* he told himself. Feeling a bit better, he pulled out a fresh sheet of paper and listed the items he could sell and for approximately how much. He soon discovered he had nothing left to sell. The house had a first and second mortgage, the Mercedes was leased, and his gun collection would only raise maybe twenty-five grand. Matt swore, threw down his calculator, and pushed himself up out of his chair.

He paced around the room like a caged animal looking for a

way out of the prison he had created. *I've been so stupid! I've wasted everything I've worked for.* He continued to pace and berate himself as the request from Sylvia popped in and out of his thoughts. The money was tempting and was enough to get the most urgent debts taken care of. It would give him breathing room at a time when a deep breath was hard to come by. He stopped pacing, returned to his desk, and picked up the phone. He consulted an address book and dialed. The phone rang three times, and Matt was almost ready to hang up when a familiar voice answered.

Matt took a deep breath. "Sylvia?"

Chapter Three

The following Friday, Matt called Sylvia into his office. He shut the door behind her and motioned for her to sit down. He resumed his seat behind his desk, as he wanted to keep a professional distance and to remind his assistant that he was still in charge. Sylvia maintained silence and waited to hear what he would say. Matt straightened his tie and assumed an upright, almost rigid posture.

"I've given our arrangement a great deal of thought," he began as his gaze shifted from his desk to Sylvia's chin and back again. He couldn't bring himself to look her in the eye. "Since we spoke last week, I've come up with different scenarios to accomplish our goal." Matt deliberately avoided words such as murder. "You have several vacation days coming to you, and I think it would be a good idea for you to go away for a few days."

Sylvia nodded but remained silent. Her heart picked up a few beats as she realized where her employer was going with his comment.

Matt continued, "Stay with a relative or friend, someone to provide an alibi; is there someone you can visit?"

Sylvia thought for a few moments before answering. "I'm sure my parents would welcome a visit; they're always asking when we can come for a few days. They live three hours away."

"Perfect, go ahead and make those arrangements," Matt

instructed. "Your husband has an appointment to see me next month to place a temporary crown on a cracked tooth; I'll work him in next Friday instead."

Sylvia's eyes widened. "You're going to kill him here?"

"Of course not, but that's all you need to know. Now, when you go back to work tell no one about this. Absolute secrecy is necessary for this to work. Do you understand?"

"Of course, I don't look any better in an orange jumpsuit than you do, Dr. Brooks," she replied, her voice dripping with sarcasm.

Matt ignored the attitude. "Good, I'm glad we understand each other. Oh, there's one more thing. I need you to sign this confession taking full responsibility for your husband's death. In case you have any ideas about pointing your finger at me and taking all the money, I'll have this as insurance that you will fulfill your part of the bargain."

He's not as big a fool as I thought he was, Sylvia thought. "How do I know you won't double cross me and give this to the police?"

Matt smiled, but the glint in his eyes was not humor. It gave Sylvia reason to fear the man sitting across from her. He pulled out a single sheet of paper and handed it to her.

"What's this?" she asked.

"That, my dear Sylvia, is *my* signed confession. We're in this together; neither of us can pin your husband's death on the other."

Sylvia opened her mouth to protest but decided against it. Dr. Brooks was right; they were in this together. She accepted the offered pen and signed her confession. Matt signed his confession and traded documents with her. Sylvia got up to leave but turned back. The full impact of what they were planning to do hit her. The risk was substantial, but she and her children would be rid of the constant threat of violence.

"How are you going to do it?"

"Do what? I don't know what you're talking about."

"Ron, Dr. Brooks. I'm talking about Ron."

"I understand, but the less you know the better. Now put a smile on your face and return to work."

It was a dismissal. Matt reached for his laptop and began to type a note in a patient's chart. He didn't look up as Sylvia left his office.

***

The following Friday morning, Sylvia packed a bag for herself and the children after Ron had left for his auto dealership. He was always the first one to arrive so he could monitor the arrival times of his employees. His controlling nature extended into his professional as well as his home life. As she packed, she pulled out Matt's confession that she had tucked away in her dresser. *I need to find a safer place for this. The police may want to search the house after... well after,* she surmised. She searched in her mind for a good hiding place the police would not be likely to find. She settled on the hidden compartment in Ron's desk. The space was not visible and couldn't be opened until a hidden lever under the desk was pulled. She carefully folded the incriminating document and placed it in the hideaway. *That should do it,* she told herself. Next, she quickly wrote a note to Ron explaining she was visiting her parents and hoped that was enough to placate him until... well, until Matt's plan was implemented. Part of her wanted to know the plan, but she knew it was best to be kept in the dark. She placed the note on the kitchen counter by the back door where she knew Ron would most likely enter that evening.

Satisfied that she had taken care of everything, she gathered her son and daughter and shepherded them to her SUV.

"Where are we going, Mama?" Sylvia's five-year-old daughter Kat asked.

"We're going to see Nana and Papa, honey."

"Is Daddy coming?"

"Not this time. Now, get in your booster seat while I help your brother."

The little girl smiled as she clambered into the back seat. Daddy wasn't coming with them; there would be no loud words or hitting at Nana's and Papa's.

Once the children were secured, Sylvia slid behind the wheel and started the car. Her hands trembled as she fastened her seatbelt and put the car into gear. *Get hold of yourself, girl; this is the only way to stop that monster.*

She hoped the note she had left behind would hold Ron off for a few days – if he was still alive. If anything, he might see it as an opportunity to drink as much as he wanted and entertain the waitress he had been seeing on the side. Sylvia had pretended not to notice the lipstick on his neck and collar or the condoms he had tucked into his wallet. She had hoped he would leave her for the unlucky waitress, but he had given no indication he wanted a divorce. With effort, she chased away thoughts of Ron and what was about to happen. She couldn't back down now; the children's safety was at stake.

When Sylvia merged onto the interstate, she relaxed a little, but she knew she couldn't let her guard down. It was a small town and Ron had many friends. Drunk and abusive at home, he was completely different with friends. No one would believe what he was really like. If murder was suspected, she had no doubt she would be hung out to dry with little sympathy from anyone.

**

Matt checked his appointment calendar on his laptop. It was Friday, the day Ron Bennett would arrive for his one-thirty appointment. He opened his top desk drawer to check on its contents. The vial of Fentanyl was still there. He had found a willing drug dealer easily enough, but finding one with Fentanyl had proved to be a more daunting task. Fatal, even to the touch, Fentanyl was created to sedate large animals such as elephants and giraffes but had found its way into street drugs. It made drug addiction much more dangerous than before and had claimed many victims. Ten thousand times more powerful than morphine, the drug was extremely dangerous even in very small quantities.

His plan was to place a drug in the new crown and have it leak out later, thus killing Ron somewhere other than the dental office. He had considered using potassium instead because Sylvia told him that Ron took potassium supplements. In sufficient quantities, potassium stops all heart function and is the main component of lethal injections. It would have been a perfect way to kill Ron, but Matt realized he couldn't put enough of it in the crown to cause death. So, he settled on the most lethal street drug he could find. This had to work the first time – there wouldn't be a second chance.

Matt's mind raced through what he was planning to do even though he had spent hours the evening before practicing each step. Ron's crown would look like any other crown, except for one very lethal exception. Matt would drill a tiny hole in it to allow the Fentanyl to leak out, but not too quickly. To delay administration of the drug, a thin layer of zinc phosphate cement would cover the hole and encapsulate the drug. This would not dissolve for several hours. The last thing Matt wanted was a dead body in his office. Ron must die somewhere else, preferably at home.

A knock on the door brought Matt back to the present. He must get through a full morning before facing his dreadful task in the afternoon. With a few deep breaths to offset a sudden queasiness, he left his office to greet his first patient.

***

Ron left work at lunchtime and drove across town to his dental appointment. He had tried to call Sylvia, but she had not answered her cell phone. He would have to deal with that bit of defiance when he got home. He had told her many times to *always* take his call. A familiar irritation grew to near rage as he tried unsuccessfully a second time to contact his wife. *She should answer; this is her lunchbreak. Never mind,* he thought, *I'll see her once I get to her office.*

Ron found a parking spot easily in the parking garage which improved his mood somewhat. He locked his Jeep and pocketed the key, unaware he was walking into danger.

He approached the dental office and held the door for a young blonde. His eyes took in the woman's curves, and he smiled his most charming smile. She took no notice of him and passed through without giving him more than a curt, "Thank you."

Undeterred by the obvious brushoff, he paused at the reception desk to flirt with the newest young female in the office.

"You must be new, darlin'," he drawled. "I haven't seen you here before. What's your name?"

The young woman smiled in response and was about to provide her name when she was interrupted by Becky, the practice manager.

"Jennifer, go to the billing office and pick up the charts which Amy has completed, please."

With a crestfallen look, Jennifer acquiesced. "Yes, ma'am." With a final flirtatious glance at Ron, she left to complete her task.

"Hello, Mr. Bennett, let's get you checked in," Becky said crisply. "Please fill out these forms and give them to the dental assistant when she calls you.

Ron glared at Becky, but didn't offer comment as he took the clipboard to complete the forms. He took a step to find a seat but turned back to the desk. "Uh, I need to see my wife; is Sylvia available?"

"I'm sorry, Mr. Bennett, she had to run an errand. I'm sure she'll return soon," she lied. Sylvia was her friend and Becky was all too happy to assist in the deception. Becky was aware of Ron's abuse of Sylvia and had seen the many bruises from the beatings. She breathed a sigh of relief when he was called back for his appointment.

***

"Now, Mr. Bennett, please just relax. We'll have your new crown in place before you know it," Matt assured.

Ron was never relaxed in the dentist's chair, no matter how many assurances were provided. "Well, just make sure I can't feel all that drilling and prodding. You dentists must love to inflict pain because you're very good at it," he said sourly. "Hey, while I'm thinking of it, I need something for my back pain; can you write a prescription for that?"

Matt chuckled. "I don't think you'll need pain medicine for this procedure. You shouldn't feel anything; I'll make sure of it. The anesthetic will cover you for the next few hours. As for your back pain, you should see your physician for that," Matt explained.

"Oh, come on, doc. All I need is a few to get me to Monday when I can see him."

Matt sat back on his stool and considered the request. Finally, he acquiesced. "Okay, I'll write a script for ten tablets of hydrocodone. Just be sure to follow the directions on the label and don't drink alcohol at the same time."

"Got it, thanks. My back should be better in a couple of days; it usually is."

The dental assistant looked up at the mention of pain medicine. Dr. Brooks almost never provided narcotics to anyone. She hid her surprise, however, behind a mask of indifference as she arranged the instruments for the procedure.

Matt injected the anesthetic and chatted amiably with Ron as it took effect. Once his patient was numbed adequately, he readied the tooth for the temporary crown with practiced precision. He excused himself to check on another patient while the assistant made the mold for the temporary crown. Ten minutes later he re-entered Ron's treatment cubicle. He was about to begin to place the temporary crown when Becky approached with a message from another patient.

"It's Mrs. Schneider. She is experiencing bleeding from the gum procedure she had on Wednesday and wants to see you today if possible."

"Thank you, Becky. I'll call her as soon as I'm finished here."

Becky nodded and returned to her office.

Matt smiled behind his mask. *Perfect!* He had been trying to find a way to distract his assistant so he could drill the pinhole in the crown to administer the deadly drug. Mrs. Schneider had given him the perfect opportunity to be alone with Ron for a few minutes.

"Beth, will you please return that call for me. I can fit her in at five this afternoon."

The assistant was puzzled that her boss had not told Becky to call the patient back, but she knew better than to question the request and simply left to make the call.

Matt continued friendly chatter with Ron as he drilled the hole quickly in the crown that would deliver the lethal dose of Carfentanil. As he worked, his mind wandered to the money he and Sylvia would share. It would be enough to buy him some time.

When his assistant returned, Matt had the crown placed and was checking the fit. Satisfied with his work, he sat back. "Mr. Bennett, we're all done here. Here is your prescription for the pain medicine; let us know if you experience any problem with that crown, okay?"

"Tanks, Doc, mush 'preciated," Ron managed to utter, his lips too numb to form his words correctly.

Matt watched as Ron was ushered out by his assistant. He

slumped against the back of his chair and felt as if he would be sick. What was he thinking? He was ready to kill another human being. Sylvia would be upset, but he couldn't kill Sylvia's husband. The Fentanyl was still in his pocket. He would dispose of it carefully later.

He took several slow deep breaths to regain composure and turned his attention to his next patient who was already waiting for him in the next booth. It was essential for his routine to continue.

Chapter Four

Ron drove away from the parking garage and ran his tongue over his new crown. *I'm glad that's over; I hate going to the dentist.* He navigated the downtown streets and turned his Jeep onto the Interstate Highway. *One quick stop at the pharmacy and I can go home. The pain pills will feel good, especially washed down with a little bourbon,* Ron surmised, ignoring Matt's admonition about drinking with the drug.

He drove to the pharmacy's drive-thru and showed his I.D. for the narcotic. Minutes later, he was driving home, and his thoughts returned to Sylvia. *Why didn't Sylvia return to work before I left? What was she doing? She'll have some explaining to do when she gets home.*

Ron pulled into his driveway and reached up to push the garage door opener button. With his vehicle put away, he retrieved the bottle of pain pills and entered his house through the kitchen door. The sudden draft of air lifted Sylvia's note and sailed it under the kitchen table, unnoticed by Ron. As expected, it was quiet. It was too early for Sylvia to be home from work, and he thought the kids were at daycare. He could have picked them up early, but decided to enjoy some peace and quiet for a change. He hadn't wanted those brats anyway.

He sat down heavily on the living room sofa and opened the bottle of bourbon and the hydrocodone. *Two should make me feel really good and relaxed,* he decided as he popped them into his mouth and washed them down with the bourbon. An hour later, the anesthetic had worn off and Ron took more hydrocodone and poured a double shot of bourbon. They made him feel good. He watched TV and drank more bourbon. Nature called a short time later and Ron headed for the bathroom on unsteady legs, He stood in front of the toilet and attempted to unzip his pants but the zipper was stuck. As he struggled, he lost his balance, fell backward, and hit his head on the bathtub. He was knocked out cold and the slow bleed in his brain worked with lethal efficiency. In an hour, Ron Bennett was dead. He lay on his back with one leg under him and the other sprawled out to the side. This would be the way Sylvia would find him when she returned in two days.

***

On Sunday afternoon, Sylvia pulled into the driveway of the two-story brick home she had shared with Ron for six years. The day was sunny, but the beautiful day didn't match Sylvia's mood. She knew what she would find inside. Ron must be dead because he had not attempted to call her since his dental appointment two days ago. Her heart beat faster as she opened the trunk to unload the luggage. She was glad she had thought to drop the kids off at her sister Claire's house to play with their cousins. She told her sister that Ron would be angry when she got home and she didn't want the kids to hear the arguing. Claire readily agreed to a visit from her niece and nephew but was concerned that Ron would do more than just argue. She had seen the many bruises Sylvia had tried to conceal. It had done no good to beg her sister to leave the creep, so she tried to be as supportive as she could.

Sylvia put her key in the lock and slowly opened the door. The stench of death attacked her sense of smell immediately, causing her to hesitate. *This is it; he's really dead.*

She entered the house but walked as slowly as one heading to her own execution. The foyer looked remarkably normal which surprised her. It was if the house was trying to deny its terrible secret. She entered the living room and saw the open bottle of hydrocodone and the half-empty bottle of bourbon. She called out for Ron as she continued walking through the house. She entered the kitchen and glanced at the counter where she had placed her note to Ron. It was gone so she assumed he had taken it. She didn't notice it lying on the floor under the table.

She continued to search room-by-room and found Ron on the bathroom floor; his face was ashen. He was obviously dead, but Sylvia walked closer to make sure. Her hand shook as she reached for a pulse. Ron's skin was cool and felt rubbery. No pulse.

Sylvia's first response was not relief as she had thought it would be; it was panic. She assumed Matt had killed Ron and the full impact of what she and Dr. Brooks had done came crashing down around her and made her nauseous. She staggered out of the bathroom and collapsed onto a chair. She fought to get her breath as she dug in her purse for her phone. She struggled to be coherent as she related Ron's death to the emergency dispatch operator. She gave her name and address and described what she had found upon returning home. The operator assured her that help was on the way and for Sylvia to leave the home without touching anything else.

After the call, Sylvia sat on the top step of the front porch until the police arrived. She didn't have to feign shock as she was questioned. She told them her carefully rehearsed story and waited for the forensic team and the detectives to arrive. They escorted her around to the back patio so the house could be processed and the body examined by the coroner. Sylvia barely remembered the interview. She answered questions numbly and sat quietly with a uniformed officer nearby. She kept wondering how her employer had pulled it off. How did Ron die? She tried to remember the scene. Ron was lying on his back on the floor and there had been a small smudge of blood on the edge of the bathtub. It certainly looked like Ron fell backwards and hit his head on the tub. Could Dr. Brooks have staged the scene to look like an accident? Terror gripped her as the full impact of Ron's death became a reality. Up until now, it had only been a plan. The reality was much worse than she had imagined it could be. Her thoughts were interrupted by someone calling her name. She looked up through swollen eyelids with tears still trickling down her face.

"Mrs. Bennett... Mrs. Bennett?" Detective Robertson queried as he watched her closely.

"Uh, oh, yes – what did you say?" Sylvia held tightly onto the now tepid cup of coffee someone had given to her. She had not taken a sip. "I'm sorry, it's just so shocking; he was fine when we left on Friday."

"Mrs. Bennett, I completely understand your shock and we're almost finished, just a few more questions. Now, did you see your husband on Friday before you left to visit your parents?"

"Uh, yes, before he left for work. I packed a bag for the kids and me and headed out right after he left. It's a three-hour drive and I wanted to get there as quickly as possible."

"Why did you visit them this weekend? Was there anything

special about this weekend?"

Sylvia looked up at the detective standing a few feet away. What did she see in his eyes? Suspicion? After all, Ron had friends on the force and some might take Ron's death a little too personally. "Special? Why no, nothing special. I had vacation time coming to me and decided it was a good time for a visit, that's all."

The detective studied the young woman sitting at her patio table. He knew she and Ron had a rocky marriage; he even knew about Ron's affairs. Was anything of that behind his death? He suspected Sylvia Bennett knew more than she was saying. The woman was obviously in shock, but there was something else he saw in her countenance – fear. What made her so afraid? He decided to let her go for now and get the autopsy results back. He also decided to find out about any life insurance policy and the financial condition of Ron's car dealership. He had a strong feeling Sylvia had a motive: money and escape from an allegedly abusive husband. Perhaps she had a lover of her own.

"Okay, Mrs. Bennett, just a couple more questions. Did your husband have a life insurance policy and what were the provisions for the auto dealership in the event of your husband's death?"

Sylvia looked up sharply. She paused and swallowed before answering. "Detective, Ron has a business partner. He has the option to buy out Ron's half of the business from his heir – me. I guess I'll go that route as I have no desire to be involved in the dealership's operations. As for the insurance policy, it's in the file drawer of Ron's desk in his study. He is a good provider and wants to make sure we are taken care of."

The detective heard the present tense in the woman's

statement. Death might be abrupt, but its acceptance often takes more time. The detective left to find the policy and Sylvia waited on the patio in the company of a female patrol officer. The detective found the policy in the top left file drawer of the desk in Ron's home office. He made a cursory search of the rest of the desk's contents, but found nothing of interest. He had no idea he was inches away from Matt's confession to Ron's murder hidden in the desk's secret compartment.

Three hours after Sylvia arrived home, Claire's husband arrived to take her to his and Claire's home. She and the children would stay with them until she was permitted back in her home.

The next several days were a blur for Sylvia. It took four days for the coroner to release Ron's body for cremation. The funeral service followed three days later. Matt closed his office for the afternoon so staff could attend, and he arrived in his best Armani dark gray suit to pay his respects. He arrived in time for the pre-service visitation and noted the nearly full parking lot. He waited his turn in line to convey his condolences and recognized many of his dental patients along the way. Sylvia was popular, as was Ron, and the crowd reflected it.

Finally, he advanced in line and approached his employee. "Sylvia, I'm so sorry for your loss," Matt offered, as he leaned over to hug his assistant. Sylvia bristled at his touch, but fought to control her response – the police were in attendance. Two detectives were watching the proceedings with interest and at least a dozen uniformed officers stood close by the coffin. Sylvia had been told that Ron had a great deal of narcotics and alcohol in his blood and likely lost his balance and fell backward against the tub. The injury to the back of his head was consistent with this scenario, so the detectives' presence puzzled her. She returned the hug from Matt and whispered, "Thank you." Despite the coroner's findings Sylvia was still under the impression that Matt had killed Ron and had made it look like an accident. After the discovery of Ron's body, there had been a steady stream of family and friends around Sylvia so Matt had not had a chance to tell her he had not killed Ron.

As the time for the funeral service neared, Sylvia found her seat on the front row and let her mind wander through the days of her years with Ron. She couldn't help but grieve for what had been between them in the early days of their marriage. A tear escaped and trickled down her cheek. She dabbed at it with a tissue and struggled to maintain her composure. Claire sat next to her and reached for her sister's free hand. Claire could feel Sylvia's hand shaking and held it even tighter. As far as she was concerned, it was good riddance to good ol' Ron. He had made her sister and her kids miserable. Claire would shed no tears for her brother-in-law.

***

Two weeks later, Sylvia was back at work and the kids were beginning to show signs of healing from the abuse they had endured. The official cause of death was ruled an accidental fall. Subsequently, the insurance check was deposited in Sylvia's account, and the police had stopped asking questions. *It's over; it's finally over,* Sylvia thought as she resumed her routine of assisting Matt with his patients.

During Sylvia's lunch break, her employer called her in to his office. The request alarmed her. Her hands were shaking as she quietly knocked on his office door.

"Come in," Dr. Brooks instructed.

Sylvia stood before Matt's desk, too uncomfortable to sit down. "Dr. Brooks, I don't think we need to speak at work about, uh, you know. I don't think it wise."

"Please sit down, Sylvia, I need to tell you something."

Sylvia complied reluctantly. She sat across from her boss and waited.

"Sylvia, I didn't kill Ron. I almost went through with it, but just couldn't do it. I was totally shocked when I heard of his death."

Sylvia's mouth gaped open. "Then how…? He had drugs in his system; the autopsy included blood work for drugs. The coroner said the combination of booze and drugs caused him to fall and hit his head. I assumed you hit him instead and made it look like an accident or you pushed him and he fell. After all, you prescribed the hydrocodone."

Matt froze. He had all but forgotten about the prescription he had written for Ron. "The drug he had in his system was hydrocodone?"

"Well, the final toxicology report hasn't come in yet, but there was a half-empty bottle of hydrocodone tablets on the table beside the sofa and a half empty bottle of bourbon. He bought both the afternoon he died; receipts proved it. Your name was listed as the prescribing physician on the bottle of pills. I thought that was your plan, but I don't know how you got him to take so many pills and drink so much bourbon."

"I only gave him a script for ten tablets. When I saw him, he asked if I could give him something for his back pain. I told him I could prescribe a few tablets, but that he needed to see his GP about his back. I even warned him not to drink alcohol with the pain medication. I did prescribe the medicine, but I didn't kill your husband, Sylvia."

"Are you just saying that to make you feel better? You agreed to kill Ron on the very day that he died. That can't be a coincidence, Doc."

"I'm serious, Sylvia. I didn't kill Ron. I had no idea he would overdose on the hydrocodone, or that he would wash it down with a half-bottle of bourbon. This means, of course, that you don't owe me half of the insurance money. It's all yours."

Matt's response finally registered with the widow. He would not say he didn't kill Ron if he had because he wouldn't give up the money. There would have been no motivation for him to kill Ron without it.

"Okay, let's say I believe you, but I know you need the money and I don't want you to lose your dental practice, so I want you to have some of the insurance anyway. Would a hundred grand save the practice? It's not just you I'm thinking of; I like the staff here and I don't want anyone to lose their job."

"One hundred grand? Yes, that would definitely give me some breathing room. I will only accept it, though, if it is a loan. I insist on paying you back. I'll take it at five per cent interest if that's okay."

Sylvia answered quickly. "Yes, that will work for me. Let's call it done."

***

Weeks passed, and although the investigation into Ron's death was closed officially, Detective Steve Robertson continued his own investigation in the background. The police were suspicious of foul play but no solid evidence could be found to bring charges against anyone. Still, there was that two-million-dollar insurance policy and why did she give her boss one hundred grand? Was it a payoff for killing Ron? Matt was questioned and he provided evidence of the money as a loan with interest. Every lead the police traced down, however, revealed no smoking gun and they were forced to officially close the case. Unofficially, Detective Robertson devoted part of every week working on the case. He simply couldn't reconcile Sylvia's words and actions with her alibi. When the house was searched, the note to Ron had been found under the kitchen table. Why would Sylvia leave a note? Why didn't she tell Ron that morning before he left for work? It didn't add up. Maybe he would get lucky if he kept at it, he reasoned. After all, Ron was a friend, one of the good ol' boys.

Unaware of the unofficial continuing investigation, Matt and Sylvia breathed deep sighs of relief as they went on with their daily routines.

***

Matt was tempted to take the money Sylvia had given him and try his luck in Vegas, but he resisted. The money was necessary to prevent bankruptcy. Over the next three months, he used the money from Sylvia and the proceeds from his lucrative practice to pay down his debts. Relieved that he was no longer on the brink of ruin, Matt managed to refrain from gambling for two more months. Then, it all began again.

Chapter Five

Matt opened the moon roof of his rented Lexus and rolled down all the windows. He wanted to feel the cool breeze as it flowed through the luxury sedan. The moon was full and Matt relished the anticipation of a weekend in Vegas. A delayed flight and a mix up in luggage combined to threaten Matt's ebullient mood, but once on the road in his rental car, Matt concentrated on strategy.

I have thirty grand to bet this weekend. If I'm lucky, I'll be able to go home with ten times that much. Las Vegas, here I come!

Twenty minutes later, Matt pulled up to the front entrance of the MGM Grand. He tossed the keys to the valet and pocketed his ticket as his bags were pulled out of the car's trunk and placed on a luggage trolley. He tipped the porter and asked for the luggage to be taken to the luxury suite he had reserved the day before. He wanted to waste no time on trivial matters, not when the tables were calling his name.

A regular at the hotel, most of the dealers knew him by sight, if not by name. He waved his hand in greeting as he passed each table, much like a monarch would acknowledge his subjects as he passed through the village. *Ah, it's good to be back,* he thought as he sought out his favorite dealer for black jack. A seat was open, and Matt slid in next to a comely blonde wearing an expensive perfume. The aroma was intoxicating and Matt had to force himself to focus on his play.

"Good evening, Dr. Brooks," the dealer acknowledged as Matt placed his chips on the table in front of him. He bet the maximum for the table – five hundred – and took his first card, an ace. *Not bad,* he thought. The ace was followed by a ten of hearts. With practiced calm, he displayed no emotion in response, but indicated he would stay pat. Additional cards were dealt to two other players. The dealer revealed his cards – an ace and a nine, followed by the blonde who turned over twenty points as well. Matt claimed the pot with his twenty-one and felt the all-too-familiar rush of adrenalin that a win always gave him.

The cards fell the right way for most of the night, and Matt walked away from the table with an additional forty thousand dollars. He was on a roll.

He awoke mid-morning on Saturday and smiled as he remembered his success the night before. A couple of women had tried to get his attention as he rose from the table, but Matt had not been in the mood for company, at least not last night. He ordered room service and showered. Wrapped in the hotel's plush white robe, he sat down to his breakfast of bacon, eggs, apricot jelly, toast, and coffee. As he ate, he savored not only the excellent meal but also his winnings. He smiled to himself and succumbed to the invincible feeling many gamblers experience. *This is my big chance and I feel lucky!*

Matt hummed a familiar tune as he dressed in his Valentino trousers and Dolce and Gabbana shirt. He looked every bit the part of a high-stakes gambler. A final brush of his hair and a quick buffing of his shoes readied Matt for the tables once again. He exited his room, removed the DO NOT DISTURB sign, and nodded to the maid he met along the hallway.

Matt pulled a fifty out of his money clip and offered it to the young woman. "Could you arrange to have the bed turned down at ten this evening and a bottle of the hotel's best champagne delivered around the same time? Oh, and make sure the champagne is on ice. I'll need two champagne glasses and an assortment of light appetizers. Tell the kitchen to charge everything to my room." He was sure he could find someone to share his night.

The maid accepted the money and nodded shyly, "Yes sir."

Matt strode down the hallway and caught a glimpse of himself in a mirror. He studied his reflection for several moments as he waited for the elevator. Pleased with what he saw, he straightened his shoulders and lifted his head an inch.

When the elevator doors opened, he was surprised to see the blonde from the night before.

"Oh, good morning, Miss... ah"

"Hodges, Carolyn Hodges. I didn't get a chance to congratulate you last night. That was quite a lucky streak you had going," she offered.

"Yeah, well... thanks. I hope my luck holds today. My name is Matt Brooks, by the way."

"You're heading to the tables now?"

"Uh, yeah; I thought I would try my luck again."

"What a coincidence! I was just heading there myself," Carolyn responded.

The elevator stopped and the doors opened. Matt stepped aside and made a wide sweep with his right arm. "After you."

Carolyn smiled and stepped out. Without looking behind, she proceeded to the nearest poker table and chose a seat with an empty chair next to it. It was a clear invitation for Matt to join her, but he leaned over and spoke low in her right ear.

"Enjoy your game; I think I'll try my luck at the slots first." Matt didn't wait for a response and made his way to the nearest bank of slot machines. Normally, he avoided the slots altogether; he considered them only for the tourists, but he wanted to keep an eye on the comely blond. The machine he chose had a perfect vantage point to observe her.

Matt dropped almost a hundred dollars of tokens into the machine over the next hour with a payout of just seven dollars. He ordered a Coke from a passing waitress and sipped it as he continued to watch Carolyn play poker. As an experienced gambler, Matt evaluated her style and had to admit she played poker skillfully. She was a bit of a risk taker, but it paid off more than once as he watched. She was certainly no novice, he concluded.

Matt looked at the nearly empty bucket of tokens and decided to move on to poker once the bucket was empty.

The next token dropped and began the spinning of the machine. One, two, three matching figures appeared in front of Matt. It took a moment for him to register that he was about to receive a payout. A light spun at the top of the machine and a bell sounded loudly. A ticket spit out and indicated winnings of five thousand dollars. Matt smiled. *I'm golden this weekend; I can't seem to lose.* With a smug expression, he pocketed the ticket and headed for the poker table.

The individuals surrounding the poker table were all serious players. Each had come to Vegas for a high stakes game and had found it. Matt sat down and was dealt in on the next hand. After a few hands where two men were big winners at Matt's expense, he suspected the men were passing signals to each other. It wasn't the amount of money Matt had lost that bothered him; it was his suspicion the men were working together.

During the next hand, Matt was sure of it. Certain signals preceded specific actions. A raised eyebrow from one of the men was always followed by the other man raising the bid. A wrinkled nose caused the second man to fold. Surely, someone from the casino noticed this.

As tempting as it was to try to win back the money he had lost, Matt realized he was at a distinct disadvantage and decided to leave the table. He tossed a fifty-dollar chip to the dealer, gathered the rest, and headed to the buffet.

Matt scooped up a mound of shrimp, added a dollop of cocktail sauce on the side, and grabbed a salad. He scanned the dining room for an empty table and saw the beautiful Carolyn Hodges. He assumed his most charming smile and approached her table.

"Is this seat taken, Ms. Hodges?"

Carolyn looked up from her salad plate and returned Matt's smile. "Well, if it isn't the elusive Matthew Brooks. Join me, I hate to eat alone," she replied as she indicated the empty chair across from her.

Matt accepted and settled himself as a scantily clad waitress approached to take his drink order. He ordered iced tea and began picking at his salad. To be polite, he made small talk.

"So, where are you from, Carolyn?" Matt asked between bites.

"Louisville, Kentucky – actually, a small town near there. I run our farm."

Great, he thought, a farm girl. He decided the conversation would be about county fairs, pigs, and prize heifers.

What about you, what keeps you busy?"

"I'm a dentist; my practice is just outside Chicago."

"A dentist? Really? I had you pegged for a plastic surgeon or maybe a dermatologist."

Matt laughed. "Nope, just an ordinary, run-of-the mill dentist." He glanced at Carolyn's left hand. "Is that a wedding ring on your pretty little finger?"

It was Carolyn's turn to laugh as she answered. "Yes, but… well, it's complicated." Matt waited for more. "Yes, I am married, but we lead very separate lives these days."

"Well, this may be a bit presumptive of me, but why don't you just divorce the guy? These days, it isn't hard to do." Matt suggested.

Carolyn chuckled, but there was no humor in it. "I'm afraid divorce is out of the question. As I said, it's complicated." Carolyn brought her napkin to her mouth and reached for her water glass.

"Sorry, I didn't mean to pry. It's just that someone as beautiful as you should be loved and appreciated. You deserve happiness." Matt was surprised by his own words, but somehow felt compelled to tell this lovely woman what he felt.

"Wow! You surprise me, Doc. Under that calm exterior lies the heart of a romantic," Carolyn said with humor in her voice. "Okay, your turn. Are you married? "

"I was, but I screwed it up. My wife left me for another man and moved to New York. It's just me now."

"Ooh, that's so sad, Doc. So, you're drowning your sorrows here in Las Vegas by gambling, drinking, and flirting with women," Carolyn surmised.

Matt responded with laughter. "Something like that. It's a

diversion for my humdrum nine-to-five job. I like the excitement of gambling, especially when I win," Matt confessed. Again, he was surprised by his candid comment. He was usually much more reserved, but there was something about this woman; he had never met anyone quite like her.

Carolyn interrupted his musings. "Hey! Where did you go? I asked you why gambling? Why not a safer hobby like fishing or golf?"

Matt considered her question. "Safer, yes, but less invigorating. Gambling makes me feel alive. Tell me, Carolyn, what is it about you that makes me tell you more than I've ever admitted to myself?"

The attractive blonde considered the question. "I don't know; you intrigue me. You have a polished and calm exterior, but under that façade is a man with secrets. What are you hiding, Dr. Brooks?"

Matt bristled. *Boy! She hit the nail on the head. How would she react if she knew he was almost a murderer?* "Wh… what do you mean?" he stuttered.

"Now, Doc, don't get all flustered; I didn't mean anything by it. You just have this, oh I don't know, this aura about you that says, don't get too close. It intrigues me… and, I find you very attractive, Dr. Brooks." Carolyn took a sip of her water as she studied Matt over her glass to gauge his response.

In spite of himself, Matt was flattered. Carolyn was delightful and very nice to look at. She was certainly more than the one-night-stand he expected to find today. Finally, he found words. "Would you like to go for a walk? I'd like to get to know you better."

"I thought you were here to gamble."

"Sometimes plans change. Well? How about that walk?"

"Sure, lead on."

The pair walked along the Vegas Strip to the Bellagio Conservatory and Botanical Gardens. The free attraction boasted beautiful flowers arranged as lions, tigers, and even a reclining woman. The walk calmed Matt's racing thoughts. Since Ron's death, he had experienced horrible nightmares in which Ron came back to life and pointed an accusing finger at him. He hadn't committed murder, but he nearly did, and that tore at his very soul. He had thought coming to Las Vegas would exorcise his demons, but until this moment, he had not found any peace since Ron's death.

Without a thought, he reached for Carolyn's hand, and the two walked together hand-in-hand through the gardens. As if by tacit agreement, they spoke very little as they took in the fragrances and colors of their surroundings. Time lost all meaning and two hours passed before they emerged.

"That was incredible!" exclaimed Carolyn as they walked out into the summer heat of the Strip.

"It was amazing; I agree. That was really nice – not just the flowers, but sharing it with you. Thank you."

"I'd blush if I were twenty years younger," Carolyn answered. "Honestly, though, I enjoyed your company as well."

Matt had never felt so comfortable with a woman. It felt so natural to be together and he wanted to extend this feeling.

"Where shall we go now? I don't want to go back inside; I feel like making an afternoon of it." Matt offered his arm. "Shall we?"

"Carolyn smiled. "Yes, thank you."

***

Matt smiled as he entered his room that night and saw the champagne and appetizers waiting for him. His plans had certainly taken a detour. He and Carolyn had spent all afternoon and evening together. He couldn't remember a day more pleasurable. With Carolyn, he felt more alive, more aware. He chuckled as he surveyed the items in front of him. He had certainly planned for his night to go differently! The meaningless one-night-stand seemed shameful to him now. Carolyn had changed all of that. He munched on the appetizers and contemplated the afternoon he had spent with the gorgeous blonde.

Matt undressed and slipped under the soft sheets. No expense had been spared in outfitting his room, but he paid no attention to the luxury as he drifted off to sleep. His only awareness was Carolyn and how she made him feel.

Chapter Six

Early Sunday morning Matt rang Carolyn's room. On the second ring, the now familiar voice answered.

"Hello?"

"Good morning, sunshine! How about breakfast?"

"That would be lovely, Matt. Give me twenty minutes; I'll meet you in the dining room."

"Perfect! See you then." Matt hung up, feeling buoyed by the prospect of seeing Carolyn again.

Matt finished dressing and walked to the dining room. Carolyn was sitting at a table and motioned him over. "Good morning! Did you sleep well?"

"Better than I've slept in a long time. I guess yesterday tired me out," Matt confessed.

"Then, have a good breakfast, it will revive you," Carolyn offered cheerfully.

The two conversed amiably over their meal and lingered as they sipped coffee. Matt suggested they spend the day together as they had the day before.

"Oh, Matt, I'd love to, but I'm returning home today. I'm so sorry."

Disappointment was written all over Matt's face as he absorbed Carolyn's words. The buoyancy he had felt the day before dissipated like the steam from his coffee.

"Oh, I see. Well, I suppose if you have to..."

"I would rather stay and spend more time with you, but something has come up at home, and I have to deal with it immediately. I hope you understand. Yesterday was wonderful. I enjoyed it very much, but duty calls."

"Duty?"

"I'm afraid so. Do you remember when I told you my relationship with my husband is complicated?"

Matt nodded.

"Well, my husband is older than I and is in ill health. That aside, our marriage turned sour years ago. Ben's obsession with his business came between us as surely as a mistress. He never had time for anything besides one wretched project after another. He didn't have time for his own daughter, my step-daughter. Celia wanted nothing more than her father's approval, but he hardly noticed her. I stayed with him for her sake. She was only ten when I married her dad and I assumed essentially a solo parent role from that time. She's in college now."

"But, what does that have to do with you needing to leave now?" Matt asked.

"I'm only trying to give you the background. My husband's medical condition is very serious. He isn't expected to live more than a few weeks. I suppose you wonder why I'm in Las Vegas considering Ben's health."

"It's not my place to judge; after all, I have only known you for a day. Your private life is none of my business."

"No, I want you to understand. It's important to me that you know my situation."

"Okay, then, I'm listening."

"I came to Vegas to close a deal for Ben. He's a developer

and he needed me to come here to make the final pitch. As I said, Ben is in ill health and could not make the trip, so I came in his place. I've been around him long enough to know what to say and how to say it to convince a seller to take our offer. I'm actually good at it. I don't necessarily enjoy it as Ben would, but I get the job done."

"I see; I had no idea I was in the company of such an accomplished pitch man... er, woman," Matt replied with a smile.

Carolyn laughed, then looked into Matt's eyes as if she were searching for something. Finally, she said, "Another time, Matt Brooks. Now, I need to catch my plane on time."

Matt rose from his seat as Carolyn pushed back from the table. "At least let me escort you to your car."

"That would be nice; thank you"

Two hours later, Matt was back at the poker table. He was up fifty grand for the weekend, but he wanted to win more before heading home.

He tried to concentrate on the cards, but his mind was elsewhere – with Carolyn. He had never met anyone so incredible. She was not only beautiful; she was smart and definitely fun to talk to. He had only intended a one-night stand, but Carolyn wasn't like that; she was special.

After several losing hands, Matt threw a tip to the dealer and admitted to himself that he wouldn't be successful at cards if his mind was elsewhere. As he placed his luggage in the trunk of his rental car, he wondered if he would ever see Carolyn again.

***

Monday morning found Matt back at work with a full day's schedule ahead of him. By eleven o'clock he was feeling a familiar ache in his low back. He stretched and took advantage of a canceled appointment to take a break.

He opened a desk drawer and opened a bottle of Tylenol. As he shook out two tablets, he heard a knock on his door.

"Come in," he said as he reached for his bottle of Evian.

Matt downed the Tylenol as the door opened. He choked on the water as he looked up to see Detective Robertson standing in the doorway.

"Dr. Brooks, have I caught you at a bad time?" The detective asked, barely concealing a smile. He had caught the dentist off-guard which was a great start to an interview.

"Uh, no; not at all. Have a seat, Detective."

Detective Robertson chose one of the two chairs in front of the desk and sat down. He didn't speak right away. He wanted to rattle the dentist a bit more.

Matt regained some of his composure. "What can I do for you, Detective?"

"I have a few more questions about Ron Bennett's death."

"I thought his death was ruled an accident and the investigation was closed," Matt remarked as he swallowed visibly. He was sweating and acting as if he were guilty. *This is ridiculous,* he told himself. *I've done nothing wrong.* Suddenly, he wondered if someone had found out about the plan to murder Ron that he and Sylvia had hatched. Had Sylvia made a careless remark?

"Officially, Dr. Brooks, the investigation is closed, but I wanted to tie up a few loose ends. Ron Bennett visited you on the day he died, correct?"

"Yes,"

"I also know you prescribed the narcotic found in his system post mortem." It was a statement not a question.

"Yes."

"Why did you prescribe the narcotic, Dr. Brooks?"

"As I've already told you, Ron was complaining of back pain and wanted something to manage his pain until he could see his doctor in a few days. I only prescribed ten tablets and I warned him to avoid alcohol use when he took the medicine. I understand that Ron had consumed a large amount of whiskey and several hydrocodone tablets. This was completely against what I advised him to do."

The Detective set aside Matt's statement and asked another question. "Why did you move Mr. Bennett's appointment up? Was there a pressing reason to do this?"

Matt took another sip of water as he thought of how best to answer the detective's question. "Mr. Bennett had requested to be put on our cancellation list, that is if someone canceled, he wanted the slot. We had a cancellation that day and the receptionist called him to see if he wanted the appointment. He said he definitely wanted the appointment and take care of the tooth that had been causing him so much trouble."

"I see, did you visit Ron Bennett that evening, Dr. Brooks?"

"Visit Ron Bennett? At his house? I've never been to his house, Detective, and I certainly wasn't in the habit of dropping in on the man. I barely knew him."

Robertson noted the vehemence with which Dr. Brooks answered, possibly too much for an innocent man. He was more suspicious of the dentist than ever. He could have easily encouraged the drug and alcohol use and pushed the unsuspecting victim, causing him to hit his head. Or, he might have hit him with an object that would leave the same imprint behind as the tub and smeared blood on the edge of the bathtub. If so, he was dealing with a very clever man. It would take a lot more than what he had to prove Ron's murder.

Robertson had a cop's instincts and his inner voice was telling him that Sylvia Bennett and her boss managed to murder Ron using his drug and alcohol habit against him. The dentist was obviously a nervous wreck about something, and he felt it wouldn't take much more pressure to discover what it was.

Robertson stood. "Thank you for your time, Dr. Brooks. Do you have any objection if I ask your staff some questions?"

"I certainly do! This is a professional office, Detective, and we are in the middle of a very busy day. I ask you to respect that and confine your questions to after office hours," Matt responded with a tint of anger.

"Of course. If you will provide a list of your employees and their addresses and phone numbers, I would be much obliged."

Matt opened the middle drawer of his desk and pulled out an officer roster and tossed it across his desk. "Good-bye, Detective."

"Good day, Dr. Brooks," Robertson replied as he reached for the roster. "I'll be in touch."

Once the door closed behind the detective, Matt sat back in his chair, unaware until then how tense he had been. Why did the detective still suspect foul play? Even though he hadn't actually committed murder, he had planned to do it and that constituted conspiracy. It was enough to land him in prison. He rued the day Sylvia had suggested the scheme, and even more, the day he had accepted. He knew his life was changed forever as a result. His reckless behavior had caught up to him and he realized he needed to make some changes.

I'm sure he believes I killed Ron, even though I didn't. Thank goodness I didn't slip up just now and say something stupid. It's over, done; I can't undo it, so let it be.

Matt took another deep breath to compose himself, pasted his professional smile on his face, and left to greet his next patient.

Chapter Seven

Carolyn Bridges sat in her husband's hospital room and stared out the window into the darkness. Three A.M. is a lonely time to be awake, but especially so in a hospital where death was waiting its turn, lurking in the corner and biding its time. Carolyn could feel its smothering presence.

A small noise caused her to turn toward her husband. He had been in and out of consciousness all evening and night. Ben was inching his way to meet death. Carolyn wondered if Ben believed in heaven and hell? Was God so forgiving as to permit Ben entry through the Pearly Gates, or would her husband spend eternity in darkness?

The noise that had caught her attention was repeated. Ben seemed to be coming awake again. Carolyn scooted closer to the bed and reached for Ben's thin, lifeless hand.

"I'm here, Ben; I'm right here," she reassured the still form, unsure if he had heard her.

As if in answer, Ben opened his eyes and turned his head to look at her. He tried to speak, but his voice was weak. He tried again and managed a word or two that Carolyn could not discern.

"What is it, Ben? What do you want to say?" she encouraged.

Ben swallowed weakly and tried to speak again. "Water… please."

Carolyn reached for the plastic cup with a straw sticking through the lid and helped Ben lift up enough to take a sip. He fell back onto his pillows and whispered. "I need to tell you something."

Carolyn leaned in closer to hear what her husband had to say. "Okay, Ben; I'm listening."

Ben coughed. "I want you to know I'm sorry... for everything. I know I haven't been a very good husband or father, but I love you more than you realize. I wasn't good at showing it, I know, and I'm sorry. Tell Celia I love her, and I regret not being there for her. When her mother died, something in me died too. It was hard to look at Celia and not see her mother. So, I turned to my work to take my mind off my grief. Before long, work was all there was in my life. That is, until you came along. You're a good person and you deserve more than I gave you. I loved you, but I simply didn't have anything left to give you or Celia. I'm just grateful that my daughter had you in her life."

Carolyn squeezed Ben's hand in response. "I understand, Ben. It's okay. We've had a good life and I love Celia as if she were my own daughter."

Ben smiled briefly but a long coughing spell brought a nurse to his bedside.

"Mr. Hodges, you need to rest," the nurse admonished.

Ben grunted, "I'll be resting for good before long. I have some things to tell my wife before it's too late."

The nurse nodded, turned to Carolyn and rested a hand on her shoulder briefly. "I'll be close by if you need me."

Once the nurse had closed the door behind her, Ben turned again to Carolyn. "There's something I need to confess to you. Do you remember Charles Blackwell?"

Carolyn nodded. "He was your partner when we were first married."

"That's right. He died about a year later. I'm responsible for his death. I didn't kill him; but I'm responsible all the same."

"Ben, I don't understand."

"Sorry, I know this is hard to understand; it's taken me a long time to sort it all out myself. I tried to ignore my culpability for years, but now I have to face it."

Ben began to cough again and Carolyn offered him water. He took a single sip and fell back exhausted. "I can't hide behind good intentions anymore. I killed Charles just as surely as if I put a knife in his heart. I pushed him hard – too hard – until he had a fatal heart attack. I expected him to keep the same hours and intensity for work that I have always had. I didn't know he had already had one heart attack that did a lot of damage. He died alone in a hotel room after closing a multi-million-dollar deal for us. He died to make the company succeed. We needed that deal. We were about to go under without it. Charles told me he didn't feel well before the trip and asked if I could handle it. I told him I couldn't and the rest is history. I can't ignore it any longer. I'll be facing my maker soon and I need to make peace with Him and you while I can. I've already confessed my many sins to God and now to you."

Silence settled over the room like a shroud. Ben waited; he had said all he had meant to say. The rest was up to the lovely woman at his side.

Finally, Carolyn met Ben's gaze. "Darling, I'm so glad you got that off your conscience and have asked God for forgiveness. As for me, there's nothing to forgive. Somehow, I always understood you couldn't fully embrace our marriage. I was no blushing bride; I pretty much knew what to expect when I married you. As for Charles, he knew what he was doing. He fought as hard for the company as you did. Perhaps you should have gone in his place, but if all it took was that trip to kill him, then another attack was probably inevitable at some point. He was as driven as you. I think you are blaming yourself more than is reasonable."

"Thank you; you have always had such a generous nature. You always look for the good in people and I've been a lucky man. I believe I can die in peace now. I only wish I had taken the measure of my life and apologized to you sooner. I love you; give my love to Celia."

Tears flowed freely down Carolyn's face as she held onto Ben's hand. She could feel life slipping away from him, and an hour later he was gone.

The funeral and business affairs kept Carolyn occupied for several weeks. Celia had come home for the funeral but it was clear she had not forgiven her father for his neglect after her mother's death. Carolyn tried to be supportive of her step-daughter but knew it was something she had to work out for herself and in her own time. Celia had drained Carolyn of her last ounce of strength. The young woman had refused to be by her father's side in the hospital, and his passing had unleashed years of regret and anger. Carolyn had held Celia for hours as she unloaded her pent-up emotions and finally achieved a sense of peace. She had left for college on time for the fall semester, and Carolyn had breathed a sigh of relief. As much as she loved her step-daughter, she knew Celia needed to go back to school and be with the friends she had made there. She planned to come home during Thanksgiving break, which would give her time to work through her feelings for her father.

Carolyn agreed to take a seat temporarily on the Board of Directors for Ben's company but turned down a more active role. She was confident the Board would choose a leader wisely and she was more than glad to sidestep that huge responsibility. The farm was more than enough to occupy her time and energy.

***

As the weeks passed, she became restless and her mind returned to the magical weekend she had spent in the presence of Dr. Matthew Brooks. Her marriage to Ben had taught her that life was short and if happiness came calling, she should embrace it completely. She thought Matt Brooks could make her happy; at least she was willing to give a relationship with him a try. She only hoped he felt the same.

After Celia had been comforted and sent back to college, Carolyn felt the need to step away from the onerous responsibilities left to her by Ben, even if only for a weekend. Matt had occupied her thoughts a lot since her trip to Vegas but she wondered if it would be appropriate to call him. After all, they had only known each other for a couple of days. What if Matt had found someone? Or, perhaps he simply wasn't interested. In either case, she would be embarrassed by the call. On the other hand, the day they had spent together had been magical. She felt she could trust him. A combination of curiosity and a desire to explore the possibility of a more lasting connection finally gave her the courage to call him. Only time would tell what would become of it, and Carolyn wasn't sure herself what she wanted from the relationship.

With trembling fingers, she punched in Matt's number.

Matt was in his office working when his cell phone rang. It had been three months since his last visit to Vegas and the day he had spent with Carolyn.

He absent-mindedly reached for his cell phone when it buzzed. "Hello?"

"Matt, it's Carolyn, Carolyn Hodges."

"Carolyn! How are you?"

"Matt, it's so good to hear your voice. I know we hardly know each other, so I hope you don't think I'm being too forward, but what would you say to a weekend at my farm?"

Carolyn's call caught Matt off guard. He had thought a lot about the lovely blonde since meeting her in Las Vegas. He had kept up with her by text a few times but this would be the first face-to-face since Vegas. He hesitated in response to her question as he knew she was newly widowed, so he didn't want to intrude on her grief. However, her call indicated she was ready to pick up from where they left off in Vegas. Matt was more than happy to do just that. He put aside his hesitation. "I can think of nothing I'd rather do," he replied with enthusiasm.

Chapter Eight

Matt rearranged his work schedule and prepared for the trip. He knew he was fond of this wonderful woman, but he was surprised by how excited he felt to be seeing her again. He finished packing and placed his suitcase by the front door. Carolyn had said to bring casual clothes, but he had packed dress clothes as well, just in case she changed her mind and asked for an evening out.

Matt checked once more to be sure he had locked all the doors and left a note and a check for his cleaning lady. He decided against driving to the airport and had called an Uber driver instead. As he stowed his luggage and slid into the back seat, he tried to capture Carolyn's face from his memory. She was attractive and very fit, for sure, but what really attracted him to her were her eyes and her smile. She listened when he spoke and had a calm demeanor which was contagious. He smiled as he remembered their special day together. Would they be able to recapture that magic both had felt in Vegas?

He arrived at Midway Airport and tipped his driver. The reality of seeing Carolyn again in only a few hours suddenly caused anxiety. He had never felt unsure around a woman until now. This woman mattered to him. The short flight to Louisville would give him time to get a drink to settle his nerves. He couldn't explain why, but he was nervous. His time in Las Vegas with Carolyn had been natural and easy-going which left him wondering why he was so jittery now.

During her phone call, Carolyn told Matt she needed some time away from death, wills, and the legal paperwork that had been part of settling Ben's affairs. She felt a weekend with him would be just what she needed. He hoped the visit would be a repeat of the easy-going day he had spent with her in Vegas, but he was aware that time and circumstances might have changed the relationship. Either way, he was eager to see the woman who had captured many of his waking thoughts.

Carolyn watched from inside the terminal as Matt's plane touched down, right on time. She had to admit to some anxiety mixed with expectation. *What is it about this man that has me so interested?* A few deep and slow breaths steadied her heart rate as she waited for the man she barely knew. After another ten minutes, she saw passengers descend the escalator to the baggage claim area, their agreed-upon meeting place.

Matt was easy to spot as he towered above many of his fellow travelers. He searched for Carolyn as he descended. He flashed a broad smile when his eyes met hers, and his uncertainty vanished as he saw genuine pleasure in her eyes. He had almost turned down the invitation, unsure of his feelings for Carolyn and hers for him, but one look at her and he was glad he had made the trip. It was definitely a relief to spend a weekend not thinking about Ron Bennett.

As Matt approached, Carolyn opened her arms to embrace him. He responded in kind and added a quick kiss to her cheek.

"Do you need to claim any baggage?" Carolyn asked, a bit breathless from the kiss.

"No, I only have my carry-on and backpack."

"Good, then let's get going; we have a bit of a drive to the farm, but I assure you it's worth the trouble."

"I'm looking forward to some down time, especially with you. Lead on."

Carolyn smiled with genuine delight. "I hope you brought jeans and casual shoes," she explained as she noted Matt's expensive loafers.

"Um, yes, I brought jeans and a pair of sneakers."

"Good, you'll need them; I have a lot planned for the weekend."

Matt wondered just what he had agreed to by accepting the invitation. He was no farmhand and had never met a horse or a cow. He hoped he didn't embarrass himself too much with his complete lack of farm skills.

A slate gray Land Rover was waiting at the curb for them with a driver behind the wheel. Matt quickly stowed his luggage and assumed his place beside Carolyn in the backseat.

"Rick was kind enough to drive today; I'm rather impatient with city traffic, and I thought it would be easier for him to stay with the car at the airport. Besides, this gives us time to catch up," Carolyn explained as she turned expectantly to Matt.

Matt held the door for Carolyn before following and settling himself against the soft leather. As he buckled his seatbelt, the driver pulled away from the curb and made his way toward the interstate. Neither spoke for a few minutes. The awkward silence was so different from the easygoing chatter in Las Vegas.

Matt watched out the window as the city retreated behind them and the landscape became more suburban. As the car sped eastward along the interstate, Matt's mind returned to Ron Bennett and his death. It seemed the guilt he carried from almost committing murder had traveled with him.

Carolyn broke the silence, causing Matt to turn abruptly to her.

"I'm sorry; I didn't mean to startle you. I asked how you've been since we met, but you seemed a million miles away. Is everything okay, Matt?"

Matt took in a deep breath and settled his nerves. "Oh, sorry; it's just a work thing, nothing important."

Carolyn considered the response. She wasn't so sure he was being completely honest but decided to let it go. She smiled and reached for his hand. It was a small gesture, but it caused a tingle to go up his spine. He smiled.

"Well, to answer your question about what I've been doing. Actually, my life has been pretty much routine since we met in Las Vegas. My practice is rather busy and consumes much of my time." Matt deliberately depicted his life as normal, even a little dull, as he tried to forget he had almost taken another person's life. This was a chance for a new beginning and he planned to make the most of it. He shifted the conversation from his life to Carolyn's. "I know you have been through a rough time with your husband's death, but how are you doing?"

Carolyn laughed. "I wish I could say my life has been as routine as yours. My world has been completely turned upside down since Ben died. Accountants, lawyers, and assuming a place as a member of the Board have consumed much of my time. Ben's business dealings were extensive. I need this time away from it all to clear my head and wind down a bit."

Matt warmed to the mood. "Well then, I'll do my best to help you do just that."

Carolyn smiled in response and the two chatted amiably for the next half hour. Both visibly relaxed and settled into the same comfortable friendship they had forged in Las Vegas. By the time they reached the farm, they were laughing and enjoying each other's company.

The SUV paused at an elaborate entrance gate. The driver pressed a button over the rearview mirror and the gates opened before them. *Some farm,* thought Matt as he caught a glimpse of the massive stone house along the drive.

"I thought you said this was a farm."

Carolyn chuckled. "I assure you it is a working farm. We have over two hundred acres and raise about one hundred head of cattle, a dozen horses – mostly for riding – and a few goats and chickens. The farm is managed by Carl Richter, a friend as well as an employee. He has worked for Ben for more than twenty years. He manages a full staff of farmhands."

Matt was clearly blown away by the wealth represented all around him. The lawn and hedges were impeccably groomed and the flower beds displayed beautiful blooms free of weeds. He sensed Carolyn was waiting for a reply.

"Well, this is certainly impressive. When you said we were going to a farm I pictured something much ah… shall we say… smaller?"

Carolyn laughed. "I had pretty much the same impression when I first came here, but I think you will find this a great retreat from the city. I hope you can unwind a bit while you are here."

Before Matt could reply, the car pulled up to the entrance of the grand home. An older man approached and opened Carolyn's door.

"Welcome home, Mrs. Hodges; everything is ready for your friend's visit."

"Thanks, Carl. Matt, this is our farm manager Carl Richter.

Carl, this is Dr. Matt Brooks."

"Pleased to meet you Dr. Brooks. I hope you enjoy your stay." Carl tipped his Cubs ball cap and excused himself. "I'll be in the barn, ma'am, if you need me."

"Thanks, Carl; I'll come by after dinner so we can discuss our prospects for the fall sale at Keeneland. I'm hoping Honey's colt will bring a good price."

"I'm sure he will, ma'am, he's a special one, for sure."

"Okay, see you later then."

Matt turned to retrieve his luggage but found it had already been removed from the car's trunk and taken inside. Rick started the Land Rover's engine and headed for the garage. Matt followed Carolyn into the house and involuntarily let out a soft whistle once inside. "I've never seen a farmhouse like this."

"I know; it's a bit much, but I have come to love this place. It is so peaceful here – no smog, no noise, no fussy people."

Matt smiled. He understood. The farm represented a retreat for Carolyn, a place to just be herself. Matt could see how happy she was here.

"Well, it suits you, and I appreciate the invitation to share this with you for a few days. As you suggested, I set aside work for a couple of days so I don't have to leave until Tuesday afternoon."

"Good, I was hoping you could stay a bit longer. You deserve a break. Now, let me show you to your room so you can freshen up, then meet me in the sunroom once you get settled. It's at the end of this hallway, through the double doors. Dinner is just the two of us, so no need to dress for dinner. We keep it pretty casual around here."

Matt followed Carolyn up the stairs to his room and found

his luggage already there. He had no idea who had removed it from the car and brought it to his room – another of the staff he assumed.

His room was large and looked out over the fields in the back of the home. From the double window he could see pastures stretching out beyond where his eyes could see. Three mares grazed on the lush pasture grass while their foals raced each other around the verdant field.

Matt undressed and turned on the shower. The warm water helped to relax him somewhat, but he couldn't shake the feeling he was out of his league. He couldn't believe the wealth all around him. As the son of a wealthy man, he was accustomed to nice things. He practically grew up at the country club of his hometown, and he had always driven an expensive car, but this was steps above what he had known. This was the kind of money that made things happen – business acquisions, political candidate influence, and much more. It made Matt a bit uncomfortable.

The shower did little to relieve Matt's unease. He dressed quickly and checked his appearance in the bathroom mirror. Satisfied with his image, he only wished he felt as confident as he looked. What was it about this woman that made him feel as if he needed to impress her? It wasn't just the obvious wealth, although that was definitely a factor. He had felt so at ease with her on neutral territory in Vegas, so why was he so uneasy now?

Matt headed downstairs to the sunroom at the back of the house. It faced east so there was only muted ambient light coming through as the sun began to set. Carolyn was standing at a window with her back to Matt as he approached. He noted with pleasure her slim figure and athletic muscle tone. A memory of walking together in Las Vegas came to mind, and he recalled how comfortable it was to be with her. That feeling, that was why he had come. She made him feel good in his own skin. He didn't have to be anyone or anything else, just Matt Brooks. So many women he dated wanted only the playboy with all the money, but Carolyn seemed to want the same thing he wanted – an honest connection with another human being with no strings attached. The memory settled his thoughts and he walked into the sunroom as Carolyn turned around.

"Hey there! Come sit down here by the window. I asked for dinner to be brought in here if that's okay with you."

"Sure, whatever you want is fine with me," Matt responded with a broad smile.

Carolyn turned back to view the rolling pastures that seemed to stretch to the horizon. "I love this time of day especially here in the sunroom. The pastures are bathed in the last rays of sunlight and the world seems perfect, at least for a little while." Matt joined her and understood what she was trying to say. The farm obviously provided a sense of well-being and comfort to her.

Carolyn turned to him, and for several moments they stood face-to-face, simply meeting the other's gaze. Each was searching for something, a recognition or a validation of the instant connection they had experienced in Vegas.

Matt reached for her hands and spoke first, while still meeting her gaze. "Carolyn, I must say I was surprised, but definitely pleased when you called. I've thought of you a lot since we first met. You made quite an impression on me."

Carolyn smiled. "I have to admit I felt the same. I wanted to spend more time with you to see if our brief time together was

73

real or simply two people away from home finding companionship with the first person who seemed interested."

Matt suppressed a grin. "I wondered the same, but soon realized that the weekend we met was the first time in a long time that I felt as if I could relax. It was so easy to talk to you. but I was afraid I had bored you to death."

Carolyn considered Matt's response and smiled. "Then, we are of like mind. I felt comfortable with you too, no that's wrong. I felt safe with you. Yes, that's it."

"Safe?"

"Yes, but not in the sense of physical safety, although I'm sure your commanding physical presence would deter any would-be assailants. No, I felt emotionally safe, connected in a way as if we had known each other for a long time. Does that sound silly to you?"

"Not at all; I felt the same. It's not a bad way to begin a friendship."

The conversation was interrupted by the appearance of a uniformed female. "Ma'am, cook says dinner is ready. Would you like it brought here?"

"Yes, Sadie, thank you."

Carolyn reached for Matt's hand and led him to a small table in a corner of the room where service for two had been laid. "I play bridge here with friends; having dinner with you is a definite improvement."

Matt chuckled, "I'm glad I could help." He pulled out a chair for his hostess and claimed the one across from her. He searched for something to say but could think of nothing. Carolyn saved him.

"So, Dr. Brooks, you said on the way here that your life has been mostly boring routine since we parted, is there nothing exciting in your life?"

The innocent question sent a shiver down Matt's spine. The memory of what he had almost done would make interesting small talk. No, he couldn't confide any of this to Carolyn; she would run the other direction and slam the door on their friendship. So, his response was generic. "Oh, the usual exciting stuff, root canals, fillings, and plaque removal."

Carolyn laughed. "Really? That exciting? Then I guess you really do need a weekend in the country so you can relieve all that stress!"

Matt joined in the laughter. "Yes, my life is pretty dull."

"Ah, that may be the case during the day, but I think I saw a more interesting Matt Brooks in Vegas, and I'd like to get to know that man a little better."

She was flirting with him, but Matt didn't care. He wanted to get to know her better too, a lot better.

Dinner was an excellent Mediterranean-style sole fillet with asparagus and glazed baby carrots. Matt ate heartily, grateful for a change from his usual takeout meal.

When the last of his dessert was gone, Carolyn smiled and said, "It seems you enjoyed your meal; I'm glad. Mary is an excellent cook and likes to show off her skills for company."

Matt sheepishly responded. "It was delicious. I hope I didn't make a pig of myself; but I don't get food like this on a regular basis. My compliments to Mary."

"She will be thrilled you liked it. Now, change into sneakers and let's go for a walk."

"Yes, ma'am! That is the perfect way to work off that dessert."

Matt hurried off to comply with Carolyn's instructions and rejoined her in the front hall. Even in an old shirt and farm boots she was beautiful and he told her so.

"Ah, you're the vision of loveliness," he said with practiced finesse.

"You charmer, you! I bet you use that line on all the women in your life."

"Well, actually, I haven't been out with anyone since our weekend in Vegas. I've been busy and, well... *am I moving too fast? He thought. Oh, heck, nothing ventured, nothing gained. ...* and, I just couldn't get you out of my mind. I knew you were married and you said things were complicated between you and your husband, but I still couldn't forget about how wonderful our time together had been." Matt wondered if Carolyn would be put off by his declaration but there was something about her that seemed to encourage his honesty.

"I see," was her only response, but he noted the smile tugging at the corners of her mouth. She looked away and hesitated a few moments before changing the subject. "I know it's dark outside but I want to show you something, then we can have a quiet evening back here."

"Okay, lead on." Matt responded with a smile.

Matt followed his hostess out a side door. Carolyn lit their way with a flashlight as they followed a cobblestone path to the closest barn, one of three large structures that he had noticed earlier. The lights were on inside the barn, and Carl Richter was visible in one of the horse stalls.

"Carl, I've brought Matt to see our newest arrival. How's she doing?"

The weathered farm manager straightened up a bit stiffly and greeted the pair. "Evening folks, well, she's still in pretty rough shape, but she's going to make it. Doc was out earlier today and changed her bandages. The infection is almost cleared up, and she's starting to eat a bit."

"That's wonderful, Carl; thank you for taking such good care of her. She will make a fine therapy horse for the children."

Matt looked quizzical so Carolyn quickly explained. "This little filly got caught up in some barbed wire. She is a nurse mare's offspring. A nurse mare is a substitute mother for a thoroughbred foal so its mother can be bred again. Her foal is taken from her and fed by a nurse mare. Of course, for the nurse mare to be available to nurse the thoroughbred's foal she must have given birth herself. Her foal is either sold for food or is adopted by a rescue organization. I'm one of the rescue sponsors. This particular little girl managed to get herself injured badly when she was separated from her mother. She panicked and ran headlong into a barbed wire fence. Her injuries were life threatening and she nearly died. The owner wanted to put her down, but Carl convinced the owner to give her to our program. It was touch and go for a while, but Carl has worked wonders with her."

"Nurse mares' babies are just thrown away?" Matt asked incredulously.

"Sadly, yes. It's a sad practice in the horse industry. Not all thoroughbred foals are taken from their mothers and given to nurse mares, but it is common practice. Racing is a huge and expensive industry and horses are a commodity. Changes are occurring in the industry, but slowly. After a horse is retired from racing, if he or she is not used for breeding, then the slaughter house is often the next destination."

Matt looked down at the beautiful chestnut foal with four white stockings and a blaze running down her nose. The dentist had never been this close to a horse before, but he felt protective of the tiny creature resting on the straw. "May I enter the stall?"

Carl answered, "Of course, just move slowly; she's had some rough treatment."

Matt was mesmerized by the tiny form as he knelt beside her. In almost a whisper he reassured her. "Hi girl, don't be afraid."

The foal watched him carefully but didn't stir. Matt reached out and stroked her gently on her neck. When he drew his hand away, the foal nudged his hand, clearly wanting more of his tender touch.

Carolyn watched with pleasure. Underneath the polished city boy image was a softie at heart. "She likes you. Are you sure you've never met a horse before? You're a natural."

Matt looked up sheepishly, suddenly aware of Carl and Carolyn watching him. "She's beautiful, and so helpless. I can't believe someone would just toss her to the slaughter house."

"Now you know why I'm part of the rescue network. We take as many as we can and sell or donate them to good homes. She is destined for an equine therapy program for special needs kids. Some have physical handicaps and others are emotionally traumatized. The horses help the children with their balance and help bring them out of their shell. Some need to learn to trust again and the teens learn responsibility as they care for their horse. Most of the kids come from very difficult home situations. For some, the counselors have to overcome behavioral issues. The kids have built up a wall around them and react with hostility whenever anyone tries to get close to them. It's a defense mechanism. The horses accept the children just the way they are and can get through the tough exterior in a way the counselors can't. It's amazing to see the transformation."

"Wow, I had no idea. I guess I've spent too much time in my own little world; I need to look around me a bit more."

Carl grunted but didn't comment and Carolyn hid a smile. "Let's head back to the house; we can visit again tomorrow. Thanks, Carl."

Matt was quiet as the pair made their way back to the stunning stone structure. Carolyn wondered what he was thinking, but she didn't intrude on his thoughts. Instead, she reached for his hand and walked on in silence.

Chapter Nine

Once Matt and Carolyn reached the side porch, they removed their shoes. Carolyn put her hand on Matt's shoulder for balance as she tugged at her right boot. Matt instinctively reached to steady her. It was a small gesture, but he realized they were becoming more comfortable with each other. He had dated his share of women, though very few since the divorce, but none of them had made him feel so at ease. This was different. The thought both terrified and thrilled him at the same time. His marriage had been a disaster from day one. He had known from the beginning of their relationship that his ex-wife was only interested in his money, not him. When the money got tight, she packed her bags and called a lawyer. The experience had left Matt unsure of himself where women were concerned, which led to his increased gambling. So why was he here with this woman? What was so different about her?

His musings were interrupted by Carolyn. "Matt, I asked if you want a drink?

"Uh, sure, sorry; I was thinking about something."

"I'll say; you were a million miles away. What has you so preoccupied?"

Matt considered a glib response but realized Carolyn deserved more. "Actually, I was thinking about my ex-wife."

Carolyn laughed as she entered the house ahead of Matt.

"Now, that is not very flattering. What made you think of her now?"

Matt followed his hostess into the hall. He reached out and held her right hand. Carolyn stopped and turned to look at him. She saw pain in his eyes. She kept silent and waited for Matt to explain.

"I was thinking about how I got here, now, with you, and how different this feels than how I usually feel around a woman." He searched her face for her response and wondered if he had said too much.

Carolyn reached up with her free hand and gently stroked Matt's face. "I don't know what caused the pain I see in you, but I'd like a chance to make that a little better," she assured as she continued to meet his gaze.

Matt let go of her hand and put his arms around her. "May I kiss you?"

Carolyn merely nodded and lost herself in the next few moments. When Matt slowly pulled away, she smiled and said, "Good, now that our first kiss is out of the way, we can relax around each other."

Matt smiled in return. "So, what's on the agenda for the rest of the evening?"

"Well, I thought we could sit by the fire and get to know each other a little better. After all, we know so little."

Matt agreed and followed Carolyn to the spacious living room. A fire had been started and was giving off a nice warmth to chase away the September chill.

"This is nice."

"I'm glad you approve. What would you like to drink?"

"Just club soda; The wine we had with dinner was enough

for me."

Carolyn brought Matt's club soda and a glass of water for herself and settled on the sofa next to Matt. "So, Dr. Brooks, what makes you tick?" Carolyn sat back against the sofa, turned toward her guest, and tucked one leg under her as she waited for the answer. She had not been able to get Matt out of her mind since the first day they met in Vegas. Now, she wanted to know more about this man who had claimed so many of her thoughts.

Matt's first reaction was to give a pat answer – name, rank, and serial number, or the civilian equivalent, but felt Carolyn deserved a more honest answer from him. He put down his drink, turned to her and immediately felt safe. He had never felt that way before with anyone, especially a beautiful woman.

"Well, uh, you know the basics. I'm a dentist, divorced, no children, and I like to gamble too much. I run for exercise and I like dogs..."

Carolyn studied him as he talked. There was no question as to his good looks; he had the appearance and physique of a male model, and he was obviously well educated and cultured. Yes, on the surface he was a real catch, but it was the inner man she was interested in. She had spent years with a man who had nothing left of himself to give her; she wasn't going to make that mistake again.

Matt finished talking and reached for his glass. He took a sip and placed it back on the table. "So, Mrs. Hodges, I've told you all about me; do I pass your inspection?"

Carolyn laughed. "Inspection? I hope I didn't make it sound like that. I only want to get to know you better, that's all. Do you like to play cards or games? We could pass the time with a game of gin rummy."

"Sure, but I warn you, Carolyn Hodges, I'm a great card player."

"Having watched you in action in Vegas I can believe it. You're on, buster!"

The rest of the visit was spent amiably. Matt learned to ride a horse and how to care for his mount when they returned to the stable. He was surprised to discover that he liked country living. Raised in an urban area, he had no foundation for the rural lifestyle and was looking forward to future visits.

They parted at midday on Tuesday, both satisfied the weekend had been a success. Carolyn drove him to the airport and stood waving until she could no longer see him as he made his way through security. A good foundation had been laid upon which a lasting relationship could develop. Both wondered if it would.

***

Wednesday morning found Matt sitting at his desk and daydreaming about Carolyn and the time they had spent together at her farm.

A gentle knock on the door brought him back to the present. "Yes? Come in."

Sylvia slipped through the door and closed it behind her. "Dr. Brooks, may I speak with you?"

"Of course, Sylvia. Have a seat. What can I do for you?"

The diminutive blonde pulled out a chair and sat down. Her gaze was directed at her lap where she was folding and unfolding her hands.

"Sylvia, what's wrong? You seem upset about something."

"I need to give my notice, Dr Brooks. I appreciate everything you've done for me, but I need to move away from here. Every time I walk into the bathroom, I see Ron lying dead on the floor. I can't stand it anymore; I'm not sleeping, and I've lost weight. With the proceeds from the sale of the dealership and the insurance money I don't need to work anymore, but I have found a part-time position near my folks. I don't think I could stay at home all the time; I would just sit around and think about what we did and it would drive me crazy."

Matt interrupted. "Sylvia, please believe me; I did *not* kill your husband. I know what we agreed to, but I couldn't go through with it."

"I know that's what you've told me, but don't you think it very convenient he died on the very day we planned that he should die?" Sylvia's voice had become sharper and louder.

"Sylvia, for goodness sake, please keep your voice down! Yes, it was, and I wouldn't give odds on that coincidence ever happening again, but it's the truth; I didn't kill Ron."

For the first time, Sylvia seriously considered the possibility. "I suppose it could have been an accident. Are you sure you didn't give him something that contributed to his death?"

"Well, of course I did. I prescribed the hydrocodone, but I had no idea he would take the narcotics and down half a bottle of bourbon. He did that on his own. Ron is responsible for his own death."

"I'd like to believe that; I have felt such guilt since he died."

Matt rose and walked around his desk and sat down facing Sylvia, who was crying.

"Sylvia, look at me." He gently raised her chin so her eyes could meet his. He spoke in a gentle tone. "Forget about our agreement; I didn't go through with it. Your husband's death wasn't my fault or yours. Let go of the guilt; you have no reason to feel guilty."

Sylvia pulled a tissue from her pocket and dabbed at her eyes. "I want to believe you. I regret the day I came in and asked you to kill Ron. I had no idea I would feel this way; I thought I would be relieved that he can no longer hurt the kids or me, and I am, but the terrible guilt is there all the same."

Matt patted Sylvia's hand then stood. "I think it will help you to move away. I'm sorry to see you leave, but I certainly understand your need to start over. When will you leave?"

"In two weeks, if that's okay with you. It will take that long to pack up and arrange movers. I'm meeting with a realtor this evening to put the house up for sale."

Matt nodded and let out a breath. "I wish you and your children the very best. I hope you finally make peace with yourself. You're a very good person. You don't deserve to let Ron take away your sense of worth and your joy. You didn't deserve what he did to you and you don't deserve to let him make you feel guilty from the grave."

Sylvia took a deep breath, sat up straighter, and wiped away the last tear. "You're right, Dr. Brooks. I'm letting Ron control me now as much as he did when he was alive. I choose to believe that you didn't kill my husband. He did drink a lot, especially whenever I visited my parents. I always found the empty bottles when I returned. I guess the combination of the liquor and the hydrocodone was too much this time. The autopsy did reveal he had suffered a heart attack at some point since his physical last year."

"That could definitely be a contributing factor. Now, why

don't you take the rest of the day off? Go shopping, or maybe see a movie."

"Thanks, but we're busy today. We rescheduled your patients so you could take the long weekend and several of them are booked for today."

"As you wish," Matt responded. "Are you okay now to work? Our first patient is due any minute."

"Of course; thanks for taking time to talk with me. It helped."

Matt nodded and smiled but didn't comment as Sylvia rose and left his office. Sylvia's doubt about his innocence disturbed him. What if she slipped up and expressed this to someone? He hoped that moving away from the house where Ron died would help her find peace – for both their sakes.

Chapter Ten

Sylvia stood in her late husband's home office and sighed. It was the last room to be packed up. Everything related to Ron's car dealership had already been passed along to the new owner of the business, but there was much more that needed to be packed or thrown away. The task seemed overwhelming, made more so by Sylvia's lingering guilty feelings. The talk with Dr. Brooks had helped, but she still had moments of sheer panic. She imagined the knock on the door that would mean the end of her freedom. She knew the police had suspected foul play; they had said as much, but they finally had to close the case for lack of evidence.

The phone rang and pulled her back to the present. The caller was Ron's sister. "Sylvia, it's Rachel; how's the packing going?"

"I'm finished except for Ron's office. I don't know what to do with everything."

"I'm sure it's very difficult for you. I'm available this afternoon to help if that would work for you."

"You've done so much already, but I could use some help deciding what to do with Ron's things. It's overwhelming."

"I'm sure it is. I'll come around 12:30 and bring lunch for us, okay?"

"That sounds wonderful, thank you!"

"You are very welcome. Would salads from Artie's Cafe work for you?"

"Perfect; you're so thoughtful, Rachel."

Sylvia hung up the phone and began pulling books off the shelves. Most of what was left, she would either donate or toss, but there were some nice volumes she wanted to keep. She had filled two boxes when Rachel arrived with lunch.

"You're a lifesaver; I'm really hungry."

"No problem. Are the kids at your sister's?"

"Yes, thank goodness! I can get a lot more accomplished without them underfoot."

Rachel laughed. "I'm sure. I love those little monkeys, but they are a handful together. I never knew youngsters had so much energy and resourcefulness. It was hard to keep up with them when they stayed with me last week, much less stay a step ahead!"

"That sounds like my little angels," Sylvia replied, causing both women to laugh. Sylvia and Rachel had always gotten along well. Rachel was the one person in Ron's family who had understood his temper and the extent of his cruelty. She missed her brother, but she didn't blame anyone but him for his death. No, she would not turn her back on Sylvia and the children even though her parents had.

The two women finished their salads and resumed sorting through the books. Rachel picked up Ron's high school yearbook and thumbed through the pages. She turned to Sylvia.

"Would you mind if I took this? It reminds me of happier times before my brother became such a brute." She looked up, and Sylvia saw the unshed tears in her sister-in-law's eyes.

"Sure, no problem. I'm glad you have some happy memories of Ron." She reached out and placed her hand on Rachel's shoulder. "I'm sorry, Rachel; I know you miss him."

Rachel wiped her eyes on her sleeve. "I'm okay; I'm angry with him for being such an idiot, but I miss him too. Does that sound crazy?"

"Not at all. I miss him, at least the man he was before alcohol stole him away from me and he became so mean. If he hadn't died, I would've had to leave him for the sake of my children's welfare."

"I know he hit you; did he hurt the children too?"

Sylvia looked away and placed more books in a box. She nodded. "Yes, during the last month of his life he was pretty rough with them. They were terrified to be around him."

"I'm sorry, Sylvia; no one in the family knew. I guess Mom and Dad only wanted to acknowledge the old Ron. They really had blinders on when it came to his faults. He was their only son and they were very proud of his accomplishments, from college football to owning his own business."

"I understand, Rachel, and I don't want to destroy the image they have of him. Once I move away, I hope they can accept Ron's death and begin to heal. I'm sorry they blame me for Ron's problems and death, but he did this to himself, and I need to think of my children's future now."

"Absolutely; I believe they'll come around in time," Rachel offered.

A few moments passed as both women continued packing small items from the office. Rachel filled a box and turned to Sylvia, "Okay, what's next?"

Sylvia looked around the room and made a mental note of the furniture she could use in the new house and which pieces needed to be given away or sold. Her eyes settled on the heavy oak desk.

"Rachel, what about Ron's desk? Do you think your parents would want it? I'll have no room for it once I move."

"I don't know about them, but I might be able to use it. It might be too big, though. If it is, I'll just send it to a local auction house.

"Of course; I'm glad you're taking it. I'll get it cleaned out tomorrow."

"Thank you; I'll arrange for movers to come get it the day after tomorrow. Will that work for you?"

"Absolutely! Is there anything else you want?"

Rachel surveyed the room. "No, the desk is all I want."

So it was that Rachel got the desk, and that was the beginning of all the trouble.

Chapter Eleven

Matt's dental practice was busier than ever. Patients of the charismatic and handsome dentist clamored for his special touch to improve their smile. Matt was amazed by how many people wanted the high-end cosmetic procedures he had to offer. Implants, veneers, and crowns were all in demand. The orthodontist who occupied the office next door worked closely with Matt to coordinate services for those who had the money to get the smile of their dreams. The result of all this was a considerable increase in income for Matt. His debts were getting paid down and would be paid off in the next few months.

Another reason for the improved financial picture was the lack of gambling. Matt had not been to Vegas for two months and he had even given up online gambling. He knew the difference in him was Carolyn. He called or Skyped her each evening and visited her at her farm as often as possible. No doubt about it, Matt was in love. The subject of marriage had not come up, but both knew it would at some point. For now, they were content with their present arrangement. Marriage would mean a large sacrifice for one of them. Either Matt would give up his practice and move to Kentucky or Carolyn would move to Illinois and give up her quiet life on the farm. It wasn't something that was discussed, but the issue stood between them like a door that neither of them was ready to step through. For now, though, Matt was on top of the world; the future would take care of itself.

He was on his way home from work one evening, enjoying the palette of colors offered by the sunset, when his cell phone rang. It was Sylvia.

"Matt, there's a problem; we need to talk."

"Problem? What problem?"

"Where are you? Nobody can hear what I'm about to say."

"I'm in the car, but what is the emergency? Why are you so upset?"

"You might want to pull over before I tell you this."

"For Pete's sake, Sylvia, what is it?" Matt demanded as he pulled his Mercedes into a parking lot and killed the engine. He switched the Bluetooth off and picked up his phone. "Okay, the car is parked and I turned off Bluetooth, now what is so important?"

"The desk, Matt; it's in the desk!"

"What's in the desk? You aren't making sense."

"The confession contract, Matt, the one you gave me, remember?"

Matt paled as he realized what Sylvia was saying. "I thought we agreed the contracts would be destroyed."

"I meant to; I really did. I looked for it and couldn't remember where I put it. I figured I'd find it when I packed up the house. It wasn't until a few weeks after the move that I remembered where I put it. It's in the desk that was in Ron's home office."

"Okay, just get it out and destroy it."

"That's just it, I can't. I don't have the desk anymore."

Matt's heart raced as he began to comprehend what Sylvia was trying to tell him. "Well, where is it?"

"Ron's sister Rachel took the desk, but she didn't want it after all, so she sent it to auction. It could be anywhere now."

Matt could hear the panic in Sylvia's voice and he fought to control his. This was bad, very bad. His mind raced as he considered the consequences if and when the contract was found. He would be on trial for a murder he didn't commit but had confessed to committing. What a mess!

"Okay, Sylvia, listen to me! Where did you put the contract exactly? Wouldn't Rachel have found it before she sent it to auction?"

"I don't think so. I put it in a drawer that isn't visible until a lever underneath is pressed."

"A secret drawer?"

"Yes, a secret drawer. I thought the contract would be safe in there. After Ron died and the police started asking questions, I was in a bad place and couldn't think straight. There was the funeral to arrange and a thousand details to manage. I almost shut down completely. I couldn't put one foot in front of the other, much less remember where I had put that contract. Rachel helped me get through it. She has always been supportive of me and critical of her brother's behavior. Apparently, she was on the receiving end of his bad temper as a child. If she had found the contract, she would have told me."

The other end of the call was quiet. "Matt? Matt, are you still there?"

"Yes, I'm here. I'm thinking. Do you know where Rachel sent the desk for auction?"

"I've no idea. I just spoke with her but didn't want to say too much. I suddenly realized this morning where I put the contract. I was going through some business papers that I had removed from the desk before Rachel took it and it triggered my memory. I called Rachel immediately and asked about the desk. That's when she told me she had sent it to auction. What should we do?"

Matt exhaled slowly. He had exchanged the contracts with Sylvia to ensure neither could lay blame on the other. It had seemed like a good idea at the time, when he had intended to actually kill Ron Bennett. After Ron's self-induced death, Matt had held onto Sylvia's confession until the police closed the investigation. Afterward, he and Sylvia had agreed to destroy each other's contract. What a fool he'd been! He should have insisted they return each other's confessions, but it was too late now for 'should haves'.

"Okay, let's think for a minute. We need to find out what auction house Rachel used. Call her and ask for the name of the company. Tell her a friend wants to sell some pieces and needs the name of a reputable business."

"I can do that." Sylvia replied with a high-pitched voice, still shaken from the situation.

"Sylvia, you need to calm down. Don't call her until you have yourself under control."

"I'm sorry; this is just terrible. It's all my fault."

"No, it's not. The contracts were my idea and I should have asked for mine back from you." Matt ran his fingers through his hair, which gave him a slightly mad appearance.

Sylvia hesitated to ask the next question, but she needed to know. "What did you do with my contract?" She asked in a tremulous voice.

"I shredded it; there's no need to worry," he assured her.

The relief Sylvia felt was immense, but did nothing to mitigate her terror of having the entire scheme to kill Ron uncovered. Tears streamed down her face. "Thank you."

"I need to tell you one more time, I did not kill your husband. I planned to do so, but chickened out at the last minute. I just couldn't do it; I couldn't take another person's life. When Ron left, he was as healthy as when he walked into my office."

"Then why did you prescribe the pain medication?"

"I told you; he asked me for it to deal with his back pain. I only prescribed ten tablets, no more. I had no idea he had a history of opioid abuse, or I wouldn't have given him the prescription." Matt began to drum his fingers, a habit of his when he was deep in thought.

"I think I finally believe you. When you refused half of the insurance settlement, I thought you were being generous, making sure the kids and I had more to live on, but now I see it was more than that. You really didn't kill him, did you?"

"No, I didn't. I was prepared to do it, but I simply couldn't take another person's life. It's really quite ironic."

"What?"

"Don't you see? I really didn't kill Ron, but somewhere, someone has my confession stating that I did. It's enough to convict me of premeditated murder and send me to the gas chamber."

"But there was an autopsy that concluded his death was due to his fall, most likely caused by a large consumption of alcohol and a narcotic."

"Yes, but the written confession will reopen the case, for sure. At the very least, I'll be charged with conspiracy to commit murder. It could mean jail time and the end of my career. If only Ron had not been cremated, his body could be exhumed and further tests would confirm the original autopsy conclusions.

"Matt, I'm so very sorry. I'll call my sister-in-law right away and try to track down the desk."

Matt nodded into his phone. "Yes, we have to find that desk!"

Chapter Twelve

Matt resumed his daily routine at his dental practice but a week later the search for the missing desk and the wretched confession hidden within had not yielded any results. Sylvia had obtained the name of the auction house, but the desk was sold for cash, and the buyer only gave his name as A. Smith and provided no address. Each day that passed only served to increase his anxiety. His behavior became surly and short tempered at work.

After a day of fitting in two emergencies in addition to his regularly scheduled patients, he removed his lab coat, donned his expensive Italian sport coat and headed for his car. He waved to the parking garage attendant as he passed his booth and was only steps away from his car when he was approached by a police detective he recognized. *Detective Robertson, what does he want?* A bead of sweat formed on his brow and another trickled down his back.

The detective addressed Matt. "Excuse me Dr. Brooks, do you have a few minutes?"

Matt swallowed hard and worried that the confession had been found. *Stay cool, Matt,* he said to himself. He took a deep breath and struggled to regain his composure. Finally, he met the detective's eyes. "Of course."

"Where's your car? We can speak there." It wasn't a choice.

Matt led the way to his Mercedes and the electronic door

locks opened as he approached with his smart key. He slid behind the wheel and the detective got in on the passenger side. Matt waited for the detective to speak but didn't have to wait long. He came straight to the point.

"Dr. Brooks, we've had an allegation from an interested party that you may have contributed to the death of Ron Bennett." He let the statement resonate in the dentist's mind. The astute detective had already picked up on his subject's discomfort and knew the silence would further increase anxiety. It was a common interrogation tactic and one he had found to be quite useful.

Matt felt his heart pounding in his chest and wondered if the detective could hear it beating. He frantically searched his memory for who the 'interested party' could be, but he came up blank.

"Detective, I assure you I had nothing to do with Ron Bennett's death. We have been all through this before, why are you asking about this again?"

"Dr. Brooks, I'm sure you know we have to follow up on all leads, especially when murder is a possibility."

"Murder? Are you crazy? I didn't murder anyone and the sooner you understand that, the better off we'll all be. Just who is this so-called interested party?"

"Now, you know we can't reveal our sources. What can you tell me about Ron Bennett's dental visit on the day he died?"

"As I have said before," Matt emphasized his words and spoke slowly. "I placed a temporary crown on a jaw tooth."

"Didn't you also prescribe a narcotic even though that is not your usual practice for this procedure?"

"Y-yes, I did, but it wasn't for the dental work. He asked for pain medicine for his back and I wrote a prescription for ten tablets of hydrocodone at five milligram strength. That is the lowest dose."

"Why did you do that? You aren't licensed to treat back pain, are you?"

"No, but I do have a license to prescribe narcotics. It was a stop gap measure to get him through the weekend until he could see his primary care physician on Monday. I saw him on a Friday, as I'm sure you're aware."

"Do you think that was wise?"

"I won't attempt to second guess my decision now. What's the point? It won't change anything. I did nothing wrong. Ron Bennett left my office in perfect health." Matt had regained his composure and was now on full offense.

The detective regarded the man next to him. Was he a cold-blooded murderer or innocent and simply caught up in this investigation? Still, there was the coincidence of Ron's death on the very day of a dental appointment at the place of his wife's job. He sensed Dr. Brooks was hiding something, and he planned to find out what it was. The dental assistant who had been present for Ron Bennett's treatment had sensed something was wrong when she was dismissed to make a phone call for her employer. What had Dr. Brooks done during her absence? Detective Robertson intended to find out.

The detective asked a few more questions, but Matt vehemently denied any part in the car dealership owner's death. Robertson didn't intend to take the denials as gospel, however. Ron had been a friend to the police and the men in blue wanted to see justice done if murder had been committed.

After thirty minutes of questions that did nothing to advance the investigation, the detective decided he would get nothing of use from the dentist, at least not today. He reached for the door handle.

"Dr. Brooks, I'll be in touch. If there is anything else you want to add to your story, call me. You know where to find me."

Matt didn't reply or even acknowledge the statement. His fear had given way to anger, and he was in no mood for pleasantries.

Whew! That was intense. I can't live my life in fear of the knock on the door that leads to my arrest; we have to find that desk! Matt pulled out of his parking place and nodded in response to the garage attendant's wave as he exited, hoping he didn't look as guilty as he felt.

All the way home he played his conversation with Detective Robertson over and over in his mind. Had he said anything to incriminate himself? He knew he had appeared flustered. *Robertson knew exactly what he was doing, blindsiding me the way he did. The man came out of nowhere. Why does he suspect me of Ron's murder?* Matt reached back into his memory to that fateful day and remembered asking the dental assistant to make a phone call for him. He had planned to place the fatal dose of Fentanyl in the crown during her absence. She had heard him prescribe the narcotic and must have told the police. She had left his employment soon after without giving notice. Yes, it had to be her.

He arrived home and retrieved a beer from the refrigerator. He downed a large gulp and picked up his phone to call Sylvia. After four rings, he started to hang up, but a small voice answered.

"Bennett residence, Jill speaking.

Matt smiled. It was Sylvia's six-year-old daughter. "Hello, is this Jill?"

A hesitant voice answered, "Yes."

"Jill, this is Dr. Brooks. Your mommy and I worked together before you moved. Is your mommy home?"

Another hesitant affirmative answer.

"May I speak with her?" He heard the phone drop and a loud, but small voice yelled, "Mommy, the phone's for you."

Matt heard footsteps approach.

"Hello?"

"Sylvia, this is Matt Brooks. I need to ask you something."

Sylvia answered cautiously. "Okay, what would you like to know?"

"Well, two things actually. Was there any talk around the office about Ron's death? Perhaps, speculation that it wasn't an accident?"

"Not that I heard, but then I wouldn't be the one they would come to with that kind of talk."

"No, I guess not. Do you know why Beth quit?"

"Beth?"

"You know, the young assistant who worked for us only a few months."

"Oh, yes, I remember her. No, I don't know why she quit, and there was no gossip about her leaving that I recall."

"Good, now one more thing. Has anyone from the investigation into Ron's murder contacted you recently?"

Sylvia felt a chill creep up her back. "Uh, no. Why are you asking? What's happened?"

"Nothing, nothing has happened, but Detective Robertson intercepted me as I left work today. He had several very specific questions. I believe Beth contacted him and planted seeds of doubt in his mind."

"What did she say?" Sylvia asked anxiously.

"I'm not sure except the detective knew about the phone call I asked her to make for me while I was working with Ron. He thinks I must have done something to your husband during that time. He's fishing; he has nothing. He couldn't have because I didn't do anything to Ron except place the temporary crown."

Sylvia's heart rate began to slow a bit and she took a deep breath. "Matt, we have to get that confession back."

"I know; It's the only thing that could incriminate me."

"I'll call my sister-in-law again and see if she has found out more on the Mr. A. Smith who bought the desk from the auction."

"Okay, but be careful what you say."

"I will be; I told her I needed to find it to recover some of the kids' baby pictures."

"Smart. Call me if you hear anything, I'll go see this buyer if you can get an address."

"Will do, and Matt?"

"Yes?"

"I'm really sorry about all of this. We're in this because of me. I never should have involved you, and I'm sorry I didn't believe you at first. It just seemed too coincidental."

"It's okay; I wouldn't have believed me either. It is incredible – and unfortunate."

"Thanks; it makes me feel better that we didn't actually – well, you know."

"Yes, I know. Try not to worry; it will all work out."

The call ended and Matt prayed what he had said to Sylvia would be the truth. He hung up the phone and ordered a pizza to be delivered. He finished off the rest of the beer while he waited for his food.

The doorbell and his phone rang at the same time. Matt answered the phone and walked to his front door holding the phone to his ear. It was Carolyn.

"Are you still at work?"

"No, I'm home; what's up?"

He handed the delivery boy money for the pizza and took it to the kitchen.

Carolyn laughed. "That's my Matt, always to the point. Well, what's *up* is an invitation to meet me in New York this weekend. I have to be there for a business meeting on Friday and thought we could spend the weekend taking in the sights and maybe a show. Monday is Labor Day holiday, so I thought we could make a long weekend of it. Do you think you could manage it?"

Matt hesitated; it would mean three lost days in the search for the missing desk and its hidden secret.

Carolyn sensed the hesitation. "Matt? You do want to see me, don't you?"

Matt sensed the slight hurt in her voice and hurried to reassure her. After all, she had just referred to him as *my Matt.* "Of course, I want to see you. This is Tuesday so I'll have time to rearrange a couple of things so I can leave early on Friday. Where and when shall we meet?"

"I have reserved rooms at The Plaza. I booked them for the weekend, hoping you could join me. I'll be finished with my meeting around four o'clock on Friday, so if you can get a flight that afternoon, we could have a late dinner together."

"Sounds perfect. Let me check my calendar and flight times and I'll call you back in an hour."

"Wonderful! I know it will be fun. I love New York City in the fall; there are fewer tourists and lots to do. I'll wait on your call."

"I'll get right on it, and Carolyn…"

"Yes?"

"I've really missed you."

"Same here; I've gotten rather fond of you, Matt Brooks."

Matt smiled. Carolyn always made him feel better. "Well, isn't that a coincidence. I've grown very fond of you too. I'll call you as soon as I know when I can get there."

The call ended and Matt placed his pizza in the oven to keep it warm while he checked his work schedule on the laptop in his office. His office manager had synced the office schedule with his home computer's calendar. He scrolled to Friday afternoon. Time had been set aside in the afternoon for a staff meeting. His assistant and office manager could handle that as there was nothing that required his input currently. Next, he checked flight times out of Chicago for New York, inputting the destination airport as both John F. Kennedy and LaGuardia. He wanted to avoid Newark on a Friday afternoon. The extra distance and weekend travelers could make that trip into the City from Newark a nightmare. He found a flight into JFK that left around two p.m. His last appointment would be finished by noon. With any luck, he would be having dinner with Carolyn around eight-thirty Friday evening.

He picked up his phone and called Carolyn. She picked up on the second ring. Her eagerness was very evident. "So, can you make it this weekend?"

Matt laughed. "Yes, I should be sitting down to dinner with you by eight-thirty Friday night."

"And, you can stay until Monday afternoon?"

"Yes, again. What should I pack?"

"Umm, let's see. No need for a tux, but bring a dark suit and dressy-casual clothes."

"What the heck is dressy-casual?" Matt asked, obviously perplexed.

Carolyn laughed. "Just bring a sport coat and a dress shirt, no tie."

"Got it; anything else? Well, you could bring some of those bourbon ball chocolates I can't resist."

It was Matt's turn to laugh, and it felt so good to laugh again. "You shall have all the bourbon balls you want, m'lady, but I warn you – they are very addictive."

"So, I've discovered!" Another phone rang in the background. "Matt, I have to take this other call, but I can't wait to see you."

"Same here. I..." Matt's response was cut short as he realized Carolyn had already hung up on her end. He helped himself to another beer and grabbed a plate from a cabinet and placed two slices of his pizza on it. He took a bite and carried the plate to his living room and sat down on the sofa. His mind wandered to the call from Carolyn. Their relationship was becoming serious. The realization made him happy. He envisioned a life with her and smiled. His smile faded, however, when the image of Detective Robertson intruded on his thoughts. *That stupid document could ruin everything. I could lose my practice, my relationship with Carolyn, even my life, and all for a crime I didn't commit. How could I have been so stupid?*

Matt finished the two slices of pizza and went back to the kitchen for another slice. His phone rang again, interrupting his meal.

Now, who is calling? He grumbled.

"Matt. It's Sylvia. My sister-in-law called me right after we hung up. I have an address for the buyer of the desk."

"That's great; let me get a pen to write down the information." Matt rummaged in a kitchen drawer and found a pen and paper. "Okay, I'm ready."

"As I said before, his name is A. Smith and he lives only twenty miles from you. I spoke with him briefly."

Matt wrote down the address. *Progress, at last.*

"That's great! Did he mention finding any papers in the desk?"

"No, he said he had cleaned up the desk, sanded and stained a couple of nicks here and there, and then sold it."

"He *sold* it? Are you kidding me? Who bought it?" Matt could almost feel his blood pressure rise in response to the news.

"Well, that's the thing; he thinks the woman's name was Hawkins, Brenda or Linda Hawkins, but he isn't sure."

"Sylvia! We have to find that desk!" Matt protested, unable to keep the desperation from his voice. "That detective is already looking under every rock for anything to tie me to Ron's death. If the confession is found before we get to it, I'm cooked!"

"I know, Matt, I know. I'm trying. I have Mr. Smith's phone number so you can follow up with him. Maybe he can provide more information now that he has had time to think about it, and he might open up more to you. He kept calling me 'little lady' and didn't seem to take me very seriously. What is it with you males? You think only men have brains?"

Matt chuckled in spite of the gravity of the situation. "We can be masochistic brutes at times. I apologize for every one of

106

my gender. Go ahead, give me his number. I'll pay him a visit before I leave town on Friday." Sylvia provided the number and Matt wrote it down under Mr. Smith's address.

"Okay, I have it; I'll let you know how it goes – and, Sylvia?"

"Yes?"

"I'm sorry I yelled at you; this is really getting to me. I have actually dreamed about being behind bars and screaming that I'm innocent."

"I understand. I'm having similar dreams myself. I know you have a lot to lose, we both do, but I have my children to think about. If this goes badly, I'll have to leave the country with the kids. I can't risk them losing both parents." Sylvia's voice caught on the last word of the sentence. Matt suddenly felt selfish for only thinking about the ramifications to him. Sylvia was right, she had more to lose. They had to find that desk.

Matt hung up the phone but kept it in his hand. It was Tuesday. He usually had Wednesday afternoons off if there were no last-minute emergency patients for him to see. His office manager had not told him of any, so he punched in the number for Mr. A. Smith and waited. After four rings, Mr. Smith's voice mail picked up and instructed the caller to leave a message. Matt cautiously crafted his message. "Mr. Smith, this is Dr. Matthew Brooks. I believe you spoke with my former dental assistant Sylvia Bennett. I'm planning to be in your area tomorrow afternoon to visit a friend and would like to meet face-to-face. I was hoping you have remembered more about the person who bought the desk you got at auction. Please give me a call back." Matt proceeded to provide his cell number and hung up.

He sat on his sofa and watched the sun progress lower in the sky, casting long shadows from the tall evergreens in front of his house. The fingers of light remaining seemed to claw at the ground around the shadows in an attempt to stop the ensuing darkness. Matt identified with the sun; wasn't he also clawing at what light he could which might help him find Ron's wretched desk? The night eventually claimed its rightful place and left Matt sitting in the dark. Two beers had taken effect and, although his muscles were more relaxed, his thoughts were still racing through scenarios – all bad.

After considering all the legal fallout the discovery of the document would cause, he thought of Carolyn. He would lose her and suddenly he realized what a devastating loss that would be. He knew he was fond of her but was it more than that? Did he love her? He thought he had loved his wife Ashley, but he soon realized their marriage was based solely on lust and money – his lust and her love of money. To compensate for what his marriage lacked, Matt started gambling, primarily to escape his unhappy home life and to feel something, anything. Winning or losing, gambling gave him a jolt of energy on which he fed. A good poker hand became more satisfying than time with his wife. The marriage had been doomed from the start, but he had been too blind to see it. There had been little in common and neither had made much attempt to reason through their differences. Ashley loved to shop – and often. She had frequented only the most exclusive boutiques in Chicago and had hounded Matt for more shopping allowance. When he refused, she simply charged what she wanted and left Matt to figure out how to pay for her purchases. When the money got tight, their arguments became more intense, and Ashley found money and comfort from another source.

The divorce had been expensive but at least Ashley's marriage to another man had ended the alimony after only four months. Matt was left with a first and second mortgage and few tangible assets. His gambling had become an addiction and his father's death had put an end to bailouts of money. Up until now, he had been trying to figure out ways to fool his father's attorney who was the executor of the massive estate. The money would only pass to Matt when he quit gambling. Until he met Carolyn, he saw no way he could do that. He loved gambling; he had *needed* gambling as much as an alcoholic craves his next drink.

Carolyn had changed all that. For the first time in years, he felt alive, with something to look forward to. Would he lose her if she found out about the pact he had made with Sylvia to kill her husband? What would she think of him? As much as he wanted to confide in her for her wisdom, he knew he couldn't bring himself to reveal his secret. It would have to be an unspoken chasm between them. Matt only hoped his stupidity didn't catch up to him and ruin everything he had with Carolyn.

He came back to his original question. Did he love her? He only knew he wanted to spend every minute of every day with her and that her voice immediately brightened any day. If that was love, he was all for it. But, what about Carolyn? She brightened *his* humdrum existence, but did she feel the same way? For the first time, Matt considered another person's perspective and not simply his own. He had been selfish all of his life. Being raised to a life of privilege without restraint led him to expect to get whatever he wanted. The best schools, the best friends, only the very best clothes, he had been given it all. The result was narcissism. He had not considered anyone else but himself. When he thought of others, it was merely to gauge how they could help him. He had never considered before how he could help them. It was no wonder he had no close friends except for Carolyn. Matt wondered what Carolyn saw in him. He was no prize; that was for sure. Was it possible that Carolyn could be his catalyst for change? Matt believed she could be his very salvation – *if* the desk could be located and the damning contract destroyed. *If* – such a little word with such pivotal potential. Everything hinged on that little word.

Matt turned on the TV. Maybe a little time with the idiot box would distract him for a bit.

He was well into his second sitcom when the phone rang. "Hello?"

"Dr. Brooks?"

"Yes, this is Dr. Brooks."

"Dr. Brooks, this is Al Smith. You called earlier wanting to meet with me tomorrow afternoon. I can do that after two o'clock if that works for you. I run my own business and foot traffic gets a bit slower in mid-afternoon. My employees can manage without me by then so I'll meet you at my house. Do you have the address?"

"I believe so." He read aloud the address Sylvia had given him.

"That's it. I'll let my wife know; she loves company," he chuckled.

"Sounds good; thanks Mr. Smith. I really appreciate that you are making time to see me."

"It's not a problem. Say, what is so important about this desk anyway?"

The question was predictable but it still caught Matt off guard. He struggled to provide a believable answer. "Important?

No, nothing terribly important but I did leave some papers left by an ancestor in this desk. They have value to me only as a memento, but I would hate to lose them."

"I understand. I have a few old papers myself. One is the original land grant for my farm. It's dated 1762. I treasure that document and will pass it along to a grandchild someday, so I understand your situation. I'll ask my wife if she remembers the name of the lady who bought the desk. I thought it was Hawkins, but I am often wrong."

"Thanks, Mr. Smith; see you tomorrow."

After hanging up the call with Mr. Smith, Matt called Sylvia and updated her on his plan to visit the hardware store owner the next day.

Sylvia, while pleased that Mr. Smith seemed willing to help search for the desk, was worried that he might become suspicious. "Matt, are you sure he didn't suspect anything?"

"No, Sylvia, absolutely not. I told him I had left an old family document in the desk and I wanted it back for sentimental value. He even told me about a land grant document dated in the 1700's he has that he plans to pass along to his grandchildren. He understands and plans to ask his wife if she could remember the name of the lady who bought the desk."

"Okay, but don't blow it when you see him tomorrow. If he asks, have a back story ready for the document."

"A back story?"

Yes, what type of document it is, how old, et cetera."

"Oh, right. Okay, I'll say it's my parent's marriage license or something like that."

"That'll do. Don't overplay it; we don't want the Smiths to become suspicious because you seem too anxious or insistent."

Matt was becoming irritated; he didn't need coaching from his former assistant. "Got it, don't worry. I'll play it down and just apply the old Brooks charm."

Sylvia was all too familiar with the 'old Brooks charm' as she had seen it in action with Matt's patients. The ladies loved him, and the men felt like old chums when Matt turned on his office charisma. It was likely one of the chief reasons his practice was so busy and successful. Matt made each patient feel special and welcome. It wasn't a bad strategy but one that was difficult to maintain under stress such as the current situation. She only hoped her old boss could hold it together as the alternative was too dreadful to contemplate.

"You do that, Matt. Good luck and call me after you meet with Mr. Smith."

"Will do. Don't worry, we'll find the desk."

"I hope you're right; I don't look good in an orange jumpsuit."

Matt laughed at the image in spite of being as worried as Sylvia.

"It's not funny," Sylvia protested. "I can't go to jail; my kids need me."

Matt sobered. "I understand."

"Which is why you should concentrate on finding that desk, not fly off for a romantic weekend with your girlfriend."

"What makes you think my trip is to meet a girlfriend?"

"Your lady friend is open office gossip. I still talk to a couple of the gals I worked with at your office. You can't keep a secret at work for long, which is another good reason to find that desk and not be distracted until you do," Sylvia pleaded, almost shouting.

"Calm down, maybe we'll get lucky and Mr. Smith will give us the name we need."

"I hope and pray that happens but stay focused, okay?"

"I'm focused, Sylvia, believe me I've thought of little else since you told me about this. Try not to worry; I'll call you as soon as I speak with Mr. Smith."

"Okay." Sylvia thought about saying more but felt she had probably said enough. She knew her former employer didn't tolerate hysteria or nagging. "I'll look forward to your call tomorrow. 'Bye, Matt."

"Goodbye Sylvia." Matt hung up the phone and wished he felt as optimistic as he had sounded on the call. He couldn't imagine being more worried than he was at the moment.

Chapter Thirteen

The next day Matt pulled up to Al Smith's home promptly at two-thirty. He turned off the car's engine and sat for a moment looking at the Smith home. There was something about it that made it a home and not merely a house. The white picket fence was part of it, but other touches such as a rose garden in the side yard, a friendly-looking dog lying on the sidewalk, and twin rockers on the porch completed the look. There was love here. Matt wondered if he would ever have a home like this. Would he have a home with Carolyn?

His thoughts were interrupted by a cheery greeting.

"Hello!"

Matt followed the voice and saw a weathered face sporting a broad smile. Dressed in worn jeans, a denim shirt, and a Chicago Cubs baseball cap, Mr. Smith walked toward Matt's car.

Matt opened his car door and returned the greeting. He exited the car and met the man at the gate. "Mr. Smith?" he asked as he extended his hand.

"The older man grasped Matt's hand with a younger man's strength. "You got him; you must be Dr. Brooks. Come on up to the porch and sit a spell. Mama's bringing out lemonade for us."

"That would be nice, thank you." Matt was clearly surprised at the friendly reception. He was being treated like an old friend, not a prying stranger.

Mr. Smith led the way to the porch and indicated that Matt should sit in the rocker farthest from the front door. Matt settled on the blue cushioned rocker and noted how comfortable it was.

"This rocker is great! I don't have one, but I believe I could become a fan."

Mr. Smith laughed. "You can't beat a rocker after working all day. Mama and I sit here most evenings in the summer and watch the sky turn colors as the sun sets. There's nothing like it."

Matt nodded as if he understood the feeling, but the truth was he had never watched a sunset beginning to end in his entire life. He decided it might be worth a try, especially if he could share it with Carolyn.

Matt started to bring up the matter of the desk when a petite woman in her sixties emerged from the house carrying a tray with a pitcher of lemonade and three ice-filled glasses. She set the tray down on a small table nearby and turned to face Matt.

Mr. Smith made the introductions. "Dr. Brooks, this is my wife Madeline. Maddie, this is Dr. Brooks."

Matt stood and reached out his hand to the smiling woman. "Please call me Matt, ma'am."

"All right, and you can call us Al and Maddie. We don't get too formal around here."

"Thank you, Mrs., I mean Maddie. I'm very pleased to meet you."

Al gave up his rocker for Maddie and perched on the porch railing facing his wife and Matt.

It was Al who brought up the subject of Matt's visit. "So, you're looking for that old desk we bought." It was a statement not a question. "Well, I talked with Maddie about it, and we think we can help you."

Matt finished his sip of lemonade and tried to hide his rising excitement, but he was aware of his heart picking up a few beats. So much was riding on finding that desk before the contract was found. He set his glass down on his right knee and smiled slightly as he waited for more information.

Maddie spoke up. "We don't know the lady's name for sure, but we think we know where she lives. She is new to the area, bought the old Palmer place, and appears to live alone. She bought the desk one day when we were not home. Our hired hand took care of it. She answered a notice I had put up on the grocery store bulletin board advertising the desk for sale. Al cleaned it up some and sold it for a nice profit. We arranged for her to have it picked up the next day by two men she hired, so our hired hand didn't hear the name. The only time we were told her name was when she called to answer the notice. I believe she said her name was Brenda or Linda Hawkins, but my memory and my ears aren't what they used to be; it could have been a name with a similar sound."

Matt was becoming excited, but he was not home free yet. "The name isn't important if you can tell me where she lives."

It was Al's turn to speak. "Well, you keep going down this road about a mile, turn left at the old sawmill, drive another mile or so and it's the blue house on the right. The last time I passed there the name Palmer was still painted on the mailbox."

Matt was not accustomed to directions so vague. A house number would be nice, but he realized the couple probably didn't know it. He pulled a small notebook and pen from his sports jacket pocket and wrote down the information. "Thank you; I'm sure I'll find it."

Matt didn't want to appear rude or give any indication of

how desperate he was to find the desk, so he sat on the porch with his hosts for another twenty minutes and talked. He discovered he liked the engaging couple. They were hardworking, generous, and hospitable, certainly a welcome change from most of the people he encountered in his practice who were wealthy and very consumed with their own lives. He doubted any of them would have taken the time to help him as the Smiths had. *Lesson learned,* he concluded.

Maddie pushed up from her rocker and stood. Matt noticed she was a bit slow getting up. Her face registered pain, but she didn't voice a complaint. *I'll add stoic to her list of attributes.*

"I could sit out here all day and talk to this nice young man, Al, but I have a lot to do inside if we're to eat dinner on time."

Matt stood in a show of respect as his hostess retreated from the porch. He thought this might be a good time to take his leave. He turned to Al who had also stood and offered his hand. Al accepted it and returned a firm handshake. Matt could feel the roughness of the older man's hand. Al was a man who used his hands to work hard. He wondered what Al was thinking about his own softer and manicured hands.

"It was nice to meet you Matt. Come out anytime, have a meal with us. Mama loves to show off her pie making skills. I guarantee you won't go home hungry."

"That is very nice of you Al; I must do that."

"Good! Bring your little lady with you. I'm sure a good-looking young fella like you has a lady friend."

Matt smiled. Carolyn would love this couple. "Yes sir, but she lives in Kentucky."

"Kentucky? Now, there's a story there. You'll have to tell us sometime."

Matt chuckled. "It is quite a story, that's for sure. Thank you again for your hospitality and the information."

"You're very welcome. I hope you find the desk."

"Thank you." Matt turned and walked to his car. Once behind the wheel, he looked up and saw Al standing on the porch. They exchanged a final wave good-bye as Matt headed down the road, with the directions he had been given.

Matt's mood was greatly improved as he navigated the curves of the country road. With any luck, he would have the confession in hand in only a few minutes. The derelict sawmill where he was to turn left came into view. *So far, so good.* After the turn, he slowed down a bit to watch for the blue house and a mailbox with the name of 'Palmer' on it. He had driven about three miles when he concluded that he had missed it. He had seen no painted mailbox and no blue house.

He turned around and made his way along the narrow road. He was careful to look left and right frequently but had found no blue house by the time he reached the corner with the sawmill again. It occurred to him that the new occupant might have painted the house, so he retraced his route and looked for signs of new paint. There were only about ten houses to consider as most properties had some acreage. He knew the house was on the right so that eliminated all but six in the two mile stretch he judged to be his target. He passed four houses on the right side of the road before he saw what he thought could be a newly painted house with a new mailbox. The mailbox was like all the others along the road, but it was new and there was freshly turned earth at its base. Bingo!

Matt parked just off the road in front of the house. He didn't want to pull into the driveway and then have to back out onto the curvy country road with its poor visibility.

There was a late model Chevy truck in the driveway, a good indication the occupant was home. Matt considered his pitch for a few moments before exiting his car.

Satisfied with what he was planning to say, he exited his car and walked toward the house. Like most homes in the area, there was a fence around the house with a front gate. Matt released the latch and proceeded up the walk.

The door of the house opened before Matt could reach the steps. A middle-aged woman with bright red hair appeared on the porch. "Hold it right there, mister! I don't want to buy anything from you or anyone else. Now, leave!"

Matt was momentarily stunned by her gruffness, in great contrast to the friendly reception he had received at the Smiths. "Ma'am, I'm not selling anything. I just want to ask you about a desk you purchased recently from the Smiths.

"Mister, I told you to leave and I mean *right now!*"

"But I only want to…"

The obviously enraged woman pulled a handgun from behind her skirt. "Apparently you don't hear too well." The woman lifted the gun and fired one shot just above Matt's head. Matt fell to the ground onto his knees.

"Hey! Are you crazy? I only wanted to ask about a lousy desk; you don't have to shoot me!"

"If I had meant to shoot you, there would be blood. I'm a good shot and the next one will definitely hit its target, now git!"

Matt slowly got to his feet and backed up a few steps, afraid to turn around and risk being shot in the back. He raised his hands up. "Okay, okay, I'm going!"

The woman kept the gun trained on Matt until he was

through her gate. Matt closed the gate and finally turned around and walked quickly to his car, his heart pounding.

Once safely inside his car, he wasted no time and drove away quickly. Sweat trickled through his expensive suit and his bowels felt unusually active. He took a few deep breaths and slowed his heart rate as he decided what he would do now. He had to get at that desk!

Several miles away from the crazed woman, Matt felt composed enough to place a call to Sylvia. He explained what had just happened.

"She actually pointed a gun at you and fired it?" Sylvia asked in amazement. "What did you say to her to get her so riled?"

"I didn't have a chance to say hardly anything. I only asked about the desk and she would have none of it. She decided to let her gun do the talking for her."

"Matt, if we can't get at the desk, how are we going to retrieve that wretched piece of paper?" Sylvia screeched.

"Sylvia, calm down. I'll think of something. Maybe the Smiths can speak to her for me. They are really nice people, salt of the earth type."

Sylvia struggled to keep the anxiety from her voice as she responded. "Okay, that's good; when will you call them?"

"I'll call them when I get home. I'm in no shape at the moment to be coherent about anything; I need some time to get over that encounter. I'm telling you, that woman is certifiably insane and a nuisance to society."

Sylvia could hear the stress in Matt's voice and decided to back off a bit until he could regain his composure.

"Okay, call me again later after you speak with the Smiths." Matt offered no response. "Matt? Are you still there?"

"Yeah, sorry, I was navigating a sharp curve as a delivery truck was passing in the other direction. I didn't trust myself to talk and drive past him at the same time."

Sylvia smiled to herself in spite of the urgent issue still pending between them. "Good call. I said, I want you to call me after you speak with the Smiths."

"Okay, will do, 'bye."

Sylvia heard the call disconnect before she could respond. She hung up her phone and turned to look out her window. Beyond, the trees were beginning to show signs of autumn as the bright green leaves were slowly changing to yellow, but she only saw the desk in her mind and the hiding place of the contract, Had the crazy lady already found the document? Had Mr. Smith? No, she assumed; Mr. Smith would have said something to Matt instead of welcoming him like a long lost relative. She closed her eyes and offered up a prayer that the document would stay hidden until it could be retrieved safely by Matt or her. *Please, God, keep that wretched paper hidden and help us find a way to access the desk,* Sylvia prayed.

Her thoughts were pulled away from Matt's close encounter by the cries of her children. Apparently, they were having a lively discussion over which television program to watch. It was fall break for her daughter's school and Sylvia couldn't wait for classes to resume. As much as she loved her children, events of the past several months had depleted her inner reserves so that even this small squabble tore at her nerves. She sighed and assumed her mommy mode to intervene before blows were exchanged.

Chapter Fourteen

Matt arrived home still struggling to recover from the encounter with the current owner of the desk. *All I wanted was to see the desk. Why did that wild woman pull a gun?* Matt asked himself as he tried to make sense of what had just happened. He pulled into his driveway, feeling fortunate to be alive. He was never so glad to be home. With a shot of bourbon, Matt settled onto his sofa to consider his next step. No matter how crazy the woman was, he had to see that desk. The amber liquid burned going down, but Matt didn't feel it. His mind was on the problem at hand. He reached for the television remote and turned on a game show. Ever the gambler, he enjoyed seeing others vie for prizes and cash.

As he watched the show, his mind wandered to the issue of his inheritance. Time was running short to claim it and he had not proven to his father's attorney that he could stay away from gambling. When was the last time he had made a trip to Vegas? He searched his memory and couldn't recall his last trip or even his last online bet. Matt stood up and walked into his study. He booted up the computer on the desk and pulled up his online wagering account. He searched for the last bet made and was surprised to discover it had been over three months since he had gambled. He could now prove to his father's attorney that he had reformed and was eligible for his inheritance. He thought it rather amusing that he would finally inherit just as he was about to be sent to prison possibly for the rest of his life. At least the money would pay for a good lawyer, he mused, and he made a mental note to call his father's attorney the next morning after he spoke with Mr. Smith.

Matt slept poorly with dreams of being arrested and put on trial. All the evidence was against him; after all, he had written out a full confession. The prosecution presented Matt's bank records showing the jury how close the high-priced dentist had been to bankruptcy. It was an easy connection from there to the plot to kill Sylvia's husband for the sizable payoff of a million dollars. The jurors in his dream sat stone-faced as the damning elements of his guilt were laid out. The narcotic prescription written by the defendant for Mr. Bennett, the written confession, the near-bankruptcy, and full access to the deceased on the day of his death, all created convincing evidence for conviction.

The prosecution was seeking a sentence of life without the possibility of parole. Conspiracy, motive, opportunity, and medical knowledge could be proven sufficient to carry out the crime. What couldn't be proven was just how Matt killed the deceased who was apparently alone at the time of his death. He had consumed the narcotic and booze of his own volition.

The defense, in Matt's dream, attempted to pass off the written confession as an office joke with no evidence that the defendant had done anything wrong.

Each time Matt awoke from the dream, he would lie awake and consider his future. Would he and Carolyn find a life together? Or, would he be sentenced to live out his life in a penitentiary – or worse, a lethal injection. He considered the procedure used for the lethal injection. He had looked up the information, just in case. Apparently, one drug was given to calm the condemned before another drug was administered to stop the heart. It didn't sound too bad, certainly nothing like the previous methods used to end the life of convicted murderers.

Around three a.m. he gave up on sleep, not wanting to continue the endless cycle of the dream and his racing thoughts of execution. He wanted to speak to Carolyn and hear her wonderful voice, but he looked at the clock and decided she would not be receptive to a call at that hour. Their visits made him feel as if he could take on the world and win. How could he tell her about the desk and its hidden secret? Would she understand, or turn and run?

Matt rose from bed and pulled on jogging shorts, a long-sleeved tee, and an old pair of running shoes. He hoped to clear his mind and find a few moments of peace. The first mile his mind was still running faster than he was. There was no middle ground; either the confession would be retrieved and he would be home free, or the confession would end up in the hands of the authorities and his nightmare would happen for real. The two extremes clashed together like rams vying for a female's attention. After another mile, he slowed his pace and allowed his exhausted mind to clear away all of the worry and fear. He knew he only had one choice – get the confession back any way he could.

At the end of five miles, Matt arrived home, showered, and crawled back into bed. It was nearly five in the morning and he hoped he could catch another hour or two of sleep. He crawled into bed, pulled up the sheet and slept soundly until seven a.m. when his cell phone rang. It was Carolyn.

"Matt? Are you there?" she asked after Matt had picked up

the receiver but had not yet found his voice.

"Um, yes, I'm here. Sorry, I just woke up."

"Oh, I'm sorry to wake you. Would you prefer I call back later?"

"No, I need to get up anyway and get ready for work. Why are you calling? Are we still on for this weekend?" Matt asked, trying hard to keep the worry out of his voice. His greatest fear, next to being found guilty of a murder he didn't commit, was losing Carolyn.

"Yes, of course I want to see you, silly, but the plans have changed. Instead of New York, would you prefer time at the farm?"

Matt considered the question for only a moment. "Anywhere you are, that is where I want to be. It doesn't matter if it's New York, your farm, or a simple walk in the park."

Carolyn smiled. She knew how Matt felt about her, but was he willing to make a commitment? She hadn't decided yet if she would remarry, but she knew she wanted a long-term relationship with Matt. He had turned her world around so that it made more sense. With him, she felt safe. No, it was more than that. He made her happy and she thought she might be in love.

"Good answer! That's settled then; the farm it is. Can you change your flight?"

I'm sure I can; I'll let you know what time my plane lands."

"Good, I'll be there to meet you."

"Carolyn?" Matt wanted to tell her what she meant to him but hesitated, not knowing if she would run in the other direction if he pushed too hard.

"Yes?"

Seconds ticked by as Matt considered what to say.

"Matt? What were you going to say?"

"Only that I miss you and can't wait to see you." There was so much more he wanted to convey to her but couldn't find the courage to say it.

Carolyn heard the fake cheerfulness in his voice, but she decided to let it pass – for now. Matt had always been vague about his personal life and she worried he was hiding something. Before their relationship could progress any further, they needed to have a heart-to-heart talk. Secrets were not a good foundation for a couple. Carolyn returned Matt's cheerful response with one of her own. "Well, Dr. Brooks, I miss you too. I'm glad we will be at the farm this weekend. We can kick back and relax. How does that sound, cowboy?"

"It sounds wonderful. I'll text my flight information later."

Matt ended the call with a smile. A weekend at the farm was just what he needed. He enjoyed being with Carolyn anywhere but he found a special peace in the country setting. He could forget everything there, at least for a couple of days.

Matt picked up his phone again and called Mr. Smith. Mrs. Smith answered on the third ring.

"Hello?"

"Mrs. Smith?"

"Yes, this is Mrs. Smith."

"Ma'am, this is Matt Brooks; we met yesterday."

"Oh yes, I remember you; how are you?"

"I'm doing well, thank you, and you?"

Mrs. Smith chuckled. "There's nothing wrong with us that shaving twenty years off our ages wouldn't fix, but you didn't call to ask about our health. What can I do for you?"

"Well, I followed the directions Mr. Smith gave me and

found the lady who bought the desk I'm seeking."

"Did she let you inspect the desk?"

Matt let out a short laugh. "Not only didn't I have the chance to see the desk, I didn't get to the front door. For some reason, the lady took an immediate dislike to me and, in no uncertain terms, demanded I leave her property. She reinforced her demand by pulling out a gun and firing a shot over my head."

"Oh, my goodness! That's terrible! Hold on, Al hasn't left for the store yet, let me get him on the phone. He needs to hear this."

Some minutes later Matt could hear footsteps and the now familiar voice of Al Smith.

"Hello, Matt? What's this I hear about a gun being drawn on you?"

Matt repeated what he had told Mrs. Smith and added, "It was very unnerving; I wasted no time getting out of there."

"No, I would imagine not. Did you say anything to her that would make her respond that way?"

"Absolutely not. Before I had reached her front porch, she came outside and started screaming and demanding I leave. I tried to tell her what I wanted but that's when she drew the gun and fired a shot over my head."

"Amazing. What can I do?"

"Well, I don't want to impose on you and Mrs. Smith; you've done enough already."

"Nonsense, now what do you need? You called for some reason, so how can we help?"

Matt was touched by the offer from someone he had met only the day before. "I was hoping you know someone who knows her. I thought if I could speak to them and explain the situation, she might reconsider and let me see the desk."

"Hmm, let me see. As you know, we didn't meet her when the desk was picked up. Our hired hand said she came with two men in a pickup truck to get the desk. I don't think names were exchanged, but I'll ask him. I do know a couple of folks who live not far from her; I'll ask them if they know her. Give me a couple of days and I'll see what I can find out for you."

"Thank you, Al; I appreciate your help. I'm going out of town for the weekend, but I'll call on Saturday."

"Okay, enjoy your weekend."

"I plan to, I'll be spending it on a farm in Kentucky – horses, cows, barns, the whole scenario."

"Sounds like heaven to me. I'll try my best to get some information for you."

"You're a great guy, Al, thanks." Matt ended the call, showered, and popped a bagel into the toaster. His automatic coffee maker signaled that it had finished its brewing cycle and Matt poured a cup. He spread the toasted bagel with jelly and consumed it quickly, followed by a gulp of hot coffee. He carried his coffee cup to his bedroom to dress for work. As he picked out clothes to wear, his mind traveled back to the desk – and Carolyn. He knew he must be honest with her about his gambling, the signed confession, and the plot to kill Ron Bennett. Their relationship might not survive, but Carolyn would not be able to trust him if he withheld something so important and she found out later. He decided to disclose everything to her but would need to pick the best time to break the news to her. Then, their future together would be in her hands.

He unlocked his car and backed out of his driveway. It was a normal Thursday morning. Neighbors were walking dogs, jogging, raking leaves. How he wished his life consisted of such mundane routine. Even a boring day was preferable to the roller coaster on which he was riding.

As he drove, he remembered to call his father's attorney to arrange for a meeting.

"Hello, Dr. Brooks; what can I do for you this morning?" Matt noted the false cheerfulness in the man's voice and mentally applauded the man's attempt to be civil considering past conversations with Matt. Most had not gone well, with Matt dishing out harsh accusations. He realized what a perfect ass he had been. The attorney agreed to see Matt immediately as he had an open spot in his schedule.

Matt thanked him and pointed his car toward the attorney's office. He parked his car on the street a block from the office and silently rehearsed what he would say to the man who held the keys to his trust fund.

He was ushered in to an inner office by a polite but frosty secretary. She obviously remembered Matt's behavior from previous visits. The attorney failed to rise in greeting. He invited his visitor to sit in one of the chairs in front of his desk.

Matt spoke without waiting on the older man. "First of all, Mr. Trenton, I want to apologize. My past behavior has been indefensible, and I'm truly sorry for it and the things I have said to you."

The seasoned attorney was taken aback. This was a different sounding Matthew Brooks from the indulged and immature person to which he was accustomed. Had he changed, or was this another ruse to get the trust fund money? He knew from the investigator he had hired to observe Matt that there had been little to no gambling for months. No trips to Vegas, no online betting, nothing. Mr. Trenton wondered what had caused the change. He was pulled back from his musing by Matt's voice.

"Secondly, I know I must show good faith by not gambling, I wanted you to know I don't intend to return to my former speculative ways. I have paid down the mortgage on my home and have nearly paid off the loan against my practice. I want my dad's trust in me to be justified, and I hope he would be proud of me if he were still here."

"Yes, Matthew, I'm aware of your changed behavior. I must say I'm very pleased, surprised, but pleased," he added albeit somewhat sardonically. "I'm curious as to what has changed to effect this new outlook on life that you now have."

Matt laughed. "A good woman, Mr. Trenton, a remarkable and beautiful woman."

"I see," the lawyer added, although the tone of his voice did not sound as if he really did. "Okay, here's what I am prepared to do. Your father's will included certain stipulations, as you know. The first, of course, is to end your spendthrift ways and show maturity in the handling of your money. Until recently, I despaired of that happening. Now, however, you have shown progress so I can loosen the purse strings a bit. According to the guidelines set forth in your father's instructions, I can release fifteen thousand dollars per month to you. Or, you can take it as a six-month lump sum, your choice."

Matt was not surprised that he was being kept on a short financial leash but was grateful for the offer. It would pay back Sylvia and give him some extra for a nice gift for Carolyn. "I would like that as a lump sum, Mr. Trenton; it will be enough to repay a debt."

The older man took some moments to assess Matt's

sincerity. Was Matt planning to pay off a debt as he had said, or was it seed money for Vegas? How Matt used the money would determine future payments, if any, from the trust fund.

"As you wish, Dr. Brooks," assuming a more formal manner. "I'll have the money deposited into your checking account by the end of business today."

"I appreciate that very much, sir," Matt responded as he rose and offered his hand.

Not able to hide his surprise at the courtesy, the attorney also rose and shook hands with Matt. After Matt left, he called in his assistant and made arrangement for the funds transfer. He was informed his next appointment was waiting and the attorney turned his attention away from Matthew Brooks.

Chapter Fifteen

In spite of the turmoil he was feeling over the missing document, Matt worked through his day and gave no indication of his inner feelings. He turned on the charm with his female patients and was the consummate professional. His office staff whispered among themselves about the new, more pleasant Dr. Brooks.

"Maybe he came into a lot of money," offered one dental hygienist, who was unaware how close to home her comment was. Matt had shared nothing about his inheritance or the strings attached to it with his staff, but most of his staff knew his father had been fabulously wealthy.

"No, I'll bet it's a woman," another offered.

"Well, whatever it is, I'm glad. His mood has improved, and I haven't been chewed out in more than a month," a third employee explained. The office manager approached the group with a get back to work look and everyone scattered to ponder the reason for the change in their boss on their own.

After work, Matt ordered takeout from his favorite pub and headed home. The barbecue platter would be a welcome meal as he hadn't eaten lunch. The day had gone well, but he was tired and he was ready for a relaxing evening. He turned on the news and pulled the plate of food onto his lap. Halfway through the meal the phone rang. Matt uttered a curse and set his meal aside.

"Hello?"

"Dr. Brooks, this is Detective Robertson." The detective paused. "I wondered if I could stop by this evening?"

Matt swallowed the bite he had just taken before the call and coughed as it stuck in his throat. He grabbed his Coke and downed a large gulp. He knew that made him look suspicious, and he struggled to recover quickly. "Of course, Detective; I'll be home all evening."

"Good, I'll see you in about twenty minutes."

"Okay, I'll be here." Matt hung up the phone and stared at nothing as his mind swirled with possible scenarios. Was he being arrested? Had they found the confession? No, he wouldn't have been given the courtesy of a phone call.

He considered the food on the table in front of him. He had no appetite for it now. He cleaned up the food, removed it to the kitchen, and washed his hands. He then returned to the living room to wait for the detective's arrival.

The doorbell startled Matt even though he was expecting the visit. He took a couple of deep breaths before opening the door and reminded himself to be calm. "Come in, Detective."

Matt led his visitor into the living room. "Have a seat." Detective Robertson chose the sofa and Matt sat in a side chair. "Would you care for something to drink?" He offered.

"No, thanks, Dr. Brooks." Robertson looked straight at Matt and held his gaze for several seconds.

Matt felt self-conscious and figured he was being assessed. With an effort, he remained silent and kept his breathing even as he met the detective's scrutiny. "How can I help you, Detective?"

"I need to follow up on some details of our investigation into Ron Bennett's death, and I think you can help me," he said amiably.

"Sure, I'm glad to help."

"Let's talk about the narcotic you prescribed for Mr. Bennett. You told me it was to treat back pain, is that correct?"

"Yes, only ten tablets of the lowest dose just to carry Ron until he could see his primary care physician on Monday."

"Do you usually prescribe pain medicine for the procedure Mr. Bennett had?"

"No, as I told you, it was for his back pain. I asked him about drug allergies before prescribing the medication and only wrote for ten tablets." Matt could feel his temper rising but couldn't afford to show it to the detective.

"Why would you prescribe for something outside of your area of expertise?" Robertson pressed.

"Ron was an acquaintance and the husband of an employee of mine. It's not unusual for physicians to write scripts for their staff. For example, one of my assistants suffers from migraines and couldn't see her doctor for another week. I prescribed Tramadol for the pain."

"I see. Now, tell me about the time you were alone with Mr. Bennett."

"Alone?"

"Yes, didn't you ask your assistant to make a phone call for you?"

Matt took a few seconds to gather his thoughts; he didn't want to say the wrong thing. "Uh, yes, I did. One of my long-time patients had called, and I told the office manager I would call her back later. Then, I remembered how impatient she was and decided to return the call right away. She can be rather bothersome to the office staff if she doesn't get immediate attention."

"So, you felt compelled to send your assistant away to call her just as you were preparing to place a temporary crown in Mr. Bennett?"

"Yes, that's exactly what I did. I didn't require a second person to seat the crown; it's an easy procedure. My more experienced assistants often do it on their own and then I check their work. The assistant who was with me that day had only been with me a short time, so I did the placement myself."

"Do you always drop everything and return calls, Dr. Brooks?" His voice dripped with suspicion and non-belief, and Matt knew he was not convincing the detective.

"You have to understand my clientele, Detective. Many of them are very wealthy and expect V.I.P. treatment. I do my very best to accommodate them whenever possible."

The detective changed his approach. "Did you see Mr. Bennett after he left your office?" The question was more of an accusation, and Matt could tell by his tone that he believed him guilty – of something – but he was fishing, he had nothing.

"Absolutely not. I finished seeing my patients and went home."

"Can anyone verify that?"

"I live alone, but I always set the house alarm when I leave home, and my security company could possibly tell you what time I returned and turned it off."

"I'll do that but what would prevent you from leaving your home later? If you didn't set the security system, it wouldn't know you left again, would it?"

"Look, what's this all about? I thought Ron Bennett fell and hit his head in the bathroom."

"He did, or at least it appears he fell accidentally. He had consumed a large amount of alcohol, but he also took half of the pills you prescribed just hours before his death."

"So? I didn't make him swallow them, and I certainly didn't prescribe for so many to be taken in such a short time. Furthermore, before he left my office, I cautioned him about drinking while on the medication. Why are you still investigating after all this time? It's been several months." Matt was becoming angry and impatient.

"There's no statute of limitations for murder, Dr. Brooks."

"Murder? Is that what you think?" Matt's voice rose in spite of his intention to remain calm.

Detective Robertson didn't answer but merely stared. It was unnerving.

"I had absolutely nothing to do with the man's death. Why would I do such a thing?"

"Why, indeed." The detective rose and walked to the front door with Matt following. "Thank you for your time, Dr. Brooks. I'll be in touch."

"Good-bye, Detective." *And, good riddance!* Matt said to himself. He didn't offer to shake hands and neither did Robertson. The detective left without further comment.

Matt closed the door, leaned against it, and exhaled. *What was that all about? If they haven't found the confession, why do the police think I'm guilty?*

Chapter Sixteen

Matt slept poorly again and rose early to finish packing for his weekend trip. He stowed the duffle and rolling bag in his trunk and headed to the office. As he worked, his thoughts returned to the unexpected visit from Detective Robertson the night before. If the police did not have the confession, why did they believe Ron was murdered? It didn't make sense unless someone voiced their suspicions during the investigation – or after. The question was who? It was obvious that Beth, his dental assistant on the day of Ron's dental visit had spoken with the police, but there must be someone else. Sylvia had sworn to him she had told no one about their plan to kill Ron. Had she let something slip? He decided to call her on his way to the airport.

When the last patient went out the door, Matt waved good-bye to his staff before hurrying out to his car for the drive to Midway Airport. As soon as he was clear of his office parking garage, he engaged the Bluetooth function in his Mercedes and requested a call to Sylvia. She answered right away.

"Sylvia, it's Matt. I need to ask you something, and I want you to think very, very carefully before answering."

"Okay, what is it?" She responded cautiously, picking up on her former employer's tone.

"Detective Robertson came by my house last night. He's fishing for something as if he's trying to put a puzzle together but hasn't all the pieces. He keeps asking about my actions the day Ron died. Have you said anything to anyone about our plan?"

"No, Matt, I swear I haven't."

"Think carefully; our futures may depend on it. Did you say anything to anyone even joking about getting rid of Ron or that you wished him out of your life?"

"No, I can't think of... oh..."

"What is it; what do you remember?"

"No, it can't be."

"What?" Matt demanded "What can't be?" He was nearly yelling.

Sylvia's voice betrayed her anguish. "I may have said to his sister that the children and I would be better off if Ron were no longer in our lives. She had asked what I meant by that. I told her I had tried more than once to leave Ron but was stopped by his threat to plant evidence that would show I wasn't a fit mother and would take the children from me. I told Rachel I didn't know a way out, that I wish there were some way we could get away from him, but I didn't say anything about murder. Besides, Rachel is my friend and hated Ron nearly as much as I did. She wouldn't have gone to the police; I'm sure of it," She added with emphasis.

"Well, someone has caused Detective Robertson to be suspicious of us, both of us. Where were you when you talked with Rachel about trying to leave Ron?"

"Let me see. It was a few weeks before Ron died. We were at his parents' home for his mother's birthday. Rachel and I were on the patio watching the children play in the backyard. Rachel told me I appeared to be tired and asked if I was getting enough sleep. I tried to play it off, but she persisted, and I confided in her about some things."

"What things?" Matt asked anxiously.

"Well, I told her about Ron hitting me and keeping me awake at night until I couldn't keep my eyes open. When I did fall asleep, he would wake me up with a punch to my ribs or a cold washcloth thrown across my face. He was cruel, and I was becoming desperate."

"Could anyone have heard what you said to Rachel?"

Sylvia thought for a few moments. "The party was in late spring and the patio door was open for the breeze into the kitchen. There was only the screen door so anyone could have heard part or all of our conversation. Ron's mother has claimed since the funeral that I killed Ron. I have been wondering why, and it wasn't until just now that I remembered that conversation with Rachel. His mother could be the one pressing the police for a murder charge against me. I suppose you are being targeted because of the pills you prescribed and the unfortunate coincidence of his death the same day as his dental appointment." Here Matt blew out a breath. It was a lot to take in, and he wasn't sure there was a solution. At any rate, the damage was already done. "That must be it. Sylvia, I'm at the airport now; I have to hang up. If you speak with Rachel, try to find out if she knows why her mother is so angry with you. Don't let on about her mother's accusations, just get as much information as you can without being too obvious."

"Okay, I usually call her once a week on weekends. I'll let you know what she says after I speak with her."

"Please don't give your hand away by being too obvious."

"Give me some credit, will you?"

"Sorry. Call me as soon as you find out anything."

"Will do."

He pressed the button on his steering wheel to end the call and turned into the airport entrance and navigated his car toward long-term parking."

Matt parked his car, gathered his belongings, and walked into the terminal. His conversation with Sylvia was still playing in his head. His recent encounters with Detective Robertson had shaken him. He thought the investigation into Ron's death was long since finished, but someone had rekindled it. He didn't want his visit with Carolyn to be overshadowed by his fear of being arrested for Ron Bennett's murder, but it was time to confide in her. His thoughts of her caused him to smile. Carolyn always brought out the best in him. In return, she deserved the best, and he knew he couldn't pursue a long-term relationship with her until he was honest about his past. His gambling and the murder pact with Sylvia were large hurdles which had to be revealed and overcome. The big question was if she would run the other way once she knew about his past. He knew he was a changed man, but he had once considered taking the life of another human being. What kind of monster does that or even thinks about it? Could Carolyn love him once she knew the truth? Even someone as loving as she would have her limits.

***

The eighty-two-minute flight touched down on the tarmac of Louisville Muhammad Ali International Airport. He gathered his belongings and became part of the crowd walking to luggage claim, where he knew Carolyn would be waiting.

He spied her first as he began his slow descent on the

escalator. Her view of him was blocked by a tall soldier in fatigues. Still unseen, Matt studied the woman who had claimed his heart and soul. Each time he saw her he was stunned by her beauty and poise. His pulse quickened as he stepped off the escalator and came into full view of Carolyn.

"Matt!" she exclaimed. "I'm so glad you're here!" Her arms opened wide to embrace him and he gladly returned the hug. He kissed her cheek and reached for her hand, his bags in the other.

"So, what's on the agenda this weekend? Riding lessons, horse grooming, baling hay, or hot chocolate in front of the fire?" Matt asked playfully.

"An interesting selection, Dr. Brooks. What would you like to do?" Carolyn teased.

Matt squeezed her hand. "Anything you want to do, dear woman, is fine with me."

"Ha, just like a man – can't make a decision. Well, in that case, how about a little of all the above, except baling hay. I'm not sure you're ready to handle that job yet, city boy."

The cheerful banter continued on the drive to the farm, and it was easy for Matt to relax and to forget for a while how he would rock Carolyn's world the next day.

Carolyn pulled her Land Rover through the farm gate. She was a good driver, Matt noted, and handled the relatively large vehicle with practiced expertise. As usual, Carl came to greet them as Carolyn stopped in front of her home.

"Evenin' Ma'am, Dr. Brooks; it's good to see you again."

"Thanks, Carl. I believe this place has rubbed off on me. Do you think you could find time to give me more riding pointers tomorrow?"

"Sure thing; just let me know when you're ready," Carl

agreed. Then, he turned to Carolyn.

"Ma'am, I thought you should know. We've had a bit of trouble again."

"Oh? What was it, Carl?" Carolyn responded, a worried look on her face.

Carl drew in a breath before speaking, clearly uncomfortable relating the incident. "Well, ma'am, it was the Simpson brothers again. They opened the east pasture gate this afternoon, and three mares got out of the pasture and onto the road. One of them was hit by a pickup truck and didn't make it. Two others were grazed but not head-on. I called the vet, and he patched up the two injured mares. There was nothing he could do for the third one; she probably died on impact."

Carolyn didn't speak at first, too stunned to respond. When she found her voice, she asked, "Was the driver of the pickup injured?"

"No, just a small bump on his head. He tried to miss the mares, but he clipped the first two and the third one took the brunt of it as his truck spun around. He ended up against a tree."

Which mares?" She prayed it wasn't Honey.

"Millie died, ma'am. She was older than the rest and a bit slower. I guess that's why she got hit." Carolyn winced at the image. "Rosie and Annie were injured."

"Are you sure it was the Simpson brothers?"

"Ninety-nine percent sure. Who else could it be? Besides, I found tire tracks by the gate that match those giant tires on Jeremy Simpson's truck, a monster truck he calls it. It isn't the truck that's the monster, it's him!" Carl's face had become red with anger.

"Easy there, Carl. Let's not lay blame yet. Did you call the sheriff?"

"I did, but we all know how far that will go, don't we? The Simpsons will provide an air-tight alibi, and that will be the end of it."

Carolyn let out a sigh. "When will this feud end? I've tried everything I know to make amends to the Simpsons, but it hasn't helped. Has the sheriff come yet?"

"He sent a deputy who took the information. He said he would follow up with the Simpsons. What do you want to do about it?"

Carolyn was silent for several moments, concern etched on her features. "Nothing, Carl, at least not at the moment. Thank you for looking after the mares and calling the sheriff. I'll be down to the barn to check on the mares in about thirty minutes." It was a dismissal.

Carl was clearly surprised by the response, but said nothing. He trusted his employer to handle it her way. His only reply was, "Yes ma'am," and he walked back to the barn to tend to the injured mares.

Matt had stood quietly and said nothing as he listened to the conversation. When Carl walked away, he turned to Carolyn. "What is going on; who are the Simpsons?"

Carolyn looked tired. "It's a long story. Let's get you settled; I'll tell you about it later." She turned toward the house and Matt followed. It seemed Carolyn's slice of paradise had a snake in it. He wasn't the only one with a lot on his mind. How could he tell the woman he loved about his own problems when she was obviously carrying a heavy load of her own?

Matt stowed his things in his usual room on the second floor of the large farmhouse, washed up quickly, and headed back downstairs. As he reached the bottom step, he heard Carolyn speaking to someone on the phone.

"Phil, you're the sheriff! You can't overlook this behavior any longer. I don't care if they are your wife's nephews, their behavior has cost a mare her life and injured two others, not to mention the danger to the driver who came along as the mares were crossing the road. He could have been killed."

Matt could hear the strain in her voice as she made an attempt to stay calm and not sound like a hysterical female. There was a pause as Carolyn listened to the sheriff's response. Apparently, she wasn't satisfied with his answer.

"I understand, but it can't go on. The Simpsons' reprisals have escalated, and I fear they won't stop until made to do so."

Matt remained by the steps, not wanting to intrude on a private conversation that was clearly not going well.

"Phil, I don't plan to just sit here and wait for the next attack from those reprobates. No, that's not a threat, it's a promise!" Carolyn slammed the phone down and stood shaking from the encounter.

Matt waited a few more seconds before joining her. "Carolyn, sweetheart, are you all right?"

Tears were streaming down her face and her hands were fisted in anger. "Oh, Matt, I'm sorry you had to witness this. I wanted your weekend to be perfect."

Matt closed the space between them and wrapped her in a gentle hug. He leaned back enough to look at her and wiped a tear away. "Carolyn, anytime I'm with you is perfect. Now, what can I do to help?"

Carolyn buried her face in Matt's shoulder. "I wish you could help, but I need to handle this on my own." She pulled a tissue from her pocket and dabbed the remaining tears from her face. "Mary has prepared a wonderful dinner for us, and we shouldn't let it get cold." She reached for Matt's hand and led him to the dining room where a candlelit table with a soft yellow tablecloth stood ready for them. Matt pulled out a chair for Carolyn and sat down opposite.

"Wow, this is quite unexpected. I would have settled for hamburgers from a drive-thru."

Carolyn laughed. "I don't get a lot of visitors out here and besides, I want this weekend to be special for you, for us."

Matt saw the yearning in her eyes and wanted more than anything to be the man she thought him to be. She deserved someone better, someone without a possible murder charge hanging over his head.

"The moment I saw you in the airport, my weekend became special. You are a wonderful woman."

Carolyn smiled. "Why Matthew Brooks, I didn't know you were such a romantic! I feel like a heroine in one of those paperback romance novels.

Matt laughed. "I meant every word. I've never met anyone like you."

Carolyn's expression sobered. "I suppose we both got lucky in Vegas. Strange, isn't it?"

"What is?"

"That we should meet in Las Vegas of all places and hit it off immediately. I certainly didn't intend to start a relationship when I went there. I doubt you did either."

"No, that was definitely not on my agenda, but we did find each other in all that mayhem."

"It was meant to be." Carolyn responded. "Now, let's eat."

Sadie appeared from the kitchen as if by magic, and Matt wondered how much of their conversation she had overheard. He had grown up with household staff but had grown unaccustomed to their presence in recent years. He made a mental note to be more aware of who might be listening to their conversations. His thoughts were interrupted as Sadie served the first course of a sumptuous meal and conversation turned to lighter topics.

By the time dessert was served, Matt was too full to accept. "It looks delicious, but I can't find room for another bite." He leaned back and patted his stomach.

Carolyn nodded. "I have to agree. Sadie, please ask Mary to put our desserts aside for later. We'll enjoy this wonderful treat more once our dinner has settled a bit."

"Yes, ma'am," the maid responded as she reached for the desserts and placed them on the serving tray. "Is there anything else you need, ma'am?"

"No, thank you."

Sadie returned to the kitchen with the desserts as the couple rose from the table. Carolyn hesitated a moment before asking Matt if he would take a walk with her. "It's a beautiful evening; would you like to take a walk?"

Matt sensed the tension within her and assumed it was because of the incident with the horses but didn't want to pry. Maybe a bit of brevity would help. He patted his belly. "Great idea, maybe I can work off a few of those calories we just consumed before they find their way to my waistline."

Carolyn laughed as she led the way to the side hallway where jackets were hanging. She handed one to Matt which he assumed had belonged to the recently deceased Mr. Hodges. He helped Carolyn into hers and slipped his arms into his before removing his shoes and donning the pair of sneakers he had left there during the last visit. The jacket had the faint scent of the barn – horses, hay, and leather. Instead of causing him to feel uneasy, it felt oddly reassuring and comfortable. Maybe he was catching on to this farm life.

Once outside, Carolyn said she needed to check on the injured mares in the barn and led the way to the large modern structure. Matt followed a few steps behind. They knew something was wrong as soon as they entered. It was too quiet, no neighing of horses or the reassuring voice of Carl as he worked with the animals. A tingle ran down Carolyn's spine and she stopped just inside the doorway. "Carl? Carl, are you in here?"

The only sound in return was a low moan. Carolyn started to move toward the sound, but Matt held her arm to stop her. "Don't, let me check it out first."

Matt stepped past Carolyn and walked cautiously toward the sound. "Carl, are you in here?"

A voice responded but the words were unintelligible. Matt walked quickly and discovered Carl lying in the doorway of a stall at the far end of the barn. He was half sitting and was holding his head. Blood was trickling down the side of his face.

"Carl!" Matt hurried to the older man and knelt down. Carolyn had caught up and bent over her farm manager.

"Carl, what happened? Who did this?"

Still too stunned by the attack, he was unable to answer.

Matt examined the head wound and looked in Carl's eyes. Blood was still oozing from the wound. A few stitches would take care of that. He used the flashlight he had carried with him to check for brain injury. Carl's pupils were equal and reactive to

147

light, a good sign. Carolyn watched Matt's practiced movements, grateful for his medical knowledge and skill. Once he finished his cursory examination, he turned to Carolyn.

"Except for the cut, he seems okay, but he'll need a few stitches, and he should have a scan to make sure his head wound isn't more serious than it appears."

Carolyn nodded and hurried to the barn office where there was a phone. She requested an ambulance and the sheriff. Both were on their way in seconds. She hung up the phone and noticed her hands were shaking. She took a few slow, deep breaths to calm down and returned to Matt and Carl.

"The sheriff and an ambulance are on their way." She knelt down next to Carl who seemed to be recovering slowly from the attack.

He looked up at Carolyn and said, "It was the Simpsons."

"Are you sure?" Carolyn asked as she searched Carl's face as if she would find another answer there.

"I didn't see who attacked me, but who else could it be? They want you to suffer and won't end their vendetta until they are forced to stop."

The effort to talk was difficult for him so Carolyn didn't respond. There would be time for details later. He needed medical attention first.

Matt looked around him and spied a first aid box on a post nearby. "Carolyn, are there bandages in that first aid kit?"

"There should be, I'll check." She hurried over to the box and opened it. "Yes, and tape."

"Good, bring them here. I'll put a temporary bandage on his head wound. Is there any saline solution?"

"Yes, we keep it for the horses to clean out their nicks and cuts. I'll get it."

Carolyn hurried away again and retrieved the solution and handed it to Matt. He used the saline and gauze from the first aid kit to clean the wound gently, then placed a butterfly bandage to hold the edges together. Blood was still seeping out of the wound, so Matt applied a non-stick dressing over the area and secured it with tape.

"That will hold you, Carl, until you get to the hospital."

"Thanks, Dr. Brooks."

"Glad to help." Matt was glad the injury didn't appear to be more serious, but he knew a head injury could be more serious than it first appeared. "I think I hear sirens, Carl; we'll have you to the hospital in no time." He turned to Carolyn. "Do you want me to go to the hospital with Carl so you can be here for the sheriff?"

"Thank you, that would help. I'll get Carl's insurance information. Tell the hospital to send the bill to me if insurance doesn't cover all of it. I take care of my own."

"Okay, sounds like a plan." He turned back to the injured farm manager who was holding his head.

"Headache?"

"Yeah, a doozy," Carl responded, not looking up.

Matt suspected a concussion, all the more reason to get him to the hospital for treatment and tests. "Hang in there, we'll be on our way soon."

Carolyn returned with Carl's wallet just behind the EMT's. The paramedics bent over their patient while Matt looked on. In a few minutes, Carl was being loaded into the ambulance.

"Here's the keys to my truck so you can follow the ambulance. I picked up your phone, too."

"Thanks, you think of everything."

"Not everything, or my farm manager wouldn't be on his way to the hospital right now." Carolyn's voice betrayed her anger and concern.

Matt leaned over to kiss Carolyn on the cheek. "Don't worry, sweetheart; Carl is pretty tough."

Carolyn merely nodded as she fought back tears.

The sheriff arrived as Matt passed through the barn door.

"What's going on, Carolyn?"

She related the events of the past twenty minutes but withheld Carl's suspicions regarding the Simpson brothers. She wanted the sheriff to come to his own conclusions.

"This is bad business, for sure. First, your mares are set loose and now poor Carl gets attacked. Do you think it was the Simpsons again?"

"I don't know; Carl certainly thinks so, but he said he didn't see who attacked him."

"This isn't good, and I don't have the manpower to leave a deputy here. Have you considered hiring a few men for protection?" The pair walked out of the barn together.

"Yes, I have Phil, and I'll take care of that in the morning. I simply can't understand why the Simpson brothers have resorted to such extreme measures. Why attack Carl? What good did it do?"

The sheriff met Carolyn's eyes. "Have you checked the horses since the attack? Maybe Carl was trying to prevent whatever they came to do."

Carolyn didn't answer the sheriff. The barn had been quiet earlier and, with the discovery of Carl, no one had seen to the horses. She turned back into the barn and ran to Honey's stall.

The gentle mare whinnied at the site of her mistress. Carolyn stroked Honey and spoke gently to her.

"Who did this, Honey? Who attacked Carl?"

The horse responded to the gentle stroking and nuzzled her. The sheriff walked up behind her.

"Don't touch more than is absolutely necessary; I'll send someone out tomorrow morning to check for any evidence of who did this. I'm really sorry, Carolyn. No matter what happened in the past, you don't deserve this."

The painful memory the sheriff had resurrected washed over Carolyn like a torrent of water after a heavy rain. The accident hadn't been her fault, but the Simpson brothers wanted her to suffer for it, as their younger brother had.

She was aware of the sheriff speaking to her and pulled her thoughts away from that fateful night when her life intersected with the Simpson family forever. "What did you say, Phil?"

Phil put his arm around her shoulders. "I know life hasn't been easy for you these past few years, but you're a strong woman and I know you'll handle this with as much courage as you have everything else. I'm here when you need me."

"Thanks, I appreciate that. You've been a good friend as well as my cousin."

Phil gave her shoulder a squeeze and turned to leave. He turned back. "Oh, speaking of friends, who is the good-looking fella that was leaving as I arrived? Got a new beau?" He smiled mischievously.

Carolyn blushed much to her own surprise. Phil noticed.

"So, it's that way is it?" He laughed. "Good for you; I hope he deserves you."

"Now, Phil, just because you're my cousin doesn't mean you

get to nose around my personal life." She smiled. "But, yes, we are very fond of each other. He lives near Chicago. He's a dentist, and I met him in Vegas."

"Vegas? Not a very good place to look for a new husband," he said wryly.

"Whoa, Phil, we're not talking marriage, at least not yet." Her eyes betrayed her feelings as she talked. "I've never met anyone like him. He's smart, kind, attentive, and the horses like him."

Phil laughed. "Well, if the horses like him, he's golden," he replied, unable to keep the amusement from his voice. He sobered. "Just be careful, Carolyn; you are a very wealthy woman, and a lot of men would go to great lengths to get access to your money."

"Thanks for the advice, but I believe he has his own wealth and doesn't need mine. We haven't talked about it, but he is definitely accustomed to the finer things in life and that comes with a large price tag."

"Well, just make sure you aren't the one paying the price, cousin."

The pair left the barn, closed the door, and walked back to the house. "I need to call Matt and check on Carl. Will you stay a while with me?"

"Sure, unless I get another call. Could I have a sandwich? I haven't eaten since lunch."

"Of course, I'm sure Mary has plenty to choose from for a sandwich."

Carolyn settled Phil in the kitchen with his sandwich and punched in Matt's cell phone numbers.

"What? You missed me already?" Matt joked when he

picked up the call.

"By the tone of your voice I surmise that Carl is okay?" Carolyn asked.

"He has a mild concussion, the head laceration, and bruises over his back in the lower rib area on the right side. His kidneys are being scanned now to see if he sustained damage there. Whoever attacked Carl kicked him in the ribs once he was down."

"How terrible, poor Carl. Have you been able to see him?"

"Off and on between tests. He should be here another hour or two, so it will be late before I get back."

"Phil can drop me off at the hospital and we can bring Carl home together. First thing tomorrow I'll hire professional security. I should have done it sooner, but I really need to do it now."

"Carolyn?"

"Yes?"

"Why are the Simpson brothers doing this?"

Carolyn sighed. "It's a long story, but it's my fault they are so bent on revenge."

"Revenge for what?" Matt couldn't believe that kind and sweet Carolyn could be the catalyst for such behavior.

"I... I caused an accident that killed their younger brother."

"When was this? What kind of accident?"

"It was after we met in Vegas but before Ben died. It took me months to get through it. Between Ben's death, his daughter's issues, and the accident, I thought I would simply fold. I was driving home from the hospital where I had visited Ben. It was raining and the two-lane road was very slick because it had been resurfaced recently. There was a thin coating of oil on the surface, and I slid into Jesse Simpson's truck as I rounded a curve. He was the youngest of their family. Even though he was speeding and driving erratically according to witnesses, I was the one who crossed the center line, so it was ruled my fault, but an accident. I was not charged with a crime given the road conditions and weather. The Simpsons didn't see it that way and pushed for charges to be brought against me. They accused me of buying the decision with Ben's money. It didn't seem to matter that there was absolutely no basis for the accusation; they still wanted me behind bars. I guess it's how they are dealing with their grief. I don't know how to make it right. Nothing will bring Jesse back. I'll live with the guilt from that night for the rest of my life."

Matt had stayed silent during her explanation. He realized he wasn't the only one carrying heavy baggage. When Carolyn finished, he offered reassurance.

"Carolyn, it wasn't your fault. Freshly applied asphalt always has a thin layer of oil."

"I appreciate your support, Matt, but I should have been more cautious and driven slower. I'm just not sure how to proceed from here. It's clear the Simpsons won't let up. They're out for blood."

"I'm sorry, Carolyn. What can I do?" Matt asked with concern evident in his voice.

"I appreciate the offer, but I don't know what anyone can do. We're almost ready to leave. We'll be there within the hour."

"Okay, be safe. I'm here for you sweetheart; I'm not going anywhere."

Carolyn laughed. "So, you're saying I'm stuck with you?"

"I guess so, unless you tell me to go away."

"Little chance of that; I'm glad you're here." Carolyn added before hanging up.

Matt thought about the exchange. He had accepted that he and Carolyn were a couple but had not resolved what that could mean logically. He lived in Illinois, she in Kentucky. A long-distance relationship wasn't feasible forever. He knew how she felt about her farm, and he would never ask her to give it up, but what about his practice? Could he willingly give up what he had worked years to build? Could he get enough from the sale of his practice to support him? The key was his inheritance. Being able to receive what his father left him would give him the ability to step away from dentistry. The sale of his booming practice would also boost his finances. He would have no need to work. It made more sense for him to move. That is, if he could get his hands on his written confession before someone else did. If he failed, the decision to move or not was a moot point and the least of his worries.

His musing was interrupted by Carl's nurse. "Dr. Brooks? Mr. Richter won't be ready to leave for a while yet, but I need to go over some discharge instructions with you."

"Certainly." The nurse sat down next to Matt and reviewed the wound care and head injury instructions. He listened carefully and agreed to follow up as instructed. He folded the paper and slipped it into his jacket pocket. He checked the time and expected Carolyn any minute. As he waited, he wondered if she would still want him to stick around if she knew about the plot to murder Ron Bennett. He let out a breath and prayed the confession letter would never see daylight. He had to find a way to get into the desk.

His thoughts were interrupted by approaching footsteps. He looked up to see Carolyn approaching. "Hey there; where's the sheriff?"

"He got another call just as we got to the hospital. What's the latest on Carl?" She asked before sitting next to Matt and handing him a decaf coffee.

"Thanks for the coffee. He's being discharged now. I have his discharge instructions." He pulled out the papers and handed them to Carolyn before taking his first sip of the hot liquid. She perused them quickly before putting them away in her purse.

"What a night! I'm sorry your weekend is being spent this way."

"I'm with you, that's all that counts." Matt wrapped his arm around her and smiled when she dropped her head on his shoulder. Her body warmth penetrated his clothing, and he realized how good it felt to have this closeness with her. She had bared her soul to him about the fatal accident that prompted the vicious responses from the Simpson brothers. Could their relationship survive if he told her his secrets? Would she feel the same as before? He was in love and was convinced Carolyn was as well. It would break his heart to lose her, but he had to tell her everything. He couldn't base their love on secrets.

A nurse arrived pushing Carl in a wheelchair. Carolyn asked Matt to get the Range Rover and bring it to the emergency department entrance. Carolyn stayed with Carl, wanting to reassure herself that he would be okay once he healed.

Matt navigated Carolyn's Range Rover to the emergency entrance as instructed and turned off the engine. He hurried to the passenger side of the vehicle and opened the door. The nurse brought Carl out and assisted him into the backseat. Carolyn helped Carl with his seatbelt before assuming her seat next to Matt. The trio thanked the nurse and headed back to the farm.

Carl was the first one to speak. "I'm really sorry about this, Mrs. Hodges; I should have expected trouble after the episode with the mares."

Carolyn turned to her farm manager. "Carl, this is not your fault. It's mine. We need more security, and we will have a professional security service beginning tomorrow. I doubt we'll have any further problem tonight, but I did ask Frank and Mark to make rounds tonight with loaded rifles. I instructed them to be cautious and not shoot unless absolutely necessary, but we need to be more vigilant. I don't want anyone else hurt. I'm so sorry you were attacked."

"Thank you, ma'am, but I'm going to be all right. A day or two to rest up and I'll be back to normal."

"The doctor wants you to recuperate a few days longer than that, Carl. Please do what he said to do. Sadie has made up a bedroom in the house for you so you can get the help you need."

"I appreciate that, I really do, but I'll be just fine in my own cottage. I'm used to my own place."

"But, Carl..."

"Please don't insist, Mrs. Hodges; I'll be fine on my own."

Matt kept silent, but he understood Carl's desire to stay in his own home. He would lose privacy and most likely suffer from a bit too much attention from Sadie and Carolyn if he went along with his employer's plans.

Carolyn considered the logistics of caring for Carl in his own cottage. After a few minutes she said, "Okay, Carl, stay in your own cottage, but someone will check on you several times a day and your meals will be brought to you. No cooking, understand?"

Carl knew he had won the battle and readily agreed to the stipulations. "That sounds good; I like Mary's cooking."

"Good, that's settled."

The three of them rode on in silence the rest of the way, and Carl eventually nodded off to sleep. Matt reached for Carolyn's hand and gave it a squeeze. He hoped it gave her some comfort as she was carrying a lot of guilt for the accident and the attack on Carl. He decided to arrange for a locum tenens dentist to care for his patients for a few days, maybe a week, so he could provide emotional support for the woman he had come to love. The decision felt right to him despite the pressing need to get his hands on the confession he had so foolishly written.

Chapter Seventeen

The next morning Matt woke early in spite of getting to bed at one a.m. He showered and dressed quickly before heading downstairs to breakfast. He hoped Carolyn was still asleep; she needed the rest after everything that had happened. He was disappointed, however, when he walked into the dining room and found her already seated at the table.

"Good morning, sleepy head!" she greeted cheerfully.

"Aren't you the chipper hostess this morning," he replied. "Did you get any sleep?" Matt asked as he pulled out the chair next to her and sat down.

"Actually, yes I did. All the excitement caught up with me. I was asleep as soon as my head hit the pillow. How was your night?"

The same. How is Carl this morning?"

"Frank and Mark reported on him before heading home this morning. They checked on him once during the night and again this morning and said he was resting well. Sadie will take his breakfast to him in a bit."

"I meant to ask, who are Frank and Mark?" Matt asked.

"They are neighbors who help us out fairly regularly. They know their way around a farm and are good shots, so I felt safe with them patrolling last night. I guess that's why I was able to sleep so well."

"It's good to have people you can count on," Matt remarked as he reached for a piece of toast. "What's the agenda for today?"

"Well, I was planning to spend a leisurely day with you, but I guess that won't be possible. We'll have to pitch in and take care of some of Carl's responsibilities. Frank and Mark have gone home to get some sleep, but they will be back this afternoon to help out. You and I need to tend to the horses this morning, especially the mares injured yesterday."

"That's fine with me. I'll be glad to help out anyway I can."

Carolyn smiled and reached for Matt's hand. "I knew you would say that. This will certainly be a weekend to remember," she said ruefully.

"It's okay. I'll enjoy the change of pace." Matt replied, returning her smile. "I dressed for farm duty, so I'll be ready for work after breakfast."

They enjoyed their meal and light conversation, a welcome change from the drama of the night before. Once both had finished eating, they went straight to the barn to begin the chores. Carolyn entered first and was surprised to see the vet examining one of the injured horses. Matt turned to the opposite end of the barn to begin mucking out stalls and to allow Carolyn privacy with the vet.

"David, I wasn't expecting you, but I'm glad you're here. How are the patients this morning?"

"Good morning, both mares are recovering nicely. It will be a while before they are permitted back out to the pasture, but I'm sure that both will recover fully. I'm more concerned about you. I heard about the attack on Carl."

Carolyn nodded. "Yes, it was quite a night, but Carl is doing well and is expected to be up and around soon. I've arranged for professional security beginning today. Frank and Mark Thompson were kind enough to provide security last night."

"I'm glad to hear you will have professional security. This feud with the Simpson's has certainly escalated. Be careful," he added.

"I appreciate your concern; I assure you we are taking this very seriously. The attack on Carl and the incident with my mares shows how much vitriol the Simpson family has toward me. I wish we could prove their involvement because I doubt they are finished with their plans for revenge."

"I believe you're right, I'm sorry to say. You don't deserve this." The vet's expression showed genuine concern. "You have friends, Carolyn, don't hesitate to call on us."

"Thank you, David. So many people turned against me after the accident and I haven't known who to trust and who to avoid. You have always been a constant I could depend on."

"Don't judge your neighbors too harshly. The Simpson boy was popular, but folks know how wild he was. Between the freshly applied asphalt and his fast driving, there wasn't anything that could have prevented the tragic outcome. You need to forgive yourself."

Tears formed in Carolyn's eyes, and she fought to get control. When she spoke, her voice reflected the emotion she was feeling. "David, I don't believe I'll completely recover from the accident, but I do appreciate your support. It means a lot to me."

The vet reached out and pulled Carolyn in for a hug. He kissed the top of her head and pulled back to look at her. "Now, walk with me back to my truck and tell me all about your new beau," he said brightly as they walked.

Carolyn blushed, causing her to cover her face with her

hands. "Oh my, you caught me off guard."

The vet laughed. "So, tell me all about him."

The beaming smile on Carolyn's face as she answered the question made it obvious how she felt about Matt. Dr. King was pleased. He had known Carolyn's husband Ben for many years and he understood how difficult the marriage had been. It was good to see her happy.

"Okay, this guy is a dentist from Illinois, right?"

Carolyn concurred.

"How in the world did the two of you meet? It seems rather odd that you found each other given the geographical differences."

Carolyn laughed. "I guess it does seem rather improbable, but I suppose it was fate. We met in Las Vegas in May. We were both looking for something, an intangible yet vital piece of ourselves. We met at a poker table of all things, and instantly recognized the attraction."

Dr. King raised an eyebrow.

Carolyn noticed the unstated question and hurriedly added, "Not a sexual attraction, but a potential friendship, a bond if you will. We spent Saturday afternoon and evening together taking in the sights, walking and talking, getting to know each other. That was the beginning. Nothing followed that until after Ben's death. Ben's illness and passing, the accident, and all I had to deal with in the aftermath kept me very focused. I was not thinking about a new relationship even though we texted a few times, first to let him know about Ben. Two months ago, I was brave enough to invite him to come to the farm. He accepted, and we've been a couple ever since."

Dr. King absorbed her story. "Wow! That is remarkable. May

I be so bold as to ask where this relationship is going? When your dad passed, he asked me to keep an eye on you and help you any way I could. I'm asking as a father would ask, not as a prying country vet."

"I know, you're a wonderful friend, and I know you miss Dad as much as I do. As for my relationship with Matt, we are just seeing where it will go. We have several hurdles to overcome if our relationship progresses, geography for one. We live several hundred miles apart and Matt has a thriving dental practice just outside of Chicago."

"And, you have this beautiful farm in Kentucky," Dr. King finished for her.

Carolyn sighed. "Yes, the farm. There would be a sacrifice, a big one, for one of us."

The vet nodded in agreement and turned to face Carolyn. He reached for both of her hands and gave a gentle squeeze. "I can tell he makes you happy, but take it slowly, okay? The last thing you need after all you have been through this past year is to suffer another disappointment."

"Carolyn returned the hand squeeze and said, "I know you're right, and we've kept it friendly so far. I sense a hesitation in Matt too, as if he has his own demons to overcome before he can commit to a serious relationship."

David pulled Carolyn in for a final hug. "I know you will make the right decision; you have a good head on your shoulders."

Carolyn smiled in response as she watched him get in his truck and drive away. She stood for several moments and watched as the truck disappeared from sight. Her thoughts were interrupted by Matt.

"Hey there," he said cheerfully. "I've finished mucking out the stalls, and I'm ready for my next assignment, ma'am," he said as he bowed and made a sweeping gesture with his right arm.

Carolyn laughed; it felt good to laugh. "Matthew Brooks, you are something else!"

"Simply at your service, m'lady," he said with an impish smile. "So, what's next? I'm here to serve the kingdom."

"My, it is wonderful to have such a gallant knight in my little kingdom," she returned playfully. "How about we check on the mares in the pasture? I want to make sure everything is all right."

"Sounds like a good idea. It will be good to be outside after mucking out stalls," Matt agreed as he rolled his eyes.

Carolyn laughed again. Everything seemed better when Matt was with her. She decided it was the shared burden that made her worries a bit lighter. For the first time in months, she didn't feel so alone. She knew David had given her wise advice, but she also knew she was falling hard for Matt. It was both disconcerting and wonderful at the same time.

After seeing to the mares, the pair checked in with two farmhands who were reinforcing fences with loose or missing railings. "Have you noticed any damage that might have been deliberate?" she asked the men.

"No, ma'am, just normal wear and tear," answered Jim, the older of the two. "We'll let you know if we see anything suspicious."

"Thank you, I'm sure you understand why I'm asking."

"Yes, ma'am. All of us are really upset about the situation. The Simpsons have no right to act like that, but I guess it's to be expected."

Carolyn raised an eyebrow.

Jim continued. "Those boys have always been trouble. They've gotten into one mess after another for years. Don't you worry about anything; we'll make sure nothing else happens."

Carolyn was touched by the loyalty. "Thank you, but the Simpsons have shown they are dangerous, be careful. Don't try to take them on, just call the sheriff."

"Now, Ms. Carolyn, you know it takes at least thirty minutes for a deputy to get here. By that time, those fellas could burn down a barn or worse. We're ready the next time they come calling." He patted his hip and Carolyn noticed the bulge for the first time under his jacket.

"Jim, don't use that gun. If you shoot one of them you could be arrested and put in prison," she responded with alarm.

"Aw, I won't actually shoot anybody; I'll just scare them a little bit. I'm a good shot; I'll be sure to miss them, but I'll shoot just close enough to put a scare into them. Until they know we're ready to fight back, they won't stop."

"Or, it could make things worse. Please leave the armed security to the men I've hired for that."

Jim wasn't buying it. "They can't be everywhere at once, ma'am. The men have gotten together, and we're ready to defend your farm."

It was a noble and grand statement, but Carolyn knew the situation had gotten out of hand. The feud had to end before anyone else got hurt. She cautioned her farmhands again to let the security guards deal with any situation that might arise and led Matt back to the house for lunch.

Carolyn was quiet as she munched on the chicken salad sandwich Mary had prepared. Matt could see she had a lot on her mind, and he remained silent until lunch was almost over. "A penny for your thoughts, pretty lady," he said gently.

She looked up for the first time since sitting down and seemed surprised to see another person across from her. "Oh, Matt, forgive me; I have a lot on my mind."

"No kidding. You're dealing with a lot right now, but I'm here and I'm ready to listen. I also have a very nice shoulder to lean on, if I do say so myself."

Carolyn smiled in spite of all that was weighing on her mind. "Thank you. You're good for me, Dr. Brooks."

"I'd say that goes two ways. You're pretty special yourself," he responded, all trace of amusement gone from his face.

Carolyn recognized there had been a shift in their relationship. There was more than friendship in his eyes, but was he ready for a real commitment? She decided it was time to find out. She pushed back from the table and announced a change in plans for the afternoon. "Let's saddle up the horses; I want to show you something."

Matt registered his surprise but readily agreed. He stood and joined Carolyn as she led the way to the barn. They saddled their horses and Carolyn led the way.

The day was perfect. The trees had turned vibrant shades of yellow, orange, and red. Some had already shed their leaves and the trail was strewn with a kaleidoscope of color. The autumn sun was warm on their shoulders, but a slight breeze foretold cooler days ahead. They rode side-by-side in comfortable silence for twenty minutes. Finally, Carolyn pointed ahead to a clearing. Beyond, but out of sight, was the sound of rushing water. "This is what I wanted to show you."

Matt nodded, but didn't offer comment. As they approached an outcropping of rock, he could hear the thunder of a waterfall.

Anticipation surged through his veins.

The trail narrowed, and Carolyn pulled her horse to a stop and motioned for Matt to go ahead of her. The sight that greeted him as he passed the outcropping was breathtaking. He pulled on the reins so he could take it all in. It was beautiful and frightening all at once. The power of the water as it plummeted to the blue pool below created a fine white mist that was almost impenetrable to the eye. He turned back to Carolyn and saw the respect for the spectacle on her face.

"Wow! That is beautiful! I have never seen anything like it outside of books or television," he exclaimed.

Carolyn smiled and nudged her horse to walk past her companion. "Follow me, there's more."

He couldn't imagine anything more magnificent, but he followed obediently.

As they neared the falls, the mist coated them. It felt good after the penetrating warmth of the sun. He turned to look at the fresh water of the stream as his horse continued walking. He turned back around only to discover that Carolyn had disappeared! He pulled his horse to a halt and scanned the area. *Where could she have gone?* he wondered.

From behind the falling water he heard his name being called. He rode on, unsure of where he was going. Just as he was passing the falls, he noticed someone on his left. Carolyn and her horse were *behind* the silver curtain of the rushing water!

He nudged his horse to join them and marveled at the dry ground so close to the falls. Carolyn smiled and gently slapped the reins to get her horse to move on. They passed to the other side of the water and up a steep hill. The horses picked their way with practiced expertise, confident of their footing.

At the top of the ridge, Matt's breath caught for the second time in only a few minutes. Spread out before them was a thick carpet of color. Autumn had put all of her glory into this special place and now proudly displayed her colorful raiment. It was magical. Matt halted his horse next to Carolyn's and both dismounted. They held the reins loosely and walked slowly along the ridge with their mounts ambling along behind. They secured the horses' reins around a low hanging branch. Carolyn approached a large rock and sat down. She patted the space next to her and they sat together in silence taking in nature's splendor as the horses grazed on the vegetation nearby. A yellow-tailed hawk soared soundlessly overhead as a rabbit, frightened by the passing shadow over her, scampered quickly into nearby bushes.

Carolyn breathed in the cool autumn air and decided it was time to discover what Matt was holding back from her. She hoped the spectacular surroundings would help him to open up.

"Okay, it's time to spill it."

He turned in surprise. "Spill what?"

"What you're not telling me. I can tell there has been something on your mind since the day I met you. What is it?"

He looked at her and searched for assurance before he spoke. He thought of playing off her concern, but he knew from the look in her eyes that she was ready for what he had to say.

He cleared his throat and took a deep breath. He looked straight ahead, afraid to see her face as he shared his secret. He began. "Earlier this year, around the time we met, I was facing financial ruin. I was about to lose my house, my practice, everything. My gambling, my ex-wife's over-spending, and a costly divorce had bankrupted me. I was desperate. The ironic part of it is that I am very wealthy. Now, that is, and you are responsible for that."

Carolyn gave a quizzical look but allowed Matt to continue without interruption.

"You see, my father left his entire estate to me. He was a successful businessman and made a lot of money in his lifetime. He died almost a year ago. His will stipulated that I had to show I had changed from my spendthrift lifestyle before I could claim my inheritance. If I had not changed to my father's attorney's satisfaction, the money would have defaulted to various charities. I had one year to prove I was worthy of such a fortune. It wasn't until I met you that I was able to bring about that change. I thought I could gamble my way out of the mess I was in and to hell with my father's money. That plan went out the window when I met you. I wanted to be the man you deserved. During the months after we met, I thought of you all the time. I didn't know if we would ever meet again, but I kept seeing you in my mind which somehow gave me the courage and direction I needed. I know this sounds too incredible to believe, but it's true. You have been the muse responsible for making me a better human being. I know I still don't deserve you, but I want to try."

Carolyn was silent several moments as she took in all he had said. "Oh, Matt, how incredible! I had no idea. And, as for deserving me, put all those notions behind you. I'd say we have found each other. Both of us are blessed by it."

Matt reached for her hand and smiled as he looked at her. "There's more. I just haven't had the courage to tell you. I've been afraid it would cause you to end our relationship and that frightened me. But, it's time for you to know the rest."

Carolyn was surprised by Matt's statement but merely nodded encouragement for what he was about to say.

"One day, when my debts were overwhelming me, I was paid a visit by my head dental assistant, Sylvia Bennett. She knew of my financial problems even though I had tried very hard to keep it private. She had a rather shocking proposal for me." Matt turned to search Carolyn's face but found no clue as to her response so far. He looked away again. "She told me her husband Ron had abused her during their entire marriage and was now turning his attention to their small children. She feared for them and wanted to be rid of her husband. She said she had tried to leave him, but he was a wealthy and well-liked man and had influence with people in high places. He told her she could never leave him. She felt the only way out of her marriage was to kill Ron."

Carolyn's eyes grew wide. "Kill him?"

Matt looked up at the clouds as they slid by over their heads. *How free they are – no commitments, no agenda, just floating over all the misery of the people below,* he thought to himself.

"Yes, kill him. She wanted me to do it and in such a way as to avoid suspicion. In exchange, she offered to share her husband's two-million-dollar life insurance policy with me fifty-fifty. I was tempted, but I felt I couldn't kill another human being. However, I sat down and looked at my debts and assets and realized I was facing financial and professional ruin and reluctantly agreed to her proposal."

"You killed her husband?" Carolyn asked with obvious shock.

"You're getting ahead of me, but no, I didn't. I couldn't go through with it. I planned it and thought I was ready to do it, but I just couldn't bring myself to kill another human being."

Carolyn let out her breath and realized she had been holding it as she waited for Matt's answer to her question. She reached for Matt's hand. "Go on."

"You won't believe the rest of this story. It turns out that Ron died that very night. He consumed a great deal of alcohol and a narcotic which caused him to lose his balance in his bathroom and fall. He hit his head on the edge of the bathtub and died from the resultant brain bleed. The police investigated and included me in their queries because I was the doctor who had prescribed the narcotic. Ron had asked for a pain killer for his back pain when he came for his dental appointment. I told him his primary care physician should do that, but he insisted. I prescribed only ten tablets of hydrocodone and cautioned him not to drink if he took the medication. He ignored my advice and consumed several tablets and washed them down with a half-bottle of whiskey. I'm surprised that didn't kill him outright, actually. In this intoxicated state he walked to his bathroom and fell. The blow to the back of his head caused bleeding in his brain and he must have died within a couple of hours after the fall."

"Then what?" asked Carolyn, now caught up in the story.

"Well, my assistant didn't believe me when I told her I didn't kill her husband. I refused the insurance money but accepted a loan instead. We put it in writing and had the loan agreement notarized."

"I'm proud of you, Matt. You resisted temptation in the face of tremendous pressure. You're no killer."

Matt was dumbfounded. Carolyn was proud of him, not screaming for him to go home to Illinois. His respect and admiration for her grew in that moment. "Before you think that was the end of it, I need to tell you something else."

"There's more?" she asked, afraid of the answer.

"I'm afraid so. When I agreed to kill Ron, I typed up two confessions. One for me and one for my assistant. I signed and gave my confession to her, and I kept her signed confession. That way, neither of us could point the finger at the other afterwards. We would both get away with it or both would go to prison, probably for life. It would be unlikely that I would be eligible for parole – ever. My assistant as a co-conspirator would probably get life in prison, too, but maybe parole in fifteen or twenty years. There was too much to lose to simply trust each other, so I created the confessions. After the police finished their investigation and ruled Ron's death an accident, I shredded my assistant's confession and asked her to do the same with mine. She didn't. She had hidden it in an old desk in a secret compartment and forgot about it in the aftermath of her husband's death and all that entailed. Throughout this time, Sylvia wasn't convinced of my innocence and she continued to have overwhelming guilt for her part in the plan to kill her husband. I finally convinced her I didn't kill Ron and asked about my confession. She responded with horror and told me she had given the desk to Ron's sister and had forgotten to remove the document before it was taken away. She explained she was moving and needed to get rid of a lot of her furniture. The sister-in-law sold the desk at auction, and I had to track it down."

"Did you find it?" Carolyn asked anxiously.

"Yes and no. I discovered the person who bought the desk, but she won't let me near it. I have no idea if the confession has been found or not."

"I'm stunned. Now I know what has stood between us all these months. I knew there was something, but I didn't imagine anything like this. What are you going to do?"

"I'm not sure. All I know is I have to look inside that desk. If someone discovers the confession, my goose is cooked."

"I see that. Well, that means we must convince that person to let you see the desk. Better yet, we'll offer her a lot of money for it, enough so she can't turn it down."

Matt laughed ruefully. "An offer she can't refuse?"

Carolyn smiled. "Something like that."

They were silent for several minutes. Eventually, it dawned on Matt that Carolyn had used a plural pronoun. "Carolyn?"

"Yes?"

"What did you mean when you said *we* need to convince her to let us see or buy the desk?"

"Just that, silly. You got yourself into a real mess, and it looks as if you could use some help getting out of it. I'm signing on."

"I don't understand; you are offering to help someone who contemplated murder for money."

"But you didn't go through with it. Your true character came through. Everyone is capable of bad things when pushed hard enough. The important thing is you couldn't do it."

"So, you aren't sending me packing?" He asked, too incredulous to believe her astonishing offer."

Her laughter rang over the ridge. "You crazy man! Don't you know I love you?"

Chapter Eighteen

The next morning after breakfast, Matt and Carolyn walked to Carl's cottage to check on his progress.

"Good morning, Carl! How are you feeling?" Carolyn asked cheerfully.

"I'm coming along, still sore, but I can move about easier."

"That's good to hear; we brought some of Mary's homemade blueberry muffins and a jar of peach marmalade."

Carl reached for the items. "Thank you, and thank Mary for me. I'm going to be fat by the time she gets through with me. I still haven't finished the pie she sent the day before yesterday," he added with a chuckle. He reached for his side and moaned. "It still hurts to laugh. My ribs took quite a beating."

"Carl, I'm so sorry about all of this. I never wanted a problem with anyone, much less a family bent on revenge."

"Not your fault, ma'am; they're just a bunch of hot heads. They only know one way to solve anything and that's with their fists. They won't catch us unaware next time."

Carolyn shuddered at the mention of a *next time*. "Please don't do anything rash, Carl. I don't want any of you hurt – or arrested. Let the security guards handle it." Her tone was slightly shrill.

The farm manager wanted to argue that the security guards couldn't be everywhere at once but decided against it. Behind his employer's words her face registered fear but also resolve. She was a strong woman, and he knew she meant what she said. He dropped his eyes and simply nodded in response.

Her tone became softer. "Carl, I'm responsible for all of you. I know you are very loyal and want to protect the farm and me, but we don't need more trouble or injury. The attack on you was bad enough. The sheriff will get this resolved."

As she spoke, she hoped she was right. She and Matt stayed with the farm manager a bit longer and left to check on the injured mares.

Upon approaching the barn, they heard the sound of horses in distress. High pitched whinnies and hoofs hitting the boards of stalls alerted Carolyn to trouble. She pulled her pistol from her jacket pocket and released the safety.

Matt's eyes widened. He had not known she had the gun. "Carolyn," he said in alarm, "What did you just tell Carl and your farmhand? You can't take on the Simpsons."

"I don't intend to start anything Matt, but I do intend to stop it," she replied with a determined look that stopped him from commenting further.

She strode forward to enter the barn, but Matt hurried to walk ahead of her. "Let me go first," he whispered.

Carolyn nodded but kept the gun firmly in both hands, ready for a quick response to any threat.

Just inside the barn lying on the ground was one of the security guards. Blood was oozing from a cut on his head, and he was moaning.

She bent down to examine him, but once she was satisfied the guard was alive and coming to, she proceeded behind Matt into the barn. The sharp metallic smell of blood permeated their nostrils and Carolyn's heart beat rapidly as she knew whatever the source, it wasn't good.

The sound of their entry alerted the intruder who emerged from the last stall with a bloodied piece of wood in his hand.

Carolyn immediately assumed a wider stance and lifted her arms to point the gun at him. "Hold it right there Jeremy!" She ordered. "Drop the wood and raise your hands!"

Jeremy Simpson looked around him for a way out. He thought he might be able to get past Carolyn, but Matt stood next to her with an angry and determined look on his face. Jeremy dropped the piece of wood and slowly raised his hands. Maybe he could get closer and get the drop on her. He eased forward. "Now, Mrs. Hodges, there's no need for a gun. I'm not armed," he said with an attempt at charm.

"Stop! Don't walk any closer," she warned.

"I just want to talk to you; there's no need for a gun," he said as he eased two steps closer.

Carolyn's response was to fire a shot just to the left of his shoulder. The sound frightened the stabled horses. Honey's stall was just behind Carolyn and the horse banged heavily against the door and dislodged the latch causing the half door to fly open suddenly. Carolyn instinctively turned toward the noise.

Jeremy saw his chance and lunged at Carolyn as he pulled a gun from the back of his jeans. He raised the gun and pointed it directly at her face. Before he could pull the trigger, however, Carolyn fired and hit him in the right shoulder. His gun fell from his injured arm and he staggered backward into a bale of hay. Unable to keep his balance, he landed on his back on the ground.

"You bitch! You'll pay for this!" He exclaimed as he writhed in pain.

"No, *you'll* pay for this." She turned to Matt and asked him to check on the injured mares who were in the last two stalls.

Carolyn kept her gun trained on the injured man but in her peripheral vision she looked anxiously for Matt's response to what he found.

A low moan from Matt and his slumped shoulders were enough to tell Carolyn it was bad. She took a deep breath to steady herself and directed Matt to call the sheriff and ask for an ambulance for the guard and Jeremy. "Then, call the vet. You'll find both numbers in my phone," she told him as she pulled it out of her jacket.

Matt returned to Carolyn's side and accepted the phone. He turned to face Jeremy as he dialed. Jeremy's bravado had vanished. Dawning realization of the trouble he was facing had subdued him.

Ten minutes later, the vet showed up and joined them in the barn. He was shocked to see Carolyn pointing a gun at a man on the ground but said nothing about it. Instead, he knelt beside the security guard to check his injuries. "An ambulance is on its way. Lie still until they arrive."

The guard nodded. Then, the vet attempted to approach Jeremy even though Carolyn's gun was still aimed at the injured man.

"Stay away from me, you horse doctor!"

"As you wish," the seasoned vet answered. He rose and walked to the end of the row of stalls. Even to an experienced vet, the sight was horrific. One mare was dead and the other had a broken leg. She would have to be put down. He asked Matt to kneel next to the mare and try to keep her as calm as possible while he administered the lethal dose.

177

Matt sat next to the mare and placed her head on his lap. He stroked her gently and talked to her until the medication took effect. In a few moments it was over. She was gone. Tears came to his eyes and he noticed the vet had shed a few of his own. "What kind of monster could do this?" He asked the vet. In reply, David only shook his head and picked up his supplies and placed them in his bag.

"I'll arrange for the horses to be picked up today."

Matt nodded numbly and rose to his feet. He extended his hand. "Thanks, Doc."

David accepted the offered hand and grasped it firmly. "I'm glad you're here, Matt. Take care of Carolyn." The words were delivered with a smile but the meaning was clear. Matt would have to deal with David if he hurt Carolyn.

"Thanks, I'm glad to be here and yes, I'll do my very best to make her happy."

Satisfied that his message had been sent and received, David picked up his bag and walked back with Matt to Carolyn.

Without taking her eyes away from Jeremy, Carolyn asked, "How bad is it, David?"

He sighed. "They're both gone; there was nothing I could do."

Carolyn struggled to maintain her composure as she kept a steady grip on her gun. It was all she could do not to shoot the man lying bleeding in front of her. In a raspy voice, she replied, "Thank you."

"I'll arrange for the horses to be removed later today. It would be best to put the rest of the mares out to pasture before they come. Let me know if any of them need something to calm them down. They understand a lot more than we credit them."

"Thank you, David; I will."

Sirens broke through the crisp morning air and became louder with each passing second. An ambulance came into view and was followed moments later by the sheriff and another ambulance. EMT's rushed to the sides of the two injured men. With practiced expertise, they assessed each man, started an IV on Jeremy and applied a blood stopping agent to stem the amount of blood loss. The status of both was called into the hospital and each man was loaded onto a stretcher and placed in an ambulance.

A deputy followed behind in a squad car intent on interviewing both men at the hospital. He dreaded, however, the inevitable arrival of the Simpson family. It would be a terrible scene, one that would likely result in the need for backup and possible arrests. The Simpson temper was legendary in the county, which had resulted in the arrest of the brothers more than once. *Born trouble makers,* he thought with a shake of his head.

The sheriff had watched as the men were treated and loaded into the ambulances. He did not ask any questions until the doors slammed on the ambulance doors.

"Carolyn, are you all right?"

"Not really, Phil." Tears streamed down her face as she spoke.

"I need to see them. May I?"

David spoke up. "They're down this way, Phil. One of them was still alive but in terrible pain from a shattered foreleg. I had to put her down, I'm afraid."

Carolyn knelt beside the first horse and stroked her neck gently, then proceeded to the next stall and did the same. Her shoulders shook with sobs as she took in the slaughter before her.

"They were just innocent mares; why did Jeremy do this?"

Matt took her in his arms and tried to comfort her. Phil approached them and suggested they return to the house. "I'll join you after I speak with David."

Matt gently guided Carolyn away from the bloody scene. "Let's go, sweetheart."

Phil escorted them out of the barn before turning back to join the vet who had returned to the dead horses. The sheriff thought he knew what he would see but it was much more than he had anticipated. There were red smears everywhere with trails of it high up on the walls of the stalls where it flew from the savage blows. Rage boiled within him. He, like many people in the county, owned horses. To him, they were more than four-legged animals. He treated his own horses with respect and kindness.

He turned back to the vet who was standing just outside the farthest stall. "How could anyone do something this vicious? I thought I knew what Jeremy Simpson was capable of, but apparently I was wrong." He could feel the prickling of tears forming and brushed them away with his hand. "I'll get my forensics team out here for photographs and all. Don't move the horses until they are finished."

"No problem. I have advised Carolyn to put the remaining horses in the pasture while the area is investigated and the mares are being removed."

"Good idea," the sheriff concurred. "David, I'm concerned about Carolyn. I've known her since she was born. Our mothers were sisters, you know." David nodded. "I realize how very strong she is, but she has had to deal with a lot in the past few months. Now, I understand she is in a serious new relationship."

David nodded his agreement. "I have spoken to her about

her new beau. He seems all right and appears to be committed to her. Their biggest hurdle is geography. Dr. Brooks lives and works in Illinois. He has a dental practice there, so it would be a sacrifice for him to move here, and I know Carolyn won't leave this farm."

"You're right about that. It may have been in Ben's name, but she has run it for the past several years. Her sweat built this up to what it is now," Phil added.

David led the way back to the house to interview Carolyn and Matt. The men found them in the sunroom. Both could see that Carolyn was terribly upset. Matt was sitting next to her on the settee with his arm around her and offering words of comfort. The sound of the men approaching caught Carolyn's attention. Her eyes held questions neither man could answer.

"Sit down, please," Carolyn instructed. "I've asked Sadie to bring a pitcher of iced tea and four glasses."

David thought, but did not express his opinion that she could use something stronger than iced tea, but he merely thanked her and sat in one of the chairs available.

Phil sat in another and took the lead. "Carolyn, tell me everything that happened – from the beginning, please."

She explained about walking to the barn to check on the mares and how she and Matt had discovered the bleeding and half-conscious security guard just inside the door. Jeremy was inside one of the stalls wielding a large piece of wood. She couldn't see the mare he was attacking but she heard the blows. The memory created such horror for her that she thought she might vomit. With effort, she fought the nausea but remained pale and obviously shaken by the trauma.

"I called out to him and he turned to me. I pulled my gun out and pointed it at him. He didn't take me seriously so I sent a shot above his left shoulder; I deliberately missed him. He still didn't think I meant business and came toward me with his gun pointed at me. So, I shot him in the right shoulder so he would have to drop his gun. Matt left to phone you, David, and ambulances. I kept my gun trained on Jeremy while Matt was gone and until you arrived, Phil."

Phil could see how spent she was. "Honey, why don't you lie down for a while? Dr. Brooks can fill us in on the rest," Phil suggested gently.

Matt regarded the sheriff with new respect and gratitude. He had been unable to convince Carolyn to lie down until Phil took her statement.

"I'm fine, just shocked is all. I'd rather get this over with." Her face was streaked with fresh tears. She looked up at the sheriff and searched his face for answers. "I simply can't understand how anyone could be so cruel. What defect lies deep within Jeremy for him to do such a thing?"

"I don't know, but this has to be the end of this issue. Jeremy will do hard time for this. With the attack on Carl and this horrendous act, he has proven his inability to let the past go."

"Won't that cause the rest of his crazy family to pick up where he let off?" She asked.

"I doubt it," answered Phil. "Jeremy is the worst of the lot and the ringleader. With him out of the way, I expect the rest of them will pull back. Oh, I expect them to rattle their sabers during the trial if there is one, but once Jeremy is found guilty and sent to prison, they will probably drown their sorrows in a jug of hooch and get falling down drunk. It's more or less their pattern of behavior."

"I hope you're right; this has to stop." Tears ran down her face and she brushed them away with the back of her hand. "There has been too much loss already. I would give anything to bring that boy back, but I can't. I'll never forget the image of him lying lifeless on that stretcher. The last words I heard before I was placed in a separate ambulance was that the boy was dead. I'll live with that the rest of my life." Her silent tears had become sobs. She placed her hands over her face and turned into Matt's chest.

"Can't we talk more about this later, gentlemen?" Matt pleaded. "She needs to rest now."

David nodded and rose from his chair. Phil walked to Carolyn's side and leaned down to kiss the top of her head. "Get some rest honey. We'll get this sorted out soon. I'll update you tomorrow."

Carolyn pulled her hands down from her tear-streaked face and looked up at her cousin. "Thanks, Phil. I'm so sorry to be so emotional."

"Now don't you worry about that. With all you've been through this past year, you're allowed your tears."

Phil turned his attention to Matt. "Take care of her." His message was clear, *Take care of her – or else!*

"I'm not going anywhere, Sheriff."

Phil nodded and followed David to the door.

"I hope that Dr. Brooks doesn't complicate her life more than it already is, Phil," David remarked once the men were outside.

"Whether it does or it doesn't, I'm afraid it's too late now; she's in love. If he does hurt her in any way, though, he will have to answer to me."

David smiled ruefully. "I'll help."

Chapter Nineteen

Matt encouraged Carolyn to lie down for a while. She had protested at first but realized the rest would help her regain composure. Her mind swirled with memories from the accident. Could she have prevented it? It had happened so quickly. Her car slid just over the center line on the slick surface as she rounded a curve. In the half second of panic before the impact, she had clearly seen Jesse at the wheel tipping a bottle to his mouth. The impact was horrific. Carolyn's Range Rover withstood the impact better than Jesse's truck, though she still suffered serious, though non-life-threatening injuries. Jesse, however, was not wearing a seat belt and was ejected through the windshield onto the pavement.

Carolyn struggled to shift her mind to other things and finally settled on the wildcard in her life – Matt. Memories from the day before on the ridge and the evening that followed slowed her racing thoughts and directed them away from the problems plaguing the farm. She remembered the joy she had felt as she and Matt surveyed the vibrant valley below, painted with the colorful brush of autumn. His arm around her had felt so comforting, so safe. The memory quieted her exhausted mind, her breathing slowed, and she fell asleep.

Downstairs, Matt was on the phone in the sunroom. "Mr. Smith? This is Matt Brooks, have you been able to talk to the woman who bought the desk?"

"Matt, good afternoon! I'm glad you called. I was able to speak to a neighbor of hers who has done some repair work on her porch. He told me she speaks very little to him – just barks orders and goes back inside. He said she keeps all the curtains shut and rarely goes out. She had one visitor during the three days he was there working on the porch. It was a young man, about thirty, with dirty blonde hair and a beard. My friend spoke to him, friendly-like, but got no response. He only stayed a few minutes and my friend could hear shouting inside the house. The man stormed out, slammed the door behind him, and drove off."

"Did the neighbor mention seeing the desk?"

"No, as I said the lady keeps her curtains pulled all the time. He tried to talk to her, but she turned away and went back inside as if she hadn't heard him. A strange lady, that one."

Matt tried to contain his impatience. How could he get at that desk? "Will your friend be going back there?"

"He thinks so. The lady asked him to come back in a few days and do some painting in her kitchen, but he hasn't heard back from her yet."

Hope sprang anew in Matt. "Please ask him to look around as much as possible while he's in her house. If he sees the desk, at least I'll know where it is."

"Will do, Matt. Now, don't you worry, we'll get that family document back for you," he said amiably.

If he only knew that the 'family document' was really a signed murder confession, he thought. "Thank you, Al; I appreciate all you and your friend have done. Call me if you learn anything more."

"Absolutely, 'bye now."

Matt hung up and punched in Sylvia's numbers. She answered right away.

"Matt! Do you have it?" She asked anxiously, not offering a polite greeting.

"Not yet…"

"Why not?" She interrupted.

"Because the lady who has it won't let anyone near it, that's why," he answered defensively.

"You told me that already and that someone else was going to try." Her voice was getting shrill and accusatory.

"Sylvia, calm down; it won't help to become hysterical. I spoke this morning to the man I told you about last week – Mr. Smith. He has a friend who has spoken with her, but he's been unable to see the desk, at least not yet."

"Not yet?"

"Yes, he is supposed to return to her house and paint the kitchen. He will look around for the desk while he's inside her home."

"Then what?"

"I'm not sure yet. I'll have to play this out one step at a time. Be patient, it doesn't help to let the pressure get to you."

"Pressure? Are you kidding? All I've had is pressure since I stepped into your office eight months ago and made you that offer you couldn't refuse."

"I did refuse it, remember?"

"Yes, but not at first, and now we're in this terrible predicament."

Matt knew there was no point in arguing with her and looked for a way to end the discussion. "Look, I'm working on it; you have to be patient. I'll call you with any updates. Good-bye." He hung up the phone before she could say anything more. She had really changed since Ron's death. She had always been so kind and cheerful around the office but was now irritable and demanding. He only hoped she was not that way with her children.

Matt set the phone down and walked outside. He needed to think. He felt as if he was caught up in a three-ring circus and couldn't find the exit. He was torn between staying at the farm with Carolyn to help her through her difficulties, or rushing back to Illinois and getting to that desk. There was one thing he could control, however – his dental practice. He had arranged for a locum tenens dentist to cover his caseload for the next week. He decided to extend the time so he could tend to more pressing issues in his personal life. Besides, his inheritance assured him income and the sale of his practice would clear all his debts. He needed to sell it; there was no point in continuing as a dentist. Carolyn needed him at the farm, and he needed Carolyn. Once the issue of the hidden confession was settled, he would be free to move to Kentucky.

Late the next morning, Matt walked down to the pasture to check on the remaining horses. Carolyn had still been asleep when he left the house. He knew the surviving mares had been traumatized by the recent violence and were having problems settling down. They were allowed out in the pasture during the day but brought to the barn at night. Armed guards had been instructed to keep a close watch over them as they grazed on the lush grass. He approached the fence and leaned on the top rail and rested his right foot on the lowest one. His thoughts turned to the day before and his trail ride with Carolyn. A smile spread across his face as he remembered it. It had been a perfect day with the autumn sun low in the sky but still spreading fingers of warmth on their faces. The gentle breeze had caught Carolyn's hair which was haloed by the setting sun. How did he get so lucky? He knew he didn't deserve her and he sensed that David and Phil thought so, too. He chuckled at their suspicion but was glad she had their protection and support.

Honey spotted him and walked over to the fence, expecting a treat. Matt fished an apple from his pocket and offered it to the gentle mare. He stroked her muzzle and spoke gently to her as she munched on the fruit. He stayed there with her for another few minutes before turning back to the house. His stomach growled, and he decided to check with Mary about a sandwich.

He walked into the kitchen and was surprised to see Carolyn there going over menus with Mary. Sophia was cutting up vegetables for a salad.

"Hello!" He greeted them. "Can a hungry fella get a sandwich around here?" His cheerful greeting and smile were contagious. The trio of women turned as one and returned his smile.

Mary stepped forward. "What can I get for you, Dr. Brooks? Sophia is making a salad or I can fix a sandwich. Oh, and we have some leftover chili if you like."

"A ham sandwich and a bowl of your delicious chili would be great, thank you."

Carolyn walked over to Matt and kissed him on the cheek. "I'll join you, Matt." She turned to Sophia. "I'll take some of that salad, please. Could you bring our lunch to us out on the patio?"

"Certainly, ma'am."

Carolyn reached for Matt's hand and led him outside. Matt seated his hostess before claiming a chair for himself.

"Did you sleep?"

"Surprisingly, I did. It helped. What did you do while I was napping?"

Matt took a deep breath and exhaled before answering. "I did a lot of thinking."

"Oh, about what?" She asked cautiously.

"About us, my practice, the damned desk I'm searching for, everything, I guess."

"That's some pretty heavy thinking. So, what did you decide about... everything?"

"Well, first things first. I have come to realize that you are the best thing that has ever come into my miserable life, and I don't want to lose you – ever." Carolyn's eyes widened but she remained silent and waited for him to continue.

"After coming to that conclusion, everything else was pretty easy to decide. I have arranged for a locum tenens dentist to handle my practice for a while. In the meantime, I'm putting my dental practice up for sale. These trips to Kentucky are not enough for me. I want to see more of you, if that's okay with you."

"Of course, it's more than okay, but what about your dental practice? Are you sure you want to sell it? You've spent years building your clientele."

"Nothing is more important than you and I've come to love this farm more than being a dentist." Their eyes met and a moment of understanding passed between them.

Sadie arrived with their lunch but the pair had left the patio. The maid turned to see them walking hand-in-hand across the yard. They stopped under the shade of a large maple and embraced. Carolyn rested her head on Matt's chest for several moments before leaning back for a kiss. Sadie discreetly returned to the kitchen with the tray of food and asked Mary to keep the chili warm. In answer to Mary's questioning look, she simply nodded toward the window for the cook to see the happiness on their employer's face.

Chapter Twenty

The sheriff returned to the farm later that afternoon to update Carolyn. He was accompanied by a deputy who parted from his boss to speak with Carl. The prosecutor wanted to nail down every detail, no matter how small, in order to get a conviction for the attack on Carl as well as the vicious assault on the horses. As bad as it was to maim and then kill the horses, the attack on Carl would bring a longer sentence. It wasn't enough to assume Jeremy Simpson was responsible for Carl's injuries, the prosecution had to prove it.

The sheriff rang the doorbell and was led by Sadie to the sunroom where Carolyn was reading mail. Matt had reported for barn duty an hour earlier.

"Phil, it's good to see you!" Carolyn greeted.

The sheriff leaned down and gave his cousin a brief hug. "You're looking better today, I'm glad to see."

"I'm glad, too! I was exhausted and a good night's sleep fixed me right up. Is there anything new to report?"

"Yes, a lot actually. Jeremy Simpson was released from the hospital this morning and is now in the medical wing of the county jail. He has a preliminary hearing tomorrow afternoon and his attorney is sure to ask for bail. It's doubtful bail will be granted, but I can't rule out the possibility. If he does make bail, I'll let you know."

Carolyn shuddered at the thought of Jeremy Simpson being released from jail. "Anything else?"

"I have a deputy seeing Carl right now. We need a more positive identification to charge Jeremy with the attack on Carl. I hope he has remembered something, anything to help us there. It isn't enough to believe Jeremy to be guilty, we have to have proof."

"I understand. What about the confrontation in the barn? Will I be charged for shooting Jeremy Simpson?"

"I spoke with the prosecution about that. You and Matt were in danger, so it was self-defense as well as defense of the horses. David and I both saw Jeremy's gun nearby when we arrived. It seemed clear what had happened, but we will have to defend your actions in court. His lawyer will try to prove the shooting was not warranted. Hang tight, this won't be settled in a week like TV trials. This will probably take a year or more to play out in court."

Carolyn sighed. A year! She hoped she could endure it without going completely crazy. "I hope Carl can give your deputy a positive identification. Jeremy's actions are becoming increasingly aggressive, and I fear for the safety of everyone here."

"Keep the doors locked and your vehicles garaged. The security guards can't be everywhere at once, and we don't know what else might be attempted."

Carolyn swallowed hard and nodded. "I will, thanks."

Phil bade his cousin good-bye and joined his deputy at the farm manager's cottage. Carl was speaking as the sheriff entered.

"I know it was him; he wears these weird boots. Nobody has boots like that around here."

"Can you describe the boots Mr. Richter?"

"Sure, I can. They're black with a decorative pattern outlined in white thread. The toes have a silver plate, real silver. They are one-of-a-kind, custom made. I hear he polishes those boots every day."

The deputy wrote the boots' description in a notebook. "What else do you remember about the person who attacked you?"

Carl rubbed the lump on his head where his attacker had hit him. "Well, let's see now. I had my back to him, but I started turning around right before I got hit. I remember seeing a tattoo on his left hand. It looked like a ball with a sword stuck in it. It was blurred though, like the tattoo artist wasn't very good."

Phil and his deputy exchanged looks. Both had seen that tattoo before; it was a prison tattoo. The sheriff made a mental note to check Jeremy Simpson's record to see if the tattoo was there when he spent time in the county jail last year. That would prove that he had the tattoo at the time of the attack on Carl.

"Is there anything else you can remember? Did you get a look at his face?"

"No, that blow to my head knocked me out cold. Did I give you enough to identify him sheriff?"

"Perhaps; it all depends on the tattoo. The boots help but they're not enough by themselves. Thank you for your time. I hope you heal quickly Carl."

"Thanks Sheriff, I do too! I'm needed around here. Mrs. Hodges needs every able-bodied man she can get right now."

"That's for sure, but in the meantime, just rest and give yourself time to heal properly. Call us if you think of anything else that might help with the investigation."

"Will do. You fellas have a good day now."

Phil and his deputy left the cottage and walked down to the barn. Matt was there cleaning out a stall.

"You'll make a good farmhand yet," the sheriff said with a laugh.

"I'm doing my best, Sheriff. I'm just trying to earn my keep," Matt replied with a chuckle of his own. "It's certainly a change from my usual work. I think I prefer this to coddling spoiled rich clients. The horses don't complain!"

"No, but I wish they could talk so we could get more evidence."

"We caught him red-handed beating the horses to death; isn't that enough?"

"For cruelty to animals, yes, but we don't have a solid identification of Carl's attacker. That would ensure a long prison sentence. Unfortunately, what he did to the horses doesn't carry the same weight."

"He drew a gun on us. What about that?" Matt asked.

"Yes, that will be taken into consideration, but his attorney will argue self-defense because Carolyn drew on him first."

"That's crazy! He was in the process of beating horses to death; what was she supposed to do?"

Phil held up his hand to calm Matt. "Exactly what she did. I'm only saying what Jeremy's attorney will do to deflect attention from his client to Carolyn." The sheriff changed the subject. "How long do you plan on staying Matt?"

"That depends. I'll stay as long as Carolyn needs me. I've arranged for another dentist to handle my patients temporarily."

"Temporarily; then what?"

"What do you mean? Are you asking me if I plan to stand by Carolyn as long as this takes? If so, the answer is yes. I plan to sell my practice and move to Kentucky. I can afford to do it; I don't need the income my practice provides."

"I see. It sounds as if you want to be a permanent part of my cousin's life."

"That is a correct assumption. We haven't talked of marriage, not yet anyway, but I love her and only want what is best for her. No offense, Sheriff, but I don't see how any of this is your business."

Phil smiled. "Maybe not, but my cousin has had a very rough time of it in recent years, so I'm rather protective of her."

"I assure you that I plan to fill that role as well, although Carolyn is a very capable woman and would argue she can take care of herself."

"That she would," agreed Phil. "I'll let you get back to your work."

Matt watched as the sheriff walked out of the barn. *He's testing me; checking me out. I only hope Carolyn doesn't mention the desk and the confession to him. That would do me in for sure.*

He fought the overwhelming urge to drop everything and return home to search for the desk, but it would be useless until he heard back from Al Smith's friend. He ran his fingers through his hair, sighed, and turned back to his chore.

***

Matt and Carolyn spent a quiet evening together after a sumptuous meal prepared by Mary. Matt pushed away thoughts of the desk and its concealed confession and gave his full attention to the woman who had turned his life around completely.

The evening was cool and the fire in the living room made for a cozy atmosphere. Carolyn sat on the sofa with her head on Matt's shoulder and his arm around her.

"This is nice. It's as if the rest of the world has gone away, and it's just the two of us."

Matt smiled and held her a little tighter. Was it time to discuss marriage? Was she ready for that? He decided to find out.

He removed his arm from around Carolyn and turned to face her. He reached for both of her hands.

Carolyn sensed the change in Matt's demeanor and met his gaze. What she saw was a mixture of love, devotion, and desire. Feelings stirred in her that had been asleep for far too long. She waited to see what Matt would say.

Matt held the moment in silence, forming what he wanted to say in his mind. Finally, he spoke. "Sweetheart, there is nothing more I would rather do than be here for you always, if that is what you want."

"Of course, I do," Carolyn responded.

"Then, how would you feel about making our relationship more permanent?"

"Permanent? What are you asking?"

Matt chuckled. "I'm asking you to marry me. I know I have a lot of baggage and I need to resolve the issue of finding that desk, but…"

Carolyn interrupted him with a kiss. "You crazy, lovable man! Yes, I'll marry you, baggage and all! That is if you can accept my own baggage. Don't you see? We are good for each other, and together we can put all those past issues aside and look forward to a beautiful life together."

Matt stared at her, taking in everything she had said. "Do

you really mean it? You want to marry me?" He asked incredulously.

Carolyn stood and reached for his hand. "Yes, I really mean it, and it's time I showed you how much."

Matt stood and followed her up the stairs to her bedroom. The rest of the night was spent in each other's arms. All the worries and trauma of the past were put aside for a few precious hours. Nothing existed but their love for each other.

Chapter Twenty-One

Matt awoke first the next morning. Carolyn was sleeping beside him and he watched her for several moments. As if aware of his attention, she opened her eyes and smiled up at him.

"Good morning!"

"Good morning, yourself. Did you really make me the happiest man on earth and agree to marry me last night?"

"I seem to remember something like that," she replied coyly. She propped up on one elbow and reached to stroke his face with her other hand. "Yes, you're stuck with me now."

"That's okay by me," Matt replied as he pulled her closer to him and kissed her gently."

"Now, that we have sealed the deal, so to speak, we can stop being so tentative with each other. We're a team."

Matt laughed. "Yes, ma'am!"

Carolyn laughed along with him. The joy of the moment lifted the heavy weight both carried and showed them a life together without the loneliness and emptiness each had experienced until now. They knew the road ahead was still filled with tremendous difficulties, but now they had each other to lean on and to share the good and the bad.

Carolyn extracted herself from Matt's embrace. "Okay, lover boy, we have a busy day ahead, so get up and leave so I can get dressed."

Matt looked up at her and said, "I have a better idea."

Carolyn laughed again. "I'm sure you do, but later. Jeremy's preliminary hearing is today, and I need to check on Carl and the horses."

"Slave driver!" He teased. "All right, I'll leave but under protest," he said with a pretend pout. "I'll see you for breakfast."

"Yes, I'm starving!"

Matt went to his own room, showered, dressed, and whistled as he entered the dining room. He was surprised to see the sheriff sitting next to Carolyn. They were speaking in low voices and turned abruptly when he entered.

"Hello, Matt, Phil and I were just discussing the hearing today."

Matt couldn't shake the feeling that wasn't all they were discussing. He felt self-conscious as he returned Carolyn's greeting and acknowledged the sheriff. Before he could sit down, Sadie appeared and took his breakfast order. She retreated to the kitchen and the trio sat at the table in an awkward silence. *They were discussing me.*

Phil addressed Matt, "So, my cousin tells me the two of you plan to get married?"

It was a question, not a statement of fact. Matt thought maybe the sheriff hoped it wasn't true. Matt forced a smile and answered, "Yes, your cousin has graciously agreed to become my wife." He emphasized the word cousin as he spoke.

"I see, and do you still plan to sell your practice and move here, to Carolyn's farm?"

"If that is where she wants to live, then yes. I have already contacted an agent to sell my practice and a locum tenens dentist is filling in until a buyer can be found."

Clearly, it wasn't the answer the sheriff wanted to hear. His protective instinct was to somehow prevent the marriage. He decided he would attempt to talk his cousin out of the idea of marrying Matt Brooks. There was just something about the man that he didn't like. He was too stubborn to admit that any man who entered Carolyn's world would be suspect as far as he was concerned.

Matt's breakfast arrived and he found it difficult to swallow in light of the close scrutiny of Carolyn's cousin. He took a few bites, decided it was futile, and concentrated on draining his coffee cup instead. "I think I'll let you finish your conversation. I feel like a walk down to the pasture to check on the horses."

He pushed his chair back, rounded the table, and kissed Carolyn gently on the cheek. "See you later, sweetheart."

In response, Carolyn smiled and nodded as Matt turned to leave. Hearing no voices behind him led him to believe Phil was waiting until he was out of earshot before he resumed his conversation.

Matt stopped in the kitchen to get an apple for Honey. He tried to put the uncomfortable silence at the breakfast table out of his mind as he approached the pasture's fence. Honey saw him and came to him immediately. "Well, at least you like me, girl. Or, is it the apple I always bring you?" He laughed as the gentle mare nuzzled his hand to get at the treat. "That's it, eat it up; you deserve it after what you've been through."

Carl called to him from behind and joined him at the fence. "She likes you. She's usually shy around new people, but she has accepted you as a friend."

"She has good taste," Matt joked and laughed as he said it.

Carl responded with a chuckle that he cut short. "Ooh, it still hurts when I laugh. How long are you stayin' this time, Doc?"

Matt turned to face Carl and hesitated before answering. He felt Carolyn should be the one to tell her employees about their engagement, so he answered with a safe response. "A few more days; I've taken some time off work."

"Good; Ms. Carolyn can use your support during all this mess."

"You're right about that. Jeremy Simpson's preliminary hearing is this afternoon. We'll know about bail after that. The sheriff seems to think Jeremy's family will back off with him in jail. He says Jeremy is the leader of the family, that no one will make a move against Carolyn or the farm with him behind bars."

Carl considered the statement. "Maybe, let's hope so, anyway."

Matt wanted to ask if Carl felt differently but was afraid of the answer. Instead, he turned his attention back to the horses. He stroked Honey's head before she decided to rejoin the other mares. Matt noticed a single stallion in an adjoining pasture surrounded by a double fence between him and the mares. He knew there was another stallion and asked Carl where he was.

"He's in another pasture behind the barn. We keep the fellas separate; they tend to fight, showing off for the girls."

"Ah, I see." Matt wondered if he and Phil were doing the same with Carolyn, not for her affection but to convince her of their own point of view. *Nature teaches us once again,* he mused.

"Carl, how are you feeling? You seem to be getting around easier."

"Yes, I am, thank you, I'm gettin' around better every day."

"May I ask you something?"

"Sure, go ahead," the weathered older man answered.

"How safe do you think it is for Carolyn right now? She has a lot of responsibility here, and then there is the stress of the attacks and her husband's death. It makes me wonder how she does it all. I'm afraid for her."

"Now, Doc, don't go worrying about Ms. Carolyn; she's stronger than you think. She's got guts for sure, but she also has good common sense. She never makes a decision in haste, so she won't now. She'll do what's right for her and this farm. Well, I'd better go and check on the farmhands. I don't want them to get too used to having me out of the picture. See you later, Doc." Carl turned and walked slowly and Matt noticed how he favored his right leg.

He's as tough as Carolyn is strong. It's no wonder the pair get along so well, Matt decided.

Matt turned back to the fence and rested his arms on the top rail. He pondered what Carl had said about Carolyn not rushing into things and making good decisions. Did Carl feel that his boss had made a good decision when she chose to date a dentist from Chicago? If so, the thought comforted him and took some of the sting out of the sheriff's obvious objection to him. He smiled, letting his gaze take in the pastoral splendor all around him. Even the violent attacks of the past few days had done nothing to diminish the beauty of the farm in its autumn splendor. It was so different from Chicago, delightfully different. He felt a peace in knowing this would be his world – Carolyn, the horses, the open spaces.

Then, he was pulled back to his dark reality. The desk. He had to find that desk. Maybe Al Smith had found out if the desk was in the woman's house. He pulled out his phone and punched in the numbers.

"Hello?"

"Al? this is Matt Brooks."

"Oh, yes, hi Matt."

"How is Mrs. Smith?"

"Doing fine, doing fine. She's baking pies to give to some of our friends. She loves to bake. Where are you? If you can, come by and have a piece of her apple pie."

"It sounds delicious, but I'm in Kentucky and won't be back there for a few days. Have you heard from your friend who is doing the work for the woman who bought the desk?" He tried not to sound too anxious, but his heart was pounding as he waited for the answer.

"Yes and no. He's going back there on Wednesday to work on her kitchen. He should be able to get a quick look around then. I'll call you as soon as I hear from him."

Disappointed, Matt thanked Al and finished the call. As he stowed his phone in his jacket pocket, he heard footsteps behind him in the gravel. He turned to find Carolyn approaching with a huge smile for him.

Matt greeted her with a peck on her cheek. "Hello, gorgeous! Have you finished talking with your cousin?"

"Yes, Phil is gone. He tried to talk me out of marrying you, but I think you already guessed he would."

"What does he have against me? I'm just this lovable guy from Chicago."

Carolyn laughed and put her arms around Matt. "Yes, you are. Don't worry about Phil. He thinks it's his sworn duty to look after me. He thinks I'm still a little girl."

Remembering their love making of the night before, Matt hugged her closely and said, "Far from it, my dear."

Carolyn laughed again and got up on tiptoes to receive Matt's passionate kiss. Honey whinnied, demanding her mistress' attention.

"All right, girl, I'm still here for you," Carolyn reassured.

The gentle mare received lavish praise and pats for several minutes before she turned back to graze on the rich pasture grass. Matt and Carolyn watched her in silence, taking in the pastoral scene all around them. Matt hesitated to intrude on the moment but he knew he needed to turn his attention back to the problem of the desk and its volatile contents. He turned to face Carolyn.

"Sweetheart?"

"What is it?"

"In the next few days, I'll need to return to tie up some loose ends in Chicago. I'll be back as soon as I can, I promise."

Carolyn sensed his unease and realized he was worried about more than a few loose ends. "Sweetheart, have you heard anything about the desk? I saw you put your phone away."

Matt let out a sigh. "No, nothing yet. Al said he may have some news for me by Wednesday. His friend is starting work on the lady's kitchen that day. If the desk is still there, I need to act quickly. That detective I told you about is snooping around like a dog looking for his bone. My former assistant, Sylvia, remembered a conversation she had with her sister-in-law at a family birthday celebration. They were on the patio watching the children play in the yard and Sylvia told Ron's sister she wished Ron weren't in her life anymore. She didn't say she wanted to kill him, but she thinks Ron's mother overheard from the open patio door and put two and two together after Ron's death. She said she can't think of another reason why the investigation into Ron's death has been reopened. If the detective gets his hands on my signed confession…"

Carolyn interrupted him and put a finger to his lips. "Hush, don't think about that. We'll leave tomorrow for Chicago and we'll find the desk – together. After the hearing today, it should be fine for me to leave the farm for a while. You've stood beside me; now it's my turn."

Matt searched Carolyn's face and what he saw there brought tears to his eyes. He pulled her close. "Have I told you how much I love you?"

She smiled. "Yes, but you can tell me as many times as you like."

Chapter Twenty-Two

"I'll meet you out front, Matt."

"Okay, I'm coming."

Carolyn left final instructions with Mary for dinner and grabbed the vehicle's keys off the hook by the kitchen door. She slid behind the wheel and drove around to the front steps where Matt was waiting.

He opened the door and folded his tall frame in the seat. As he buckled his seatbelt, he looked at Carolyn's profile. He sensed a tension in her. "Nervous?"

"Terribly!"

He wanted to reach for her hand, but decided the death grip she had on the steering wheel was best left alone. "Try not to worry; there's no way he'll get bail after what he did."

"I hope you're right."

The rest of the trip to the county courthouse was spent in silence. Each was left alone with their thoughts. Matt knew he needed to go back to Chicago and was glad of Carolyn's offer to accompany him, but he was concerned about getting her involved in the investigation. He didn't want anything about that sordid business to attach itself to her. She had enough problems.

Carolyn pulled into a parking place a block from the courthouse. She killed the engine and pocketed the keys. She hesitated before opening her door as she braced herself for coming face-to-face with Jeremy Simpson and his family.

Matt got out and came around to her side of the Range Rover and opened the door for her.

"Thank you," she said absent mindedly.

Matt reached for her hand to offer his support as they joined others lining up for entry into the building.

Once past security, they found the courtroom designated for the hearing. The Simpson family was present in full force and stared at the couple as they walked up the aisle to join Phil on the front row behind the prosecutor's table. The two men acknowledged each other with nods but didn't speak. Carolyn sat between them and was glad of the support on either side of her.

Waiting seemed to take an eternity, but Jeremy Simpson was finally led into the courtroom in an orange jumpsuit, his right arm in a sling. His ankles were manacled and his left arm was secured to a chain around his waist. He shuffled to the defense table with his chains clattering with each step. Once at the table, a jail employee unlocked the left wrist restraint but stood close by.

Carolyn stared straight ahead but could feel Jeremy's eyes on her. Why was the judge taking so long? She thought. She wanted to get this over quickly.

Eventually, she heard the command to rise for the judge's entry. Feeling numb, she stood along with the rest of the room and waited for the command to sit back down.

The judge called the proceedings to order and each attorney made his case to hold or release Jeremy on the charges of attempted murder of Carl, cruelty to animals, and wanton endangerment for pulling a gun on Carolyn.

He pled not guilty as expected, but the judge ruled there was sufficient evidence to hold Jeremy over for trial. The defense attorney requested Jeremy's release until the trial and the prosecution argued against it, citing Jeremy's criminal history and the malicious nature of his attacks at Carolyn's farm. The judge ruled a compromise. Bail was granted but was set at one million dollars. His family would have to come up with at least ten per cent of that to release Jeremy. There was no way they could raise that amount as their home was rented and the members of the family who worked had never developed the habit of saving. So, Jeremy was remanded back to the jail to await trial in two months.

Carolyn let out her breath. She had held it while waiting for the judge's ruling on bail.

Phil hugged her, "I told you he wouldn't be released before trial."

"Yes, you did. It's a great relief. Now that Jeremy Simpson is in jail and there is less threat at the farm, I've decided to accompany Matt to Chicago for a few days."

Phil was shocked by Carolyn's plans. "Why would you…"

Carolyn continued as if he had not spoken. "We're leaving tomorrow morning. Will you stop by the farm occasionally and see that everything is okay? I would feel better knowing you were keeping an eye on things."

Phil looked from Carolyn to Matt, who he eyed suspiciously. He wanted to ask why she was going to Chicago, but his cousin's expression indicated she would not welcome the question. He sighed. She was a grown woman, so he grudgingly admitted he needed to back off. His gaze shifted to Matt and gave the impression he wasn't pleased. Matt half-smiled nervously in response.

"I'll be glad to check on the farm while you're gone," he

answered with obvious displeasure.

Carolyn pretended not to notice her cousin's demeanor. She gathered her coat and purse and turned to see if the Simpson family had left yet. She didn't see them, so she felt it was safe to leave. No sooner had she emerged from the courtroom, however, than she was surrounded by the Simpson family yelling and cursing at her. Phil had remained behind to check his phone but rushed to join Matt and Carolyn in the hallway. His uniformed appearance was all the Simpson family needed to fall back and rush toward the courthouse exit.

Carolyn was visibly shaken, so Phil and Matt walked on either side of her until they reached her Range Rover. Matt asked for the keys and gently guided Carolyn to the passenger side of the vehicle. She offered no objection and got in without comment.

Matt walked to the driver's side while Phil secured Carolyn's seatbelt and gave her a hug.

"Don't worry about the farm, honey; I'll check on it every day."

"Thanks, Phil."

The sheriff made eye contact with Matt. His look conveyed a strong warning: *Take care of her – or else.*

Matt read the sheriff loud and clear and gave a slight nod before he engaged the car's motor and pulled out of the parking space. Once clear of downtown, he glanced over at Carolyn. He had never seen her so affected by anything. He reached for her hand and gave a light squeeze. "It will be all right, sweetheart."

"I hope you're right. The hearing brought back all the terror and pain from the night of the accident with Jesse. I know I'll never be able to forget I took a life that night." Tears streamed down her face as she rummaged in her purse for a tissue.

Matt had no idea what to say, but Carolyn's situation was very close to his own memories of planning to murder another human being. Even though he hadn't gone through with it, he knew he would live with the guilt and shame for the rest of his life. They both shouldered a heavy burden, but maybe that's why each could understand the other and accept who they were. He was glad he had told Carolyn of the plot to kill Ron. His revelation had not altered how she felt about him, which made him love her even more.

Carolyn stared out her window, but all she saw was the dark road the night of the accident as she relived the horror. Matt reached for her hand to reassure her.

"Honey, I don't know what to say to make this better, but I do want you to know I'm with you every step of the way. I'm not going anywhere, not without you."

Carolyn stopped dabbing at her eyes with a tissue. "You don't know how much that means to me, Matt. I have felt so alone for a long time."

"Well, you're not alone anymore," he answered.

"Neither are you."

In that moment, both felt a shift in their relationship, a kinship or bond between them. Whatever the future held for them they would face it as a team.

That evening after dinner, and after packing for the trip to Chicago, Matt and Carolyn sat on the living room floor with their backs supported by the sofa. A half-empty bowl of popcorn was on the floor between them. Both were content to sit quietly and enjoy the warmth and soft glow of the fireplace.

Carolyn broke the silence. "I wish we could freeze this

moment and feel this peace all the time."

Matt set the bowl of popcorn aside and pulled her into an embrace. "That would be wonderful. No matter what we have to face we'll know we have the support of the other. Nothing is more precious than that. It will provide us with a sense of peace even in the midst of the worst life can bring."

"What a romantic philosopher you are, Matt Brooks! There are certainly many sides to you."

Matt laughed. "Tell that to your sheriff cousin. He only sees a man pushing his way into your life, probably for the money," he added with sarcasm.

Carolyn leaned back to look at Matt. "I've tried to tell him differently, but I think you're right. He is and has always been very protective of his younger cousin. Maybe he's a bit jealous as well."

"Jealous, of me?"

"Not in a romantic way, but maybe he feels that you are replacing him as my protector. I don't think he believes it's the money; I told him about your inheritance." Carolyn snuggled closer and put her head on Matt's chest. "He'll come around; you'll see."

"I hope you're right," Matt answered as he silently finished the thought, *He'll come around as long as he doesn't know about the plot to kill Ron Bennett.*

As if reading his thoughts, Carolyn pulled free and turned to face Matt. "Okay, what's the game plan for the next few days?"

Matt was surprised at the sudden change but decided to go along with it. "First of all, I will call Al Smith tomorrow evening, if he hasn't called me by then."

"Then, what?"

"Well, if the desk is in the lady's home, we need to find a way to see it. Maybe the presence of another woman will change the owner's demeanor. She certainly didn't like me, for whatever reason."

Carolyn laughed. "Did you forget to turn on the charm?"

"She didn't give me a chance to do or say anything. She let her gun do the talking. I heard the message loud and clear."

"She sounds lovely."

It was Matt's turn to laugh. "Yeah, a real peach."

"And, if the desk isn't there?"

"I haven't thought that far ahead. The desk has to be there, it just has to be."

Carolyn heard the note of desperation in Matt's voice and reached out to stroke his hair. "Okay, we'll take it one step at a time, but tonight belongs to us."

Matt looked deeply into her eyes. "Yes, it does."

Chapter Twenty-Three

Wednesday morning found the newly engaged couple on a plane to Chicago. Matt was quiet during the flight, and Carolyn gave him the time to work out what he needed to do about the desk. Her own thoughts turned back to Kentucky and her farm. What if the Simpsons tried to do something else to the animals or her staff? She felt torn between her desire to help Matt access the desk and the hidden signed confession and her responsibilities to the people and animals of her farm. Maybe they would be able to get the signed confession back quickly. That would remove one huge obstacle to their future happiness. But what if they were barred access to the desk? From what Matt told her, the present owner of the desk wasn't the type of person to negotiate or grant favors. *Please God, help us get that wretched piece of paper back,* she prayed.

The plane's landing was delayed due to heavy storms over Chicago. The waiting only served to intensify their anxiety. Carolyn noted how Matt gripped the armrests of his seat. "Sweetheart, it's going to be all right; try to relax a bit."

"I'm fine," he answered.

"Yes, I can tell by your white knuckles," she teased.

Matt looked down at his hands and realized how tense he was. He chuckled. "I guess you're right. What would you suggest to help me relax?"

Carolyn blushed and looked down. She leaned closer to Matt and whispered, "Let's at least wait until we get off the plane. I have no intention of joining the mile-high club."

Matt laughed, catching the attention of other passengers.

"For heaven sakes, don't draw attention to us!" Carolyn begged.

Matt laughed even louder causing her to retort, "You're impossible!" His laughter was infectious, however, and she couldn't help joining him. Life was never boring with Dr. Matt Brooks!

***

The plane landed nearly an hour late. Matt and Carolyn gathered their carry-on items and followed the herd of people to the checked baggage claim area. While waiting for the rest of their luggage, Matt heard his name and turned around. Detective Robertson!

"Detective, to what do I owe this honor? Are you here to pick us up? How thoughtful of you!" He said cheekily.

The detective was not amused. "I think you know why I'm here, Dr. Brooks."

Carolyn stood off to the side and watched the exchange, hardly able to breathe. *Is he here to arrest Matt?* She wondered.

"I have no idea, Detective; I've told you everything I know. How did you even know where I would be?"

The detective studied Matt for several moments before answering. If Matt was guilty, he was one cool character. "I've made it my business to know where you are – at all times, Dr. Brooks."

"Why? As I've said, I have nothing further to tell you. Now, if you will excuse us, we need to retrieve our luggage." Matt turned his back on the detective and pulled his case off the carousel. Carolyn's bag came next and Matt pulled the handles up on the rolling bags and turned to leave. He was surprised to find the detective still standing by the carousel.

"Is there something else, Detective?" Matt asked with more confidence than he felt.

"Yes, one more thing. Why are you looking for Ron Bennett's desk?"

Matt felt the blow as surely as if he had been struck by the detective. His face gave away his shock. "What did you just say?"

"You know exactly what I said, Dr. Brooks. What secret does that desk hold? You've been a very busy man, but my men have been able to follow your movements step by step. You're hiding something and I'm going to find out exactly what that is." The detective smiled his best Machiavellian smile and turned toward the exit.

Matt was left standing in place, unsure what had just happened. How could the detective know about the desk?

Carolyn moved to stand next to him, unsure if she should speak or stay silent.

Matt decided for her. "Let's go." He led the way to where his car was parked in the garage and opened the passenger door for Carolyn, his shock still evident. He stowed their bags in the trunk and slid into the driver's seat. Carolyn reached over to take his hand in hers. Matt looked at her as if just then remembering she was with him. What had he done? How could he have involved the love of his life in this disaster? "Carolyn, you shouldn't have come with me,"

"Nonsense! We're a team, remember?" She squeezed his hand and gave him her best smile. Matt said nothing else, but he planned to have a frank discussion with her once they were alone in his home. Or, were they alone even there? Was his house bugged – his phone? How did they know about the desk? Did the police know about the confession, too? Matt found it hard to breathe as if his chest was wrapped tightly. *Relax Matt,* he told himself, *if they had the confession, I would be in handcuffs in the back of a patrol car right now.*

The remainder of the trip was spent in silence. Matt navigated the route to his home with practiced skill, but his thoughts were still consumed with his airport encounter with Detective Robertson. He entered his neighborhood and pulled into his driveway. He walked to the passenger side and opened the door. Matt led the way, but still remained silent. Once inside his home, he put a finger to his lips and guided Carolyn to the patio.

Once outside, on the far side of the spacious backyard, Matt explained. "At the risk of sounding paranoid and possibly out of my mind, I'm afraid my home and phone could be bugged. How else could the detective know about the desk? I wonder what else he knows."

"Honey, calm down. This only gives us more incentive to find the desk before the detective does. There is one problem, however."

Matt raised his eyebrows in question.

"As your fiancé, I can be forced to testify against you, but as your wife I cannot."

"So, what are you saying?"

"I'm saying we should get married – now."

Matt stared at her without comment.

Carolyn became impatient. "Well, what do you say?"

"Carolyn, I… I don't know what to say. I want to marry you, of course. I proposed to you only yesterday, but I've been thinking about your involvement in this, and I don't want to drag you into the investigation. Your name will become associated with mine and ruin your reputation. Shouldn't we wait until we find the confession? There would be nothing to stand in the way then."

She gave him a hard push. "You proposed to me, Matthew Brooks, and I accepted. I'm only saying I want to be your wife sooner rather than later. I'm already involved, willingly. Are you saying you don't want to marry me; you're having second thoughts?"

"No, not at all…"

"Then what is it?" She demanded.

"You're only doing this so you don't have to testify against me. I can't let you ruin your life this way."

"Ruin my life?" She asked incredulously. "I love you. Can't you get that through your thick skull!"

"It's just not fair to you. I could go to prison – soon. I don't want to drag you through all of that. I want to marry you, it's a dream come true. Ever since I saw you in Las Vegas, I have dreamed of you, but…"

"Then, marry me. I want to get married. Besides, you need to make an honest woman out of me," she teased.

"Are you sure? Do you know what this could mean? You could wind up being married to a man who has been sentenced to life in prison."

"Shh, that's not going to happen. We're going to find that paper, destroy it, and live happily ever after. You're not the only one with dreams, buster, and you just happen to be in mine too."

Matt searched her face and found only love and raw honesty there. Could he be so lucky? "Okay, we'll get married, but you can get out of it any time you wish or need to. I'll understand," he added.

A slow smile spread across Carolyn's face. "Now, you're coming 'round. I know I shocked you but this is the only way. We were planning to get married anyway, so this way I can't be forced to tell the police what you told me about the desk and the false confession. It just makes sense."

Matt finally regained some measure of composure and seated her at the patio table. He pulled a chair out and sat down across from her. "I wanted our wedding to be special; all the hoopla associated with an event worthy of you."

"Matt, I don't need that; I just need you." She thought for a few moments and added, "If you want a big party, then we'll have a small wedding here and throw a big reception later at the farm after all this mess is cleared up. How does that sound?"

"I want what you want, dear woman. For the hundredth time, how did I get so lucky?"

Carolyn stood and pulled Matt up to face her. She buried her head in his chest. "It was meant to be."

***

Matt decided he should check on his dental practice before anything else, so he departed for his office while Carolyn used her cell phone to find someone to perform the ceremony. She didn't want a courthouse wedding, but she would settle for that if no one else could be found quickly.

Matt's phone rang on the table by the sofa. He had forgotten it when he left. The screen identified the caller as Al Smith. She remembered Matt's fear that his phone was bugged, so she answered the call, briefly explained to Mr. Smith that Matt had forgotten his phone but could be reached at another number in about an hour. She provided her own cell phone number, thanked Mr. Smith, and hung up.

Matt walked through his front door just as Carolyn's phone began to ring. "It's Al Smith, for you. I told him to call this number. Take it outside," she whispered.

Matt was somewhat confused but did as directed. He answered the phone as he passed through his back door. "Hello Al, thanks for getting back to me."

"No problem. I have news for you. My friend was called back to that lady's house a day early to give her an estimate before he starts work tomorrow. He saw a desk and it sounds like the one you're looking for. It's sitting in a hallway. He overheard her say she was getting it out of the house. She may be getting rid of it, so you might want to get out there sooner rather than later."

"Sure thing, I'll do that. I can't thank you enough, Al. I'm back in town so I'd like to take you and Mrs. Smith out to dinner this evening if that would work for you."

"That would be nice. My wife would love to eat someone else's cooking for a change. Al laughed. "You have just rescued us from leftovers. I love my wife's cooking, but some leftovers are better than others. Tonight's fare is not one of the tastier ones."

"Good, I'm glad to be of service."

"Let me check with Maddie and call you right back."

"Okay, we'll be waiting for your call."

Ten minutes later, Carolyn's phone rang and Al confirmed the dinner plans. "Maddie and I appreciate the invitation. It's very generous of you."

"It is my pleasure. I'll have a surprise for you as well."

"Now that sounds even better. Where shall we meet you and what time?"

"We'll pick you up around seven o'clock."

Al caught the plural pronoun. "We?"

"Ah, yes, my lady friend, Carolyn Hodges, is visiting Chicago this week. She's anxious to meet both of you."

"We'll be happy to meet her, too," Al replied with good humor. "Should we dress up a bit?"

"No tie, just a jacket. I think you'll like where we are going this evening."

"I'm sure we will; thanks for inviting us."

"You are very welcome, see you at seven."

Carolyn joined Matt on the patio. He looked at her in admiration. "That was pretty smart having Al call me on your phone."

"See what an intelligent wife you'll have?"

"I'm learning more about you all the time. By the way, I invited the Smiths to dinner this evening as you suggested. I told them we would pick them up at seven."

"Perfect. Now, let me update you on our wedding plans."

"Um, okay. I'm not good at this sort of thing. All I did for my first wedding was show up on time. I hope you don't expect much more from me. I would probably have the minister go to the wrong church and tell the organist the wrong day of the wedding," Matt joked.

"Be serious a few minutes, I found a minister who will marry us a week from Saturday in his church."

"Wonderful!"

"Whom do you want to invite?"

"Hmm, I hadn't thought about that. I don't really have any close friends. All our friends were couples and my ex-wife got them in the divorce."

Carolyn laughed. "I understand. Some people I considered as friends fell away after Ben's death. It's as if I ceased to exist when Ben did."

"Do you want to have your step-daughter come?"

"I thought of her, but her college is a thousand miles away and I don't want to interrupt her studies. I'll call her to make sure, but I think she'll be fine with coming later to the party at the farm."

"Well, that leaves a very short guest list," Matt said with a rueful smile.

"What about your office staff? I'm sure they'll want to come if only out of curiosity."

"I'll invite them if you wish, but don't expect much of a turnout."

"We only need two witnesses and the pastor said the organist and the church secretary could stand up with us if necessary."

"It's settled then. What do I need to do?"

"Just get me to the church. I'll take care of everything else. Do you have a good suit or a tuxedo?"

"I have a tux and it might even still fit. We used to attend a lot of charity fund raisers, so I got a tux for those."

"Good. I'll arrange for the flowers, the music, and food for the reception. I'm sure we can find a local restaurant or hotel banquet room that can accommodate our reception."

"You sound as if my office staff will actually come."

"I think you'll be pleasantly surprised. They might come if for no other reason than to see who you are marrying. We'll plan for them to attend anyway. We can always give the food away if no one comes."

"I leave it all to you, my dear. Now, I need to see if I can get access to that desk."

"I'm coming with you; maybe she will respond better to a woman."

Matt started to argue but realized it would be futile, so he simply nodded.

An hour later, Matt turned off the engine of his car fifty yards from the woman's house. He turned to Carolyn with amazement. "In the last hour, you have ordered the flowers for the wedding, written the content of the wedding invitations and sent it to be printed, and arranged for the food. How did you do it? It takes most people months of planning to pull off a wedding and reception and you did it in one afternoon!"

Carolyn laughed. "As Ben's wife, I planned dozens of get-togethers for business associates, clients, and friends."

Matt protested. "You have never been here before; how did you know where to look?"

"It was easy. Have you heard of the internet and a cell phone? I read online reviews of various florists and caterers and made a few calls. From past experience, I know the right questions to ask. And... doubling their fee takes away some of the objections they might have concerning our short timeline."

"You are incredible, simply incredible, even if your lightning efficiency is a little scary."

"It's just who I am," she responded. "Do you have a problem with that?" She knew she sounded defensive, but she needed to know if Matt could accept her as she was, not how he might want her to be.

Matt chuckled. "I wouldn't change a thing about you. You're perfect."

Just then, they noticed movement at the woman's house. Two men had pulled up to the front of the house in an old pickup truck. Matt and Carolyn watched as the men approached the front door. A single knock brought the woman to the white door. She stood aside to admit the men and quickly closed the door behind them.

A few minutes later, the men emerged carrying a desk! Could it be the one they were looking for? Where were they taking it? They watched from Matt's car as the men carried the desk down the front porch steps. They lost sight of the desk as the two men carried it around the back corner of the house. Matt guessed the desk was headed for the barn as he couldn't remember any other structure behind the house.

They waited until the men exited the barn with a large box which was obviously very heavy. They loaded the box in the back of the truck and walked back behind the house. Matt and Carolyn speculated as to the box's contents to pass the time. In a few minutes the men reappeared carrying a heavy box similar in size to the first and placed it in the back of the truck next to the first one.

The taller of the two slid behind the wheel while the other man closed the tail gate. He claimed the passenger seat and the men drove away.

Carolyn looked at Matt. "What should we do?"

"That's a good question. It's tempting to wait until after dark and check out the barn as I would rather not come face-to-face with that woman if I can prevent it. I have no desire to have a gun pointed at me again."

"Ordinarily, I would object to trespassing and goodness knows what other crimes we would be committing, but I agree. Let's come back tonight."

"I don't know whether I feel like a sleuth or a criminal," Matt joked.

"I choose sleuth. It definitely sounds better. It's a bit exciting, isn't it?"

"If you say so," Matt responded. We have a little time before we pick up the Smiths so would you like a tour of the countryside?"

"That would be lovely," Carolyn agreed. It would get their minds off the desk for a while.

Matt drove through the area with no specific destination in mind. Carolyn noted the difference in Illinois weather. Autumn had marched along faster here than in Kentucky. All the bright colors of fall were gone, replaced with barren skeletons of trees asleep for the winter. She asked about winter weather in the state.

"It gets very cold by mid-autumn here," answered Matt. We get a lot of snow, around twenty inches a year, on average."

"That's a lot more than most of Kentucky. It all depends on which part of the state is considered. Eastern Kentucky is part of Appalachia and gets a lot of snow, probably close to that of Illinois. Central Kentucky, where I live, gets about twelve inches average. The best part is the snow is rarely very deep and melts quickly. I love to see snow fall. Everything is so beautiful after a snow. Sounds are muffled, and the world seems so peaceful. Then the snow melts and everything is muddy and ugly again."

Matt laughed. "I like to hear you talk about life in Kentucky. I'm becoming fonder of the Bluegrass State every day."

"I guess if it will soon be your home, you should like where you live. I love my Kentucky farm, and I'm grateful that you volunteered to be the one to move away from the familiar. You're even giving up a lucrative and fulfilling career to marry me. That means more to me than you'll ever know."

"It was a no-brainer. I enjoyed helping my patients achieve better dental health, but I would rather be unemployed and by your side than to keep my practice and live alone. Besides, I have fallen in love with your farm. I had no idea I would enjoy it so much as I was raised a city boy. The extent of my exposure to wildlife was at the zoo."

"Then it worked out for the best, didn't it? I'm glad you love the farm. I wouldn't want you to regret your decision down the road."

"Never. I'm looking forward to tending the horses, mucking out stalls, and going for rides with you."

"Sounds heavenly. What is that up ahead?"

"If memory serves, it is a statue dedicated to the soldiers from Illinois who fought for the North in the Civil War."

"Really? I didn't know there were Civil War battles in Illinois."

"There weren't, but Illinois contributed significant numbers of soldiers to fight for the Union. It may seem strange to find the statue here but it was funded by local wealthy parents of three sons killed in the War. It is a famous landmark around here. I haven't been here since I was a child when I came here on a school field trip."

"How sad to lose three sons to the war. I hope the memorial gave the parents some comfort," Carolyn remarked. They drove on a few more miles, and Matt pointed out areas of interest.

Carolyn checked the clock on the dash and suggested they make their way to the Smiths as it was getting close to seven o'clock.

On the way, he told Carolyn what he knew of the couple and how helpful they had been. "You'll like them as soon as you meet them; they're honest and hardworking, but they're a lot of fun, too."

"They sound delightful. I'm looking forward to spending time with them before we become amateur sleuths later tonight."

"When put that way, it sounds almost respectful. Breaking and entering might be a more apt description of our intentions this evening."

"It's just a barn, for heaven's sake. We'll find the desk, get the paper, and get out."

Matt didn't reply but hoped it went as smoothly as she said. Experience had taught him that nothing was ever as easy as it seemed at first. He would relax when he had the confession in hand, and not until then.

The couple pulled up to the Smith's home twenty minutes later and had not reached the front porch before Maddie came through the door to greet them. "Matt! It's so good to see you again, and this must be Carolyn. What a lovely lady friend you have!"

"Thank you, Maddie. Yes, this is Carolyn Hodges."

Carolyn reached out her hand to Maddie who pulled it

toward her for an embrace instead. "We're huggers around here. Come on in and sit down for a few minutes. Al will be ready soon."

The couple followed Maddie into the spacious farmhouse. Carolyn marveled at the pristine appearance of the living room and decided this was for guests only. They sat beside each other on a camel back style sofa in a light shade of beige.

"May I offer you something to drink? We have soft drinks, iced tea, and water."

Matt looked at Carolyn who replied she would like to have a glass of water. Matt asked for the iced tea. Maddie returned with the drinks and sat down across from her guests. "Now, tell me all about how the two of you met."

Matt was a bit bemused by the question, but Carolyn answered for both of them. "We met accidentally in Las Vegas. We both had business there and literally ran into each other on an elevator. We shared a table later for lunch and then spent an afternoon walking around the Vegas Strip. We hit it off immediately." Matt was grateful that Carolyn had provided a somewhat whitewashed version of their meeting. He really didn't want to get into questions or judgments about gambling in case the Smiths were strict about such things.

Mrs. Smith responded to Carolyn's narrative with nods of her head and a final, "How wonderful!"

Carolyn went on to describe her farm in Kentucky and how Matt had come to love it almost as much as she did.

"Does that mean Matt is moving to Kentucky?"

"Yes, but we are getting married in Illinois, a week from Saturday, and we'd love for you and Mr. Smith to attend. We're putting it together rather quickly, so please forgive the short notice."

"Oh, my! Congratulations! Is that the surprise you promised, Matt?"

"Yes, I'm proud to say this beautiful woman has agreed to put up with me for the rest of her life. We decided to have a short engagement and get married right away."

"Goodness! That's only ten days away! How will you manage it? When our daughter got married, it took her a year to get everything together."

Carolyn laughed. "Yes, we are cutting a few corners, but we want to be married now and we want Matt's friends and employees to come so we decided to do it while visiting Illinois."

"Well, I admire your spunk and optimism. Most brides make their wedding day a huge production even though when it's all over, they are no more married than a couple who elope."

Al walked in during the laughter that followed Maddie's astute observation. "What did I miss?"

Maddie told Al of the impending nuptials and the invitation to be part of the fun.

Matt exchanged a look with Carolyn and made a request. "As a matter of fact, would the two of you stand up with us?"

"Really? You want us to be your attendants?" Maddie asked with obvious surprise.

Carolyn set her glass of water down and leaned forward. "Of course; I can't think of anyone I would rather have than the two of you."

"It would be our honor, wouldn't it, Al?"

"Absolutely! Just tell us where and when and what to wear."

"Thank you. Carolyn hasn't shopped for her dress yet, but I plan to wear a tuxedo, that is if it still fits me," Matt explained.

"Al, you can wear a dark suit if you want."

"I still have the tuxedo I bought for my daughter's wedding. She insisted I have my own instead of a rented one. It has come in handy a couple of times since then."

Carolyn turned to Maddie. "Please don't go to any expense or trouble with your dress. As the only bride's attendant, you can wear whatever you want without worrying that it won't match anyone else."

"Well, like Al, I still have my wedding clothes from Allie's wedding. It is a ballerina length dress in a light rose shade."

"That will match perfectly with the white and pink flowers I have ordered. I'll call the florist and have them add your bouquet and Al's boutonnière. You are both so gracious to agree to do this for us."

"It sounds like fun! We have grown fond of Matt in the short time we've known him, so it would be an honor to do this for you."

Matt stood. "Thank you both for your friendship and generosity. Now, it's our turn to do something for you; We've made reservations at Tony's Restaurant and we need to get going so we aren't late."

"Tony's?" Al exclaimed. "How did you get reservations on such short notice at Tony's? We've tried to make reservations there several times but were told we should have called at least a week in advance."

Matt grinned. "It just so happens the owner is a patient of mine, his whole family actually. I've made a couple of after-hours trips to the office to care for dental emergencies, so in return he waives the reservation list for me whenever I want to eat there."

"Wow! That's amazing!" Al said. He turned to his wife, offered his arm, and followed their guests outside. Matt offered to drive.

Twenty minutes later, a parking attendant took possession of Matt's Mercedes and handed him a claim ticket. The hostess recognized Matt as he approached and signaled a server.

"Good evening, Dr. Brooks," she said. Your table for four is ready. Please follow Jason. We hope you enjoy your meal."

"Thank you, Erin, I'm sure we will."

Dinner conversation was light among the four friends and the food was excellent, but Matt and Carolyn found it difficult to conceal their tension within. In a couple of hours, they would first surveil and then enter another person's property. Both knew the importance of their success or failure.

Tony came by the table and was introduced to Carolyn, Al, and Maddie. Matt assured him he would receive an invitation to their wedding soon.

"I know it's short notice, but I hope you and Rose can come."

"Of course! I'm sure Rose would love to come. She will be so excited and happy for you. How about a special bottle of wine to celebrate your engagement? I'll send your waiter out with a complimentary bottle of our finest."

"That's very generous of you Tony, thank you."

After Tony left to arrange for the wine, Carolyn turned to Matt. "See, you do have friends."

Matt smiled. "I guess I do after all."

After the meal, Matt drove Al and Maddie back to their home. "Won't you come in for a while for coffee and dessert?" Maddie offered.

Carolyn reached out for Maddie's hands and smiled. "Thank

you, but we are very tired after traveling; maybe another time?"

"Of course, anytime. If there is anything we can do to help you prepare for your wedding, please let us know. We'd be glad to help," Maddie offered.

"Thank you, we will."

After a final wave good-bye to the elderly couple, Matt turned to Carolyn. "Ready for this?"

"I'm as ready as I'll ever be," she answered with more confidence than she felt.

"Good girl." Matt let out a breath and put his car in gear. They rode in silence until they reached their destination. Matt drove slowly past the house and saw no lights except for exterior ones on the front porch and above the barn door. Matt turned his car around and pulled into a stand of trees just off the road. He hoped the car's dark color would keep passersby unaware of its presence. "There's a flashlight in the glove compartment that we'll need." Carolyn retrieved the flashlight and Matt placed it in his jacket pocket.

They waited in the car for another fifteen minutes to determine if their arrival had raised suspicions with neighbors. If someone had called the sheriff, they were prepared to say they were covert lovers merely seeking a remote spot to be together away from jealous spouses. Fortunately, they didn't need to tell the lie and were able to slip away from the car unnoticed.

Matt insisted on walking ahead of Carolyn. "If there's trouble, I don't want you to encounter it first."

"Very chivalrous of you," Carolyn joked. Inside, however, she was glad of the courtesy.

They swung wide behind the house and barn, looking for any signs they had been discovered as they crept in the shadows.

Once in position directly behind the barn, they waited in the tall weeds bordering the property line. Carolyn shivered as the cold dampness of the autumn night penetrated her light coat. She pulled up her collar and dug her hands into her pockets but couldn't stop shivering.

Matt noticed her discomfort and put an arm around her. He offered his jacket for an added layer, but Carolyn refused.

In whispers, they discussed their best option. There was a window about four feet off the ground on the back side of the barn that looked promising but a side door just around the corner seemed to be a better choice. It was in view of the house, however, so it posed a greater risk.

Matt directed Carolyn to stay hidden while he checked the door. "I'll wave to you if I get the door open. Don't come until I signal, okay?"

Carolyn nodded.

Matt crept slowly to the side door and paused outside to listen. He put his ear to the door but failed to hear voices. As he reached for the latch to open the weathered wooden door, he noticed his hand was shaking. *So much for the brave and dashing sleuth,* he thought wryly. Slowly, he lifted the latch and pulled the ring handle. The door creaked and, to Matt, it sounded loud enough to rouse anyone in the house. He stopped and listened again to determine if anyone was responding to the noise. No lights came on in the house, and he didn't hear anyone around, so he motioned to Carolyn.

"That door made a lot of noise," whispered Carolyn.

"Yeah," was Matt's only response as he reached for her right hand and led her into the barn. The moon light offered little illumination through the single dirty window. Matt pulled the small flashlight from his pocket and turned it on, careful to keep the beam low. They looked around but only saw old tools and a mouse who ran from the intruding light. Matt scanned the room and found a door with a padlock. The barn was apparently divided into two separate sections. He looked to Carolyn to see if she understood and she quietly suggested they try a window she saw on the other side of the barn. "It would give us access to the other room and just might be open," she suggested with a bit of optimism in her voice.

Matt nodded and led her back through the door but didn't close it. He didn't want to alert anyone to their presence until they were ready to leave. Carolyn guided Matt to the window she had noticed earlier. It was covered by shutters but they were secured with very loose and rusty nails. Matt was able to pull the nails out completely and set them aside to replace them later.

The window opened with some effort as both of them pushed to keep a balanced pressure on the old structure. The last thing they needed was the window to break loose and come crashing down. Matt helped Carolyn through the window using an old milk crate as a step. Carolyn squeezed through the opening and dropped to the ground on the other side. She could make out shadows of large objects but couldn't identify them. Matt followed her and turned on the flashlight. He quickly scanned the area, and both were surprised to find not only the elusive desk but a large whiskey still and dozens of gallons of home brewed alcohol tucked tightly into large crates. A bootlegging operation! No wonder the woman was so inhospitable.

Carolyn whispered to Matt. "I know Kentucky has an active bootlegging community, but I never expected it in Illinois!"

Matt chuckled softly. "I guess a lot of people enjoy this stuff

– even here!" His face took on a more serious appearance as he directed his light back to the desk. "There it is." He walked quietly and carefully toward the desk, making sure he didn't disturb anything on the ground. He handed the flashlight to Carolyn and opened the roll top and found the hidden lever underneath the desk. Sylvia had explained to him how to open the hidden compartment and he pulled those instructions from his memory. He pulled and then twisted the lever to the left and heard a click. As if by magic, a slotted façade rolled away and revealed the place where Sylvia had hidden Matt's confession. He reached in and felt all around the space. The paper wasn't there! He let out a low moan as he began searching every part of the desk. He found a ledger of past moonshine clients, the quantity bought, and the amount paid. He kept searching and found nothing else of interest, just some receipts and other items related to the bootlegging operation.

He turned to Carolyn and whispered, "It's not in the desk; let's get out of here." He put everything back where he had found it in the desk and returned to the window. He helped Carolyn through and followed seconds later. He returned the milk crate to the place he had found it while Carolyn shut the window and replaced the nails to the shutters. Last, he shut the door on the other side of the barn. The creaking of the rusty hinges was followed by a light coming on in the house. Carolyn saw it and ran to Matt and grabbed his hand. She began to run and held a finger to her lips. Matt understood and followed her lead.

They reached the car and got in quickly, both breathing hard. Matt turned the car's lights from auto to off and started the car. He pulled out slowly to prevent revving of the engine. Once they were safely a mile away, he pulled over and killed the engine. He hit the steering wheel with his right hand and cursed. Carolyn knew the source of his rage. The confession, where was it? Who had it?

Carolyn sat and waited for Matt to regain control. He leaned his head back and closed his eyes as if he could shut out the reality of what they had just discovered. Someone had found the confession already. Could it be Detective Robertson, the Smiths? No, not the Smiths; they wouldn't be so friendly if they had read it, and Detective Robertson would have already arrested him. Besides, the detective wouldn't even know where to find the desk. Would he?

Matt slumped, as if all the air had been released from him. Without looking at her, he spoke to Carolyn. "We can't go through with the wedding; it wouldn't be fair to you. You'd be visiting me once a month in a penitentiary somewhere, and I don't want that for you."

"Matthew Brooks, you listen to me! You are not a quitter; we will find it. If someone had that confession, you would know it by now. We can't give up! As for the wedding, nothing has changed as far as I'm concerned. I refuse to believe you won't grow old with me on the farm. I'm not letting you off the hook that easily."

Matt turned to look at her, unable to speak at first. Even with only the moon for illumination, he could see the love in her eyes. No one had ever looked at him that way before and he was humbled by it. "You really mean that, don't you?"

"Of course, silly. I told you I was in this with you, that I would help you find the desk and the confession, and I meant it. I love you, Matt Brooks. Get used to it because I'm not going anywhere."

"I don't know what to say except to say I don't deserve you."

Carolyn laughed. "Who said we should deserve love? It should be freely given with no strings attached."

Matt stared at the beautiful woman next to him for several moments before leaning forward and wrapping his arms around her. "You are the best thing to ever happen to me," he whispered into her ear. "I can only try to be the man you think I am."

Carolyn pulled back enough to meet his gaze before pressing her lips to his. She held the kiss for several seconds. "That's better, now let's go figure out our next move. Someone took that paper out of the desk. It's significant, I think, that whoever it was has not brought it forward. It wasn't the police, you, or Sylvia. Maybe whoever found it is planning to blackmail you. Or, it could be someone who doesn't know what they have or who to connect it to."

"Your last suggestion seems the most likely. If it was blackmail, surely I would've been contacted by now."

"Probably, but we can't rule anything out. We need to trace the path of the desk. Who has had access to it from Sylvia's house to this barn? Call Sylvia tomorrow morning and have her help with that. Maybe a mover or the auction company found it, or a child, or…"

Matt interrupted her. "Okay, I got it. I'll call Sylvia in the morning." He looked around at their dark surroundings. "Let's get out of here."

***

The next morning, Matt waited until after he and Carolyn had eaten breakfast before he called Sylvia. By the fourth ring, he was convinced she was not at home and started to hang up when he heard the familiar voice of his former assistant.

"Hello?"

"Sylvia, it's Matt Brooks."

"Goodness, Matt! I've been on pins and needles waiting to hear from you. Have you found the desk?"

"Yes, I found the desk, but I didn't find the confession. Are you sure you placed the paper in the secret compartment of Ron's desk?"

"I'm positive. Are you sure you looked in the right place and in the right desk?"

Matt sighed. "Yes, I'm positive. The scratches on the side of the desk were exactly as you described, and the crayon marks on the underside also matched. Sylvia, we need to trace the desk again. I know the desk's path to where it is now, but I need to know who had access to it along the way. I thought I would start with you. Besides you, who had access to the desk before it went to Ron's sister's house?"

"No one. Several people visited to offer their condolences, but no one went into Ron's office."

"Did anyone stay with you from the time of Ron's death until you gave the desk away?"

Sylvia thought for a few moments before answering. "No one except my parents and they were too busy with the children while I made funeral arrangements to go rummaging through Ron's desk."

"Okay, I'll check with the auction company next. Don't worry; if the confession hasn't turned up by now, it probably won't," Matt assured Sylvia with more confidence than he felt. Who was he kidding? He was in deep trouble and he knew it.

"I wish I could believe that," Sylvia answered with doubt evident in her voice. "Keep me posted; I have as much invested in this as you."

"I understand and I'll let you know the second I find it. Oh, by the way…"

"Yes?"

"I'm getting married a week from Saturday," Matt stated with a lilt in his voice.

"Married? Are you kidding? You just got out of a very bad marriage, you are hunting for a piece of paper that could cost you your life, and you tell me you're getting married?"

Matt chuckled and reached for Carolyn's hand. "Yes, I'm getting married, and she is the most wonderful person in the whole world. You're invited, by the way. The invitation should get to you in a couple of days."

"I can't believe it! Does she know about the rather precarious situation you're in?"

"Of course, and she loves me anyway," Matt replied as he turned and smiled at Carolyn.

"She is either a saint or a fool, and I can't decide which is worse," Sylvia responded with sarcasm.

Matt would not be put off. "I understand your skepticism, but we love each other madly. She is the best thing to happen in my whole life. I'm a better man because of her."

"Well, will miracles never cease!" Sylvia answered. "Now, go find that confession before you find yourself getting arrested as you leave for your honeymoon!"

"Yes, ma'am!" Matt hung up the phone and restarted the car. "I have my marching orders from Sylvia – find the confession, or she may kill me herself!"

Carolyn suppressed a smile. "Well, we can't have that, can we?" Her face became more serious and she patted Matt's right knee. "We'll find that miserable confession Matt and then have a wonderful life together."

Matt responded with a slight nod and a smile that didn't quite reach his eyes. He appreciated Carolyn's support more than he could put into words, but he knew the consequences if he failed to find the confession before Detective Robertson.

Chapter Twenty-Four

Matt sat down in his home office and began the process of speaking to everyone he could track down who had access to the desk until it reached its current location. He wasn't able to reach everyone which he had known would be nearly impossible. He felt as if he was looking for the proverbial needle in the haystack.

After three fruitless hours, he looked up to see Carolyn standing in the doorway. Her smile eased his tension a bit as she walked toward him. "How about some lunch? You've been at it a long time."

"Lunch sounds good; what did you have in mind? There isn't much food in the house, I'm afraid."

"So, I discovered, but it's not a problem. I ordered groceries and our lunch, and both will be delivered soon."

Matt looked at her in amazement. "Beautiful and efficient too, what a package!" he teased.

"It comes from necessity, I assure you. Running a farm business requires ingenuity, efficiency, and a lot of hard work. Getting food is nothing compared to that." Carolyn walked behind Matt's chair and began to knead his neck and shoulders. "Ooh! You are so tight, Dr. Brooks. I think you need a break."

"I've hit a brick wall with contacting anyone who had access to the desk, so this is a good time to take a break. What has kept you busy all morning besides organizing and resupplying my kitchen?"

Carolyn's face lit up. "I have been a very busy bride-to-be this morning. I finished making arrangements for the wedding and I can pick up the invitations this afternoon. If you'll help me address them this evening, we can get them in the mail tomorrow."

"Sounds like a plan even though my handwriting is atrocious!"

"No handwriting needed. We're going to address them on the computer using software for that purpose. Your printer can handle the envelope size and the writing will still look like handwriting."

"Amazing! Is there anything you can't do?"

Carolyn laughed as the doorbell rang. "Sounds like lunch is here!" She paid the delivery person and set out their lunch in the breakfast room. Matt walked in and sat where Carolyn had placed his food.

"What are we having?" he asked as he opened the Styrofoam to-go box.

"Mexican. I got enchiladas for both of us; I hope you like it."

"No problem here, if it doesn't move, I'll eat it,"

Carolyn sat down across from him and reached out her hand. "Let's say grace for this meal and our many blessings. We've gotten this far, and I believe God will get us the rest of the way."

Matt nodded, took her hand, and prayed. It was cathartic, and he realized he wasn't alone. He hadn't taken the time to ask God for help but had received it anyway. He finished the prayer and looked up with tears glistening in his eyes. Carolyn understood and answered with an affirmative nod of her head before opening her meal and reaching for her fork.

Matt dove into his food appreciatively. "This is really good! I didn't realize how hungry I was."

"I decided you needed something substantial especially since you skipped breakfast," Carolyn reminded as she scooped a dollop of guacamole onto her food. "Have you had any luck with your inquiries?"

"Yes and no. So many different people have had access to the desk since it left Sylvia's that it's proving impossible to track them all down. Anyone of a dozen or more people could have taken the confession from the desk," Matt replied with a sigh of resignation.

Carolyn reached for Matt's hand and gave it a squeeze. "Don't be discouraged; if someone were planning to use the confession against you, it would have happened by now."

Matt looked up with a half-hearted smile. "You're probably right but it's gut wrenching to not know where it is and who has it. It's like waiting for a bomb to drop but not knowing when or from where."

Carolyn wanted so much to help Matt, but she knew he would have to work out his own peace with the situation. If the confession was never found, he would have to find a way to live with that uncertainty. She took in a breath to comment further but decided against it and returned to her food instead. They ate in silence for several minutes, and the food appeared to improve Matt's mood somewhat.

"Sweetheart, there's something I need to discuss with you," Carolyn began. Matt looked up from his food with a raised brow but offered no comment and she continued. "I need to go back home for a few days to take care of some things there. Everything is ready for the wedding here and I'll be finished with farm business in time to return for our big day."

"I see. Is this something you want to do on your own or do you want me to come with you?" Matt asked with some hesitation, afraid that Carolyn was getting cold feet.

"Of course, you can come. In fact, I hope you want to come with me. I will understand if you need to stay here and work on finding the confession, but now that we are engaged, I don't want to spend time away from you."

"I'd love to come. I'm not getting any closer to finding that confession in spite of the hours I've spent looking. I can make phone calls from the farm as easily as here. When do we leave?"

Carolyn rose from her chair, walked around the table and threw her arms around Matt's neck. "First thing in the morning, but I have other ideas for the rest of today," she said with a glint in her eyes.

***

The next morning, they rode in the back of a cab bound for Midway Airport. It was mid-November and the landscape had continued its march toward winter. Most of the leaves had fallen from trees preparing for their winter's nap and streets were littered with a colorful carpet. Even as homeowners raked their yards, more leaves fell where others had been cleared only moments before. The scene depressed Matt as he realized the parallel. Like raking leaves, his quest had been one of intense effort followed by a disappointing result.

"A penny for your thoughts," Carolyn said, hoping to pull Matt out of the obviously low feeling.

Matt didn't want to go over ground he had trodden so many

times he saw the resultant ruts. He turned back to her and forced a smile. "They're not worth a penny; I was only daydreaming. So, what's so important you had to come back today?"

Carolyn's face took on a pained expression. "Jeremy made bail. I'm worried what he will do next. I didn't want Phil and my staff to face him without me."

"What? How did he make bail? I thought his family didn't have the money to bail him out."

"I don't know; all I know is he's no longer behind bars, and that frightens me."

Matt blew out a breath. This was the last thing they needed. "What are you planning to do?"

"Do? I'm not sure I can do anything to help, but I can't be hundreds of miles away if Jeremy picks up where he left off."

Matt sat in silence, unable to voice the terror he felt for Carolyn's welfare. His bad feeling continued after they boarded the plane. Even Carolyn's attempts at cheerful banter did nothing to relieve his mood. The flight passed in silence as each contemplated the challenges they faced.

Chapter Twenty-Five

Carl picked up the pair from the Louisville airport and helped stow the bags in the back of the Range Rover. "Good to see you both. It's been a bit too quiet around the farm since you left."

"Quiet should be a good thing after all the excitement we had last month," Carolyn quipped.

Carl chuckled. "For sure. Oh, by the way, I hear congratulations are in order."

"Thank you," Carolyn and Matt chimed together.

"I'm not sure I can make it to the wedding, but will you have a celebration here afterwards?"

"Of course, we will. Mary is already working on the plans so it should be fantastic," Carolyn replied.

Carl glanced in the rear-view mirror at the couple riding behind him. They were in love; it was easy to see. He had held back his opinion of Dr. Brooks, afraid that his employer was moving too quickly and had been taken in by a smooth talker. But they were very happy, and he could see how Matt Brooks looked at Carolyn. He clearly adored her and she him. She had found true love at last. Beneath the surface, however, he sensed tension in both of them. He suspected the reason was Jeremy Simpson and his family, which was in reality only half of the source of unhappiness. He would have been very surprised to know that a second dark cloud hung over the pair. He knew nothing of their quest for the desk and its all-important contents. He had no idea that their new-found happiness could be crushed in an instant if the confession fell into the wrong hands. Conversely, if fate was kind and the confession was destroyed, Carl and the rest of the world would never know how close the pair came to disaster.

Similar thoughts ran through Matt's mind even as he smiled and held Carolyn close. This new life was almost in reach with all its promises of happiness and the contentment he had always sought. He knew how fragile it was and cursed the day Sylvia had walked into his office with her desperate proposal. He didn't blame her for the mess in which he found himself. He was stupid to even consider the offer, much less write that confession. He had thought he was so smart. Now, he knew he had only outsmarted himself.

Carolyn sensed Matt's dark mood and knew the cause of it. She decided to try to lighten his mood. She squeezed his hand. "Hey there, cowboy, how about a ride this afternoon?"

Matt pulled himself from his dark thoughts with difficulty. "You're on. We should have enough sunlight to make it all the way to our favorite rock overlooking the valley."

Carolyn smiled in return and let her head rest on his shoulder. It was all going to work out, she just knew it. Life would not be so cruel as to destroy the happiness they had found.

They drove on through the late fall countryside with mostly barren trees holding onto a few brave golden leaves. The birds who had not migrated south watched from treetops as they passed, silent sentries of the countryside.

When they pulled into the entrance to the farm, Carolyn could see several cars in the drive. She recognized her cousin's official car with SHERIFF painted on the side and its rack of blue and red lights on top. A shiny black truck was parked just beyond and a gray sedan completed the group. She wondered if there was trouble with the Simpsons again. Her heart rate picked up as she reached for the door handle and stepped out.

Her cousin stepped out of the house and walked forward to meet her. "Carolyn, how good to see you!"

"Phil, is something wrong? Who else is here?" she asked fearing the answer.

"Now, sweetheart, everything is okay. There's just something we want to discuss with you."

"We?"

"Yeah, David and I. Your attorney is here also."

For a few moments, Carolyn thought of the lost confession and if it might be connected to this unexpected visit. Was Matt in trouble? Was she? "I don't understand…"

"It's the Simpsons. They're trying to cause trouble again," Phil explained as David met them at the door.

"Carolyn, Matt, come in. It's great to see both of you. Carolyn, you look absolutely wonderful! I have no doubt Matt has something to do with that," David said as he leaned in for a hug.

"It's wonderful to see you too, but what is happening now with the Simpsons?"

Phil stepped forward. "Let's sit down. I believe Brandon is waiting for us in the living room."

Matt and Carolyn followed Phil into the living room and sat together on the sofa, each anxiously awaiting the reason for the impromptu visit.

Phil sat down and cleared his throat. "Well, this is the situation. The Simpsons have filed a lawsuit claiming you shot

Jeremy because you have a vendetta against the family. They claim Jesse's death was not an accident, that you are attempting to kill off members of the family one-by-one."

"But, that's absurd! Jesse's death was an accident. I only shot Jeremy because he pointed a loaded gun at me after beating my horses to death!" exclaimed Carolyn.

Phil held up his hand. "We know; we're on your side. Try to stay calm and hear us out, okay?"

Carolyn nodded. "I apologize; I know you are here to help. She turned her attention to her attorney. Brandon, what can we do?"

"Well, first of all, welcome home and congratulations on your engagement to Matt here." He said as he inclined his head toward Matt. "We know this is nonsense, but the intention is not for them to win, it is to discredit you in the eyes of the community. Apparently, they have decided to come after you in a way that will do the most harm. If people in this community and even outside of it believe you to be violent and vindictive, then your farm business will suffer. This could drag out for a long time. Their attorney has agreed to take this case on a contingency basis. In other words, their attorney gets paid only if he wins their case. This gives him a lot of motivation to get a judgment favorable to the Simpsons.

"Would I go to jail?" Carolyn asked with a tremulous voice.

"No, this is a civil case, but courts have been very sympathetic with the plaintiff in these situations. They're after money, lots of it. Even if they lose, their attorney can drag the case out a long time, although it wouldn't be in the attorney's best interest to do that if he thinks he will lose."

Carolyn didn't speak for several moments as she digested

this news. "What can we do?"

"We're already doing it," Brandon answered." We have counter-sued and requested a speedy resolution in the courts. The Simpsons have a slim chance of winning, but they are determined to cause chaos in your life as reprisal for Jesse's death."

"What a mess! I would give all the money I have if it could bring Jesse back, but it can't. Even if we win the civil case, the Simpsons are not going anywhere; they'll be a thorn in my side for the rest of my life." Carolyn's emotions were betrayed by the tremor in her voice. "I don't know how all of this will end – or if it ever will."

Matt reached over and put an arm around her shoulders in an effort to console and show his support. Carolyn managed a weak smile.

"Do we have a hearing date yet for the civil case?" She asked.

"Yes, that's why we wanted you here," her attorney answered. "It's scheduled for tomorrow at one o'clock."

"So soon?"

"Yes, we pulled a couple of strings to get this past us. If it is decided that there is no basis for the suit, there will be no trial. If that happens, we will continue our lawsuit and stipulate that we won't expect any monetary damages if the Simpsons obey a restraining order to leave you, this farm, and your employees alone. If any one of them violates the order, they will be paying for it for the rest of their lives. They need to know we mean business."

Matt turned to Phil and interjected. "Do you think the Simpsons can be scared off this way? They seem very determined to punish Carolyn for Jesse's death regardless of consequences."

"I share your concern Matt, but it's all we've got. If the judge comes down hard enough on them, I think the plan has a chance to work."

The attorney stood and reached for his leather portfolio. "Well, I have to go; I have to be in court in an hour. Thank you, everyone, for meeting. It helps to present a united front in these situations. The last thing we want the Simpsons to think is that Carolyn is alone and easy prey like a calf who has wandered from the herd."

Matt winced at the metaphor but remained silent. After all, this was a working farm and the comparison was very understandable from that perspective.

"Brandon, thank you for meeting with us. Should we arrive early to the hearing tomorrow?" Carolyn asked.

Brandon closed the flap on his portfolio and tucked it under his arm. "If you're in your seats twenty minutes before the hearing starts, that should be sufficient time to get a good view of the proceedings. I doubt this hearing will draw much attention, especially with such short notice."

Phil wasn't so sure about the community's lack of interest in the upcoming hearing. Recent local gossip had consisted of little else but the Simpson feud with Carolyn, so he expected the courtroom to be standing room only. Once the attorney was out the door, he gave his own advice. "Cousin, I would go earlier than what Brandon suggested."

"So, you believe there will be a lot of people there tomorrow?" Matt asked.

"You got it, City Boy. This situation with the Simpsons and Carolyn has created a lot of interest and gossip," Phil explained.

"How wonderful to be the subject of local gossip," Carolyn

commented wryly. "I'd rather be in the background of local news, not the headline."

David reached for his denim jacket and put it on. "Well like it or not, you're the star attraction around here at the moment."

"I'm glad Matt and I have spent time away from here lately. At least we've avoided the gossip."

Phil stood and reached for Carolyn's hands to pull her to standing. "Hang in there, sweetie; this too shall pass."

"Thanks, Phil; I'll get through this." Carolyn said, then turned to David. "I appreciate both of you more than I can say. You've always been there for me."

"Our pleasure; we've known you all your life and want the very best for you. Your parents would never forgive us otherwise," David added.

Both men turned to Matt who had stood also. "We're happy for you both," David said as he shook hands with Matt.

"Yes, we wish both of you, health, happiness, and many years together," Phil added as he also shook hands.

"Thank you; that means a lot to me, and I'm sure it means even more to Carolyn. You are her friends and family. I'm honored to join this wonderful group of people My life has already been transformed more than I can say," Matt declared with feeling. "Now, can we interest you fellas in something to eat? I can't speak for anyone else, but I'm starved!"

Everyone laughed and followed Carolyn to the dining room where Sadie was ready with lunch.

Chapter Twenty-Six

After lunch, Matt and Carolyn changed into jeans and warm jackets for their horseback ride. Carolyn led the way along the narrow trail around the top of the ridge and past the waterfall. Once they reached the rock where Matt had confessed his darkest secret a week earlier, they dismounted and let the horses graze on the grass nearby.

Their view had changed drastically since their last ride to the rock, and the chilly breeze foretold winter's inevitable arrival. The couple cuddled into each other to keep warm and remained silent as they surveyed the valley below. Even with the colorful autumn display almost spent, the valley was beautiful. Pine, cedar, blue spruce, and other evergreens stood out against the stark landscape, more noticeable by the absence of their deciduous neighbors' leaves.

Carolyn sensed Matt's pensive mood and asked, "Penny for your thoughts?"

Matt chuckled. "I was just thinking how wonderful it would be if we could freeze time. I would capture this moment and replay it over and over."

"Like Groundhog Day?" Carolyn asked with a giggle.

"Yeah, just like that. Looking down at the valley and being here with total quiet except for the wind, it seems as if the rest of the world has gone away, and we are the only two people in the world."

Carolyn agreed. "Yes, it is nice to find an oasis in the middle of our chaotic lives. Each of us has an issue that threatens our happiness and our future together. Is it too much to believe that both situations turn out positively?"

Matt was thoughtful for several moments before answering. "No, I don't think it's too much to wish for or even to believe in, but we must be ready to face whatever the future holds – good or bad."

Carolyn sighed and snuggled even closer. "At least we're facing things together. We can lean on the other's strength when our own begins to fail. It is easier to be brave together than alone I think."

"Absolutely! Now, what should we do this evening to take our minds off things?"

"Hmm… how about spending some time in the barn? That little filly is almost ready to adopt out, so I'm sure Carl could use some help."

Matt smiled. "A few months ago, I wouldn't have believed that spending the evening in a barn with horses would be something I would enjoy, but I think that's a wonderful way to take our minds off our problems. Lead on!"

***

Matt placed fresh straw in the filly's stall while Carolyn walked her young charge around the barn. Matt indicated he was finished, and called to Carolyn. The little one had taken a liking to Matt and missed no chance to nuzzle him or whinny for his attention. This evening was no different as she nipped at his pants as she passed by him.

"Hey! You're getting pretty fresh young lady!" Matt laughed. "Watch out or you'll get a reputation as a man chaser!" The filly reacted by whinnying as if to say, "I don't care!" Matt laughed and reached out to stroke the beautiful creature. "So, where is she going?"

"Carl told me he hasn't lined anything up yet, but it shouldn't be difficult to find her a home. Don't worry, we'll keep her until then," Carolyn assured.

"Would it be possible to keep her?" Matt asked.

"Keep her? Well, I guess so, but we really don't have a… oh, I get it; you've become attached to her, haven't you?"

"I'm afraid so. It's funny; I've never connected with an animal before. I didn't even have a dog when I was growing up, so I haven't had much experience with animals. This little girl has definitely captured my heart. There must be something about this place that casts a spell on unsuspecting men to make them fall in love."

Carolyn laughed. Yes, that's exactly how I landed you; it was magic for sure."

"I knew it!" Matt picked up a handful of fresh straw and threw it at Carolyn who ducked and reached for some straw to throw at Matt.

"Okay, buster, it's war!"

Outside the barn, David Fields overheard the playful banter and smiled. It had been a long time since he had heard Carolyn laugh. The vet approached the barn as Matt and Carolyn were preparing to send another missile the other's way. Carolyn had straw in her hair and Matt's shirt was peppered with small pieces.

"Hey, you two! What's going on here?"

"Oh, hi David, we were just deciding who would back down first. I'm sure Matt would have given in soon if you hadn't arrived."

"Uh huh," Matt responded as he rolled his eyes. "I think I had the upper hand and it was you who were about to give up."

"I'm glad to see something fun happening here. It's been a while since there has been anything about which to be joyful," David said as his face crinkled into a wide smile.

"We decided to break some of the tension and clean out the barn for Carl. I guess we got a little carried away."

"Oh, I don't know; the mares seem to be enjoying themselves."

Matt and Carolyn looked around at the eyes trained on them. Four mares were watching the shenanigans from their stalls. Both burst out laughing at the sight. "I guess they're waiting for Act II," Matt quipped, which brought on more raucous laughter.

"Please stop," Carolyn begged. "I'm laughing so hard I can't catch my breath!"

"Okay, truce. Come here and I'll get the rest of the straw out of your hair," Matt offered.

"What brings you out this evening, David?" Carolyn asked.

"I promised Carl I would bring out medicine for the filly. It's a supplement, really, to add to her feed. Her blood work showed anemia, so we're helping her along a bit."

"Whatever you and Carl are doing is working; she's doing really well. In fact, Matt can't seem to part with her."

"Matt, farm life seems to have rubbed off on you after all," David remarked.

"Amazing, isn't it? It has come as a surprise to me as well," Matt replied.

David shook his head. "Who would have thought a city boy dentist and a business savvy farm girl would meet in Vegas of all places and fall in love in one day? It's rather a remarkable story but it seems to have a happy ending for the two of you. I know Carolyn has never looked happier."

"I'm happy, David. It's as if I have been sleep-walking through a terrible dream, but now I'm awake, and I have found myself in the most wonderful place."

David looked fondly at her. "Then, I'm happy too. Phil and I might seem a bit over protective, but I assure you we only want what's best for you and that appears to be this young man here."

Matt spoke up. "I did feel the scrutiny from both of you, but I understand why you would want to protect this beautiful lady. I assure you I share that feeling. I've come to discover, however, that she can stand up for herself rather well," he remarked as he shot a mischievous grin Carolyn's way.

Carolyn laughed. "I am rather competitive. David, can you stay a while? We're finished in here and I could use a hot cup of something."

The vet glanced at her and then at Matt and was satisfied the invitation was sincere. "I'd like nothing better. A hot cup of cocoa would hit the spot."

The trio walked together and entered the house through the side door. They shed jackets and boots in the mudroom where Carolyn caught her image in the mirror over the sink as she washed her hands. "Oh my! I am a sight." She pulled out more straw and ran her fingers through her hair but it did little to tame it.

She emerged laughing and caught up with the men who were washing up in the kitchen. Both looked up at her approach.

"What's so funny?" David asked.

"Me! I'm a sorry sight after the battle in the barn."

"Ha! Do you concede defeat?" Matt asked impishly.

"Never!" She laughed.

"Okay, you two, the kitchen is neutral territory. You don't want Mary's wrath if she finds her kitchen less than spotless in the morning."

"You're right about that," Matt agreed.

Carolyn heated water in a tea kettle and placed three cups on the table along with cocoa mix and a tea assortment. Once the water was hot, she poured it into each cup. "The rest is up to you, just pick out what you want."

They chatted amiably for several minutes until Carolyn brought up the court hearing they would attend the next day. "David, what do you think will happen tomorrow?"

"If the judge has any sense, he will dismiss the lawsuit as baseless. Otherwise, this mess will continue for some time. I'm sorry you're going through this, and especially right before your wedding to Matt. This should be a time of joy not meetings with your attorney and hearings before a judge."

Carolyn reached out for David's hand. "I'm sorry, this has affected more than just me. I appreciate all your support though this."

"Glad to do it."

Carolyn became pensive as the two men discussed the filly Matt had decided to adopt as his own. Neither was aware that Carolyn was working out a possible solution to the Simpson's feud with her. By the end of the visit, she had formulated a plan of her own and was determined to put it into action.

David drank the last of his cocoa and bade the couple good-night and promised to meet them at the courthouse for the hearing the next day. Carolyn turned down Matt's offer of a game of Scrabble.

"I'd love to any other night, but I think I'll turn in early tonight and be rested for tomorrow."

"No problem; I'll read a while then. Good-night sweetheart, sleep well," Matt said as he hugged and kissed his fiancé.

"Good night, see you in the morning."

As Carolyn showered and dressed for bed, her plan to end the feud began to take shape in her mind. By the time she climbed into bed and pulled up the covers, she knew exactly what she needed to do.

Chapter Twenty-Seven

The next morning, Matt appeared for breakfast later than usual and found the dining room empty. Sadie appeared and asked if he would like the oatmeal and banana bread Mary had fixed earlier.

"That's sounds good. By the way, Sadie, do you know where Mrs. Hodges is at the moment?"

"No sir, but I do know she put on a jacket and asked for the Range Rover to be brought around. She hasn't come back yet."

"I see, thank you."

Matt sipped hot coffee as he waited for his breakfast and wondered where Carolyn could have gone.

***

Carolyn's heart pounded as she turned off the engine. She sat for a minute longer before emerging from the Range Rover and walking toward the Simpson's home. She had momentary second thoughts about the wisdom of what she was about to do but decided this was the only way to end the year-long feud.

The front door opened before she reached the porch steps, and Mrs. Simpson emerged wearing a dirty apron over her dress and her hands firmly resting on her ample hips. Her face was etched with the trials of raising four sons with too little money and too many challenges. Widowed at thirty-five, she had had hungry mouths to feed and a run-down home to keep warm. Life had dealt her a bad hand and her face reflected the hard life she had led.

Carolyn hesitated as she saw the mistrust and hate in the older woman's eyes and wondered if she would be safe if she entered the Simpson home.

"What do *you* want? You ain't welcome here!"

Carolyn took a deep breath to settle her nerves and recited her practiced speech. "Mrs. Simpson, I only want to talk. I believe I have a solution to this situation if you will just hear me out."

"Why should I? You don't care about us. You killed my Jesse and tried to kill Jeremy; what could you possibly have to say that I'd want to hear?"

"Mrs. Simpson, I have thought of little else since the accident last year and I would give anything to bring Jesse back, but I can't. As for Jeremy, he beat two of my horses to death. Another was hit by a car and killed when she ran into the road after Jeremy cut the pasture fence wire. Even worse, he beat my farm manager badly and aimed a gun at me. I had no choice but to stop him. I deliberately shot him in his arm to disarm him. I'm a good shot; if I had meant to do more than wound him, he would be dead. Please, Mrs. Simpson, hear me out. Can we sit on your front porch and at least let me tell you how I believe we can resolve our differences?"

The older lady stood still and glared at Carolyn as she considered the request. Finally, she gave a sharp nod and turned back toward the house. Carolyn thought she had failed, but Mrs. Simpson sat down heavily in one of the rockers on the porch and jabbed a finger at Carolyn which she interpreted to mean that she should take the other rocker beside Mrs. Simpson.

Carolyn proceeded up the worn steps and sat down in the rocker. She waited for Mrs. Simpson to speak first, not wanting to say anything until the woman was ready to hear it.

"Well? What did you come all the way out here for?"

"I… I was hoping we could resolve our differences in a way that would be beneficial for both of us. I can't bring Jesse back, and I'm terribly sorry about the accident. I lost control of my car when I hit an oily patch of pavement. It was raining hard and water was collecting on the road. I honestly don't remember what happened next except I saw headlights coming at me. I was knocked unconscious for a few minutes and woke up when paramedics pulled me from the car. You know the rest. I won't cause you more pain by recounting it, but I wasn't speeding when it happened, and I hadn't been drinking as some have said. I swear to you it's the truth."

Mrs. Simpson wiped a tear from her eye before it could fall onto her cheek. She looked out in front of her as if seeing the accident played out. "Jesse was a good boy until he got in with a bad bunch his last year of high school. It was a gang of sorts. They introduced him to drinking and drugs. His brothers did nothing to help. They just laughed at him when he came home drunk or high. I tried to get him help but nothing worked. He needed a man's firm direction – they all did. It's been easy to blame you for his death, but I know the accident wasn't your fault. Jesse would still be alive if he hadn't been speeding and had put on his seatbelt."

"Thank you, Mrs. Simpson. That means a lot. I will always carry the pain of that night with me, but I'm relieved to know you understand how it happened."

Mrs. Simpson did not respond as she fought to control her emotions.

"As for Jeremy, you do understand there is nothing I can do to help him, don't you? He committed several serious crimes and will have to pay for them. I can, however, recommend leniency if I believe this feud can end, and both of us can get back to living our lives in peace."

At this, Mrs. Simpson raised her head, and Carolyn saw a glimmer of hope in the woman's eyes. She then realized that Mrs. Simpson wanted the feud to end as much as she did. "We shouldn't live this way, as enemies, and I want to help you any way I can."

The woman's head shot up and she became angry. "Are you trying to buy me off? Is that the reason you came?"

"Absolutely not. I want to help you so you can provide for your boys. I can offer them jobs on my farm and I have an empty cottage that I have been renting out that you could have to live in. It's roomy enough to accommodate your family. The kitchen is newly renovated and it has three bathrooms and four bedrooms."

"I don't want charity, Mrs. Hodges; I've always taken care of my boys on my own."

"This isn't charity. You would be doing me a favor if you took the cottage. It would provide more security for my horses if someone lived there who would keep an eye on things, especially when I'm gone. My farm manager can't be everywhere at once, and he would be glad of the help."

Carolyn continued. "I have also spoken with my attorney about the insurance settlement for the accident. I understand you have not received that money."

"Not a dime."

"Well, that has been taken care of. My insurance company has been instructed to release that money immediately. They were trying to stall but they have no choice but to pay what they owe you, Mrs. Simpson. You should have that money in your hands within forty-eight hours. I apologize it took so long."

Mrs. Simpson was beginning to show more interest in what Carolyn had to say. "That would certainly help; we haven't had much coming in since Jeremy went to jail."

Just then, a high-pitched shriek came from the house and startled Carolyn. "Is that a baby?"

Mrs. Simpson nodded and rose from her chair, leaving Carolyn on the porch alone. A few minutes later the older woman appeared at the door with a baby in her arms and asked her guest to come in.

It took a few seconds for Carolyn's eyes to adjust enough to the dark room so she could find a chair. Mrs. Simpson followed her, sat down in a worn chair, and offered the baby a bottle.

"I didn't know you had a baby."

"I didn't until last week. This is Jesse's daughter. She was born six months after the accident. Her mother brought her to me last week and left her. She was on drugs, out of money, and said she couldn't take care of the 'brat' anymore. I didn't know Jesse had fathered a baby. I'm not sure he knew before he died, but here we are."

"Is the mother coming back?"

"No chance of that; she's dead. She overdosed the day after she dropped off the baby."

Shock registered on Carolyn's face as she looked at the

innocent pink bundle in Mrs. Simpson's lap. "What are you going to do?"

"I don't know. I could let her be adopted; there are a lot of young couples unable to have a baby of their own who would love to have her. That's probably the best thing for her. It would be selfish to keep her when I have nothing to offer. I'm not as old as I look, only fifty, but it wouldn't be easy to raise a baby."

"Oh, Mrs. Simpson, I'm so very sorry; I had no idea of all you were going through. Is there anything I can do for her? Would you accept some money from me?"

"If you had walked in here two weeks ago and made that offer, I would have slammed the door in your face, but now…"

"Please let me help. The cottage I offered has a small room you could use as a nursery. It's a snug home and all utilities are on my account. You would have nothing to pay. I could outfit the nursery if you decide to keep the baby."

"Why are you being so generous, Mrs. Hodges?"

"I want to help you, but I have selfish reasons as well. I'm getting married next week and I don't want to start my new life with this feud hanging over us. I have had to hire security guards, my farm manager is still recovering from the attack on him, and I've lost three good mares in a cruel and vicious way. This discord between us needs to end. I can help you and your family. I assure you I want nothing in return except your assurance that there will be no further attacks."

"What about Jeremy?"

"Jeremy has to face the charges that have been brought against him. As I said, I can recommend leniency, but there is no guarantee that will even be considered."

"I see. Mrs. Hodges…"

"Please, call me Carolyn."

"Carolyn, you aren't what I expected. Our paths don't exactly cross very often. I'll consider what you've offered, and I'll speak to my other two sons. I think I can promise you there will be no further attacks on your farm. Jeremy was the one behind all of that. Now, I need to tend to the baby's diaper. I'll get back to you."

Carolyn rose to leave. "Thank you, Mrs. Simpson; I appreciate the time you took to hear me out. I wish you the very best with everything, especially the baby."

The women walked to the front door. "Oh, Carolyn."

"Yes?" She responded and turned back around.

"You can call me Mae."

"Thank you, Mae," she answered and smiled warmly.

***

"Where have you been? I was worried about you," Matt greeted as Carolyn emerged from her vehicle back at her farm.

"Hello to you, too."

"Sorry, but I was worried."

"So, you said. I had something to take care of this morning. Have you had breakfast?"

"Yes, ages ago. You're changing the subject."

"That I am."

"You're being rather mysterious," Matt stated with a smile. "Well, whatever it is, it has made you happier. You seem more relaxed, and there is a hint of a smile that you are trying hard to suppress. Let's hope the hearing today makes you even happier."

"Yes, I hope so, and speaking of, I need to get dressed for

court. I'll see you in the sunroom around noon, okay?"

"Okay, mystery woman." Matt gave her a quick kiss and decided to take a walk while she got ready.

Carolyn chose her outfit carefully; fully aware she would be scrutinized closely at Jeremy's hearing. She donned a navy-blue dress with a matching jacket and chose a low-heeled pair of navy-blue shoes. As she dressed, the memory of Mae Simpson and the enormity of the burdens she shouldered reinforced Carolyn's decision to help that family. She only hoped the offer was accepted.

One last check of her appearance in the mirror reassured Carolyn that she was ready for the court appearance. Matt had returned from his walk and was waiting for her in the sunroom.

"I'm ready," she announced.

"Okay, let's go. Would you like me to drive?" Matt offered.

"Yes, please; I'm more nervous than I thought I would be."

Matt helped Carolyn into the passenger seat and assumed his position behind the wheel. He gave her a last encouraging pat on her shoulder and started the engine. He was curious as to where she had gone that morning, but he didn't want to be the type of guy who controlled everything. Carolyn was an independent woman and deserved to have her own space.

After a few miles, Carolyn broke the silence. "I spoke with Jeremy's Simpson's mother this morning."

"Really?" The revelation alarmed Matt, but he waited to hear what she had to say before offering any further comment.

"Yes, I went to see her actually. She is a nice but rather overwhelmed lady. She still has two teenage sons at home and is now caring for a baby."

"A baby? I would think she is a bit too old for a baby."

Carolyn chuckled. "You're probably right, but she is caring for a granddaughter, Jesse's child. She didn't know the baby existed until a week ago when the baby's mother dropped her off for Mae to raise. The mother experienced a fatal overdose the next day, so Mae has limited options."

"Wow, that is terrible; poor woman."

"Exactly."

"Why did you go to see her?"

"I thought maybe we could work out our differences without the involvement of the legal system. It turns out Mrs. Simpson wants the feud to end as much as I do. I made her an offer that I hope she accepts. If she does, the suit against me will be dropped."

Matt whistled. "You are some kind of woman. Not many people would be brave enough to go into the lion's den, so to speak, and meet the problem head-on. How did it end with her?"

"She is considering the offer I made and said she would get back to me. I know it is a last-minute effort, but I felt I had to try."

Matt wanted to ask about the offer that Carolyn had made to Mrs. Simpson, but they had arrived at the courthouse. He found a parking spot with some difficulty and noted a line of people waiting to enter the building. *I hope there is a proceeding today for someone else, and not all of these people are here for the Simpson-Hodges proceeding,* Matt thought.

Once they passed through security and walked into the assigned courtroom, Matt's hopes were dashed. The place was filling up fast and the room was buzzing with conversation.

Carolyn was aware of the stares as she passed the crowd. She walked to the first row and joined Phil and David who had saved seats for her and Matt.

Her attorney walked in and assumed his seat. He nodded to Carolyn and she rose and joined him at the defense table.

What seemed like an hour later to Carolyn, but was only ten minutes, the court was called to order. The judge made his opening comments and was ready to hear both sides of the argument when the Simpson's attorney asked for a sidebar conversation. Brandon joined them at the bench, already aware of what the other attorney would say.

The judge listened carefully as he covered his microphone with one hand. He nodded once and asked, "Are you sure?"

Both attorneys spoke again to the judge and resumed their seats.

Phil leaned forward and asked, "Carolyn, do you have any idea what's going on?"

She smiled. "I believe so, and it means we can all live in peace again."

Phil started to ask what she meant by that when the judge banged his gavel and asked for quiet. The crowd had begun to speculate among themselves.

Once the room was silenced, the judge announced that the case had been dismissed. He rose and left the courtroom leaving a stunned crowd behind.

Phil remained seated and turned once again toward Carolyn. "Okay, what just happened? By your smile, I believe you know something about this."

David and Matt also stood close, waiting to hear what caused the dramatic outcome they just witnessed.

"Fellas, I'll tell you everything but not here. Can we find someplace private?"

Phil led the group through a side door to a hallway with three small consulting rooms. He chose the first one and the foursome entered and sat around a small table. The men were silent as they waited for an explanation from Carolyn.

"I decided to be proactive about all of this so I paid a visit to Mrs. Simpson."

"You what? Do you realize how dangerous that was?" Phil protested, ever the protector.

"It really wasn't at all. We sat on the porch, just the two of us, and I assured her she would be receiving a check from my auto insurance very soon. They had been dragging their feet, but I had my attorney make it clear to them the money must be paid out immediately. They reluctantly agreed."

"What did Mrs. Simpson say to that?" David asked.

"She simply thanked me. I also offered her free use of the rental cottage. She still has two teenage sons at home and is now caring for an infant."

Phil reacted the same way Matt had earlier. "She has a baby?" He asked incredulously.

"It's Jesse's baby, apparently. He died before he knew he was to be a father. The mother gave her to Mae last week, then promptly died of an overdose the next day. Mae is trying to decide what to do with the child. She could use some help right now. I assured her we could use her boys part-time around the farm; they could keep an eye on that part of the property."

"Amazing," Phil responded.

"By the time I left, we were on a first name basis, and she assured me there would be no further problems from her family."

David chuckled. "You could have been a successful diplomat."

Matt looked on with pride in his eyes. His lovely fiancé was not only smart, she was kind and thoughtful as well.

David and Phil said good-bye as they emerged from the courthouse.

"Will you be heading back to Illinois?"

"Yes, Matt has some things he has to finish related to the sale of his business before the wedding on Saturday."

"Have you settled on the honeymoon yet?" David asked.

Matt and Carolyn chuckled. "Not yet; we'll have to let you know where we're going in a few days. We've been so busy we haven't had time to think about it," Carolyn explained.

Phil shook his head. "Well, anyway, I hope you have a wonderful wedding. We'll see you back here in a couple of weeks for the reception Mary has planned. I understand she and Celia are putting together quite a shindig."

"So, I hear," Carolyn said. "We'll let you know about the honeymoon, but wherever we go, you can always reach me on my cell."

"I hope that isn't necessary, but good to know. Good-bye, sweetheart," Phil said as he pulled Carolyn into a hug. He looked up at Matt and mouthed the words, "Take care of her – or else."

Matt's eyes widened a bit in response, but realized it was Phil's way of passing responsibility for Carolyn's welfare to him. He nodded in response.

Chapter Twenty-Eight

Carolyn napped during the short flight to Illinois as Matt wracked his brain for more places to look for the confession. It had to be somewhere, but who had it? He concluded it must be a stranger as no one had taken it to the police or contacted him for blackmail money. It wouldn't be hard, however, for the police to track down the original owner of the desk. Time was slipping away, and Matt felt the pressure mounting.

He glanced at the sleeping woman next to him. Was it fair to marry her when his future was so uncertain? He wanted to marry her more than anything in the world but knew it was selfish of him to do it now. It wasn't too late. Somehow, he had to find the courage to insist they wait to marry.

That evening they ate a take-out dinner of herbed chicken with roasted potatoes and asparagus. Carolyn pulled a carton of Rocky Road ice cream from the freezer and dished up two scoops for Matt.

"Aren't you having any?"

"Not if I want to fit into my wedding dress."

Matt reached for her hand and led the way to the living room. He placed the ice cream on the table in front of the sofa and turned to face Carolyn. "Sweetheart, I want to try again to convince you we should wait to get married. It isn't fair to you to get married now."

A tear escaped one eye and trickled down Carolyn's cheek as she gazed beseechingly at Matt. With some effort, she regained control of her emotions and her face took on a determined look. "I want you to get this through your thick skull, Matthew Brooks; I'm hopelessly in love with you and will marry you on Saturday whether we find that blasted confession or not. You may not like it or agree with it, but you are meeting me at the altar in three days. I know you are making a noble gesture, but I'm a big girl and I know what I want… and that is you!"

"Now, for the next three days we will not discuss the confession or the desk. Together, we will make final preparations for the happiest day of our lives. For instance, I need you to help me with the table favors for the reception, and we still have to shop for Al and Maddie's gifts."

Taken aback by her forceful response, all Matt could manage was a weak, "Yes, ma'am."

"Good, that's settled."

Matt ate his ice cream and marveled once again at the inner strength of this woman he had asked to be his wife.

While he ate the delicious dessert, Carolyn gathered items she had chosen as favors for each guest. She collected the items and passed them to Matt who placed them in small decorative bags and tied a ribbon to secure each one.

"That's the last one; what's next?" Matt asked.

"Have you tried on your tux to make sure it fits and there are no repairs needed?"

"Uh, no," he admitted. "I'll go do that right now."

In a few minutes, he reappeared looking very dapper in his tux. Carolyn checked it over for any stains or repair needs and found none. "Okay, that passes inspection. Now, have you given any thought to the gift for Al?"

"Yes, I thought I might give him a case of good wine. He seemed to enjoy the wine we had at dinner last week, so I thought that might be a nice gift."

"I agree but let's give him something in the jewelry line. I'm buying a pearl necklace for Maddie; we can look for cuff links or a watch while we're picking up the necklace."

Matt thought for a few moments. I think a watch would be good. The one he is wearing has a leather band that is quite worn."

"Perfect!"

***

The jewelry store had a plentiful supply of watches and assured Matt they could have it inscribed and ready by Friday. Maddie's pearl necklace was placed in a protective pouch and placed in a velvet case.

"We'll pick them both up on Friday," Carolyn instructed. Please gift wrap them for us."

"They'll be ready," the clerk assured her. "Thank you for your purchase."

They left the jewelry store and walked a block to the liquor store to order the wine. They picked out what they wanted and gave the clerk the Smith's address.

"We'll send this out today," they promised.

"Is that everything on the list?" Matt asked.

"Yes, except for picking up my dress. If you'll window shop for about thirty minutes, I'll meet you at the car." Carolyn suggested.

"I can manage that," her fiancé replied.

Carolyn tried on her dress and was pleased that the alterations had been done. It was a short-sleeved sheath style with a chapel train and lace overlay. The elbow-length veil would attach to the back of her chignon hairdo. Everything was ready for the big day.

*****

Saturday arrived and the weather had cooperated with sunny skies. Even with a temperature of forty degrees, it was a relatively warm day for mid-November.

Maddie was with Carolyn at Matt's home in an upstairs bedroom helping her get dressed. "You are a beautiful bride, my dear; you will take your groom's breath away."

"Thank you, Maddie; you and Al are very generous to be with us today."

"We are glad to do it, and speaking of generous, thank you for our gifts. My necklace is beautiful and goes well with the neckline of my dress."

Carolyn smiled. "I checked with Al to see if you had a pearl necklace, and he told me how yours was lost two years ago."

"Yes, it slipped off my dressing table into a waste basket and was thrown away accidentally. Al offered to replace it, but I insisted on using the money to help one of our children who was newly married instead. We just never got around to it. Now, I have a new one!"

Al's voice called from downstairs. "Hurry up, you two; we'll be late for the wedding!"

The women laughed. "Well, they can't start without the

bride!" Maddie joked. She helped Carolyn down the stairs, and Al whistled as they came into view.

"I've never seen two lovelier ladies. Matt and I will be the envy of all the men there."

"Thanks, Al; will you help me with my coat?"

Al reached for the mink coat draped on a chair in the foyer and slipped it onto Carolyn. He retrieved Maddie's coat and did the same. "Your chariot awaits, ladies."

Al offered an arm to each lady and escorted them down the front steps and to a waiting limousine. The chauffeur held the door open for them as Maddie helped Carolyn secure her train.

The short ride to the church helped to calm Carolyn's nerves as she anticipated the moment she had dreamed of for weeks. The car stopped and the chauffeur again held the door as Al emerged followed by the women. Maddie held the train as they ascended the stone steps of the church.

Inside, Maddie and Carolyn were escorted to a side room to wait and Al went in search of the groom to let him know they had arrived.

Carolyn and Maddie's bouquets were waiting for them and they picked them up as they heard the organ music begin. Maddie made a final adjustment to the train before stepping out to begin her walk down the aisle. Once she reached the altar and assumed her position, the music changed; it was time for Carolyn to walk forward. Al offered his arm and everyone stood as they anticipated their first look at Dr. Brooks' bride.

As Carolyn entered the back of the sanctuary on Al's arm, she was surprised and pleased to see the sanctuary nearly overflowing with guests. She was glad she had increased the catering order, just in case everyone showed up.

Matt turned toward her as she approached, his face showing admiration for the lovely woman who would soon be his wife.

Al stepped aside when they reached the altar and assumed best man duties beside Matt.

The ceremony started with opening remarks from the pastor followed by confessions of love from Matt and Carolyn.

Scripture was read and *The Lord's Prayer* sung. Maddie dabbed at an escaped tear as Al produced the rings.

Once they were pronounced husband and wife, the couple turned to walk back up the aisle. They nearly stopped in their tracks, however, when they spied Detective Robertson sitting on the back row!

Both of them wondered if they would even get to their reception before Matt was taken away in handcuffs.

Unaware of the drama unfolding before her, the wedding planner escorted the pair to the room where Carolyn and Maddie had waited before the ceremony. They would wait here while the guests were dismissed to wait outside for the bride and groom.

They heard the crowd's footsteps pass by their door as they waited for Detective Robertson. Eventually, the guests had all exited and the door was slowly opened. Sylvia entered carrying a large envelope.

"You two look as if you've seen a ghost!"

"We thought you were someone else," Matt explained.

"Oh, you must mean Detective Robertson. We just had a nice chat. It seems Rachel called yesterday to tell him her mother-in-law had been admitted to a nursing home with dementia. She is becoming forgetful, but the facility is a very upscale senior living village where she will play bridge with friends who live there. I wouldn't say she has dementia exactly, but Detective Robertson said he is now convinced Ron died accidentally as the result of a fall. Rachel must have been very convincing. By the way, will you please introduce me to the woman who caused such a remarkable change in you."

Matt struggled to take in what Sylvia had just said as he made the introductions.

"I'm very pleased to meet you. I wish you both a very long and happy life together. Here's a little wedding present from me and there is a picture my daughter drew that I think you will enjoy. Now, there are a lot of people waiting outside for you with handfuls of rose petals."

Sylvia left as quietly as she had come. The couple looked at each other for reassurance that the other had heard the same thing – the investigation was over!

"But the confession is still out there," Matt cautioned. "This could all change in an instant if that comes to light."

Carolyn put her fingers to Matt's lips. "Shh, it's our wedding day; let's enjoy the moment."

Matt kissed his bride and offered his arm as they walked outside to a cheering crowd and a hail of rose petals.

Detective Robertson approached just before they reached their limousine. "I want to wish you both congratulations; I hope you have many happy years together." He turned and walked away, leaving the pair open-mouthed.

The chauffeur coughed into his hand to signal the couple to enter the car. Matt helped Carolyn in and followed. The car pulled away from the church to take them to the reception a few miles away. The guests had already started to leave ahead of them.

"I don't know what to say; I thought that would turn out quite differently," a still stunned Matt declared.

"I must confess I thought the worst as well. How remarkable!" Carolyn looked down at the envelope Sylvia had handed to them and broke the seal. She pulled out a child's picture of a dog and a little girl playing in a field of flowers. Carolyn smiled at the child's gift. She held it up for Matt to see and noticed as she did so that there was writing on the back. Could it possibly be?

"Matt! Look at this!"

"What?"

"On the back... see?" She said as she turned the picture over.

Matt's face registered first surprise and then excitement as he realized it was his confession! How did Sylvia come to have it and why was there a picture done in crayons on the back?

Carolyn fished in the envelope and extracted a folded note from Sylvia.

Matt, I can only imagine your joy and relief to be holding the very piece of paper you have looked for all these weeks. As it turns out, my daughter knew the secret of the desk and used it to hide her 'treasures' from her younger brother. After Ron died, and I was busy with so many things, she opened the secret drawer and found your confession. She can't read yet, so she had no idea of its significance. She knew I had cleared the desk of her father's other papers so she assumed the paper wasn't important. She used the blank side of the paper to color a picture. In a twist of irony, the paper was attached to the front of my refrigerator with a magnet for weeks. I passed by that paper several times a day unaware of what was on the other side. When we packed to move, she removed her picture and put it in a box with some of her other things. It sat in that box until yesterday when I thought to ask her about the desk and the secret drawer. She denied knowing about it at first, afraid she would get in trouble. I assured her I wasn't angry if she knew about the desk's secret hiding place. With a little more prodding, she told me the whole story. She went right to the box where it had been packed and pulled it out. Imagine my surprise and delight!

Happy Wedding Day, Dr. Brooks!"

P.S. There's more in the envelope.

Sylvia

Matt took the confession and tore it into little pieces as Carolyn examined the bottom of the envelope. She pulled out two airline tickets.

A twinkle came in her eyes as she handed the tickets to her new husband. "Matt, I know where we're going on our honeymoon."

Carolyn handed Matt the tickets. A smile brightened his face as he looked from the tickets to his new bride. "Well, my dear, I guess we're going to Paris!"